ALSO BY GINA L. MAXWELL

Seducing Cinderella

Rules of
Entanglement

GINA L. MAXWELL

St. Martin's Paperbacks

This is a work of fiction. All of the characters, organizations, and events portrayed in this novel are either products of the author's imagination or are used fictitiously.

RULES OF ENTANGLEMENT

Copyright © 2013 by by Gina L. Maxwell.
Bonus scene copyright © 2014 by Gina L. Maxwell.

All rights reserved.

For information address St. Martin's Press, 175 Fifth Avenue, New York, NY 10010.

ISBN: 978-1-250-05036-6

Printed in the United States of America

Entangled Publishing edition / March 2013
St. Martin's Paperbacks edition / March 2014

St. Martin's Paperbacks are published by St. Martin's Press, 175 Fifth Avenue, New York, NY 10010.

10 9 8 7 6 5 4 3 2 1

For my readers, who waited so patiently—
and sometimes not so patiently—for this book. I can't
begin to tell you how truly grateful I am for each
and every one of you. By making a space for me on your
shelves, you've made a space for yourself in my heart.
Thank you.

VANESSA MACGREGOR'S "LUCKY 7" RULES TO LIVE BY

7. Never take your responsibilities lightly.
6. Never indulge in the poison of lies.
5. Never let a fling last more than three days.
4. Never date a man who chooses fists over words.
3. Never date a man who lacks a stable future.
2. Never relinquish control.
1. Never fall in love.

Day 1: Sunday

"He's now officially an hour late."

And talking to yourself out loud makes you crazy as well as hungry and stranded.

Vanessa MacGregor sat on a bench next to her suitcase and carry-on outside the Honolulu airport, trying to ignore her grumbling stomach. She'd finished gaping in awe at the picturesque scenery about forty minutes ago when she realized her best friend Lucie's brother, who lived on the island, was running more than just a tad past the arranged pickup time.

Drumming her manicured fingernails on the back of her cell, she debated whether or not to call Lucie, but she didn't want to worry her friend the week of her wedding. She was already stressed out to the max. And that was before some bad sushi had her praying to the porcelain God from severe food poisoning.

Instead, Vanessa had kept trying Jackson's phone several times, but her calls went directly to voice mail. She was starting to worry something might have happened to him. And if he didn't show up soon, he might wish something had.

Vanessa pressed a button on her cell phone again to illuminate the screen and check the time. She couldn't spend all day at the airport. She'd flown down to the über-posh Mau Loa resort four days early, an entire week before her friend's wedding, to meet up with Jackson and stand in for Lucie and her fiancé with some crazed wedding planner who insisted on the happy couple being on site during the preparations.

If it weren't for the potential clusterfuck of missing Jackson while she was en route to the Mau Loa, she'd have taken a cab by now. Staring at her cell and releasing a heavy exhale, she decided to try his phone one more time. Hitting redial, she checked her manicure and listened to the rings mocking her.

"You must be Vanessa."

She looked up at the sound of a sexy baritone voice, but the sun instantly blinded her. Squinting from the sharp pain to her retinas, she shielded her eyes to try and make out the features of the man in front of her, wearing a pair of navy board shorts and a skin-tight wifebeater.

Dark and delicious. Those were the first words that popped into her head. His short, dark hair was damp, and his beard looked like it had at least a day of growth. Starting mid-bicep on his left arm, a Polynesian tattoo of ocean waves in black ink stretched up to the top of his shoulder. His skin was tan, but not the typical golden shade. It was just a tinge darker, almost like he'd lived here so long his body had adapted to the native heritage. The only part of him that didn't fit the dark motif was his topaz eyes, reminding her of caramels rimmed with thin lines of dark chocolate . . . Shit, she needed to get something to eat before she tried licking his eyeballs.

She'd never met Jackson in person, but she'd seen plenty of pictures. Enough to recognize that the owner of the sexy voice was indeed Lucie's brother and champion MMA fighter. Hearing his voice-mail message come through her phone snapped her out of her momentary stupor long enough to take the phone away from her ear and end the call. The airwaves didn't do his vocal chords justice, she decided as she stood and held out her hand.

"Jackson, it's so nice to finally meet you."

He looked at her outstretched hand with what seemed to be an amused smile before finally grasping it in his own. His hand was rough with calluses and deliciously warm.

"Nice to finally meet the infamous best friend of my sister," he said with a boyishly charming smile.

Oh, he was definitely doable. Did Hawaiians have the saying "Save a surfboard, ride a surfer"? If not, she was totally starting it. She wondered if he even surfed.

Getting her head back in the game, she asked, "Is everything okay?" At his questioning look she added, "You said you'd be here at eleven and it's past noon. I tried calling but only got your voice mail."

Jackson shrugged. "Yeah, my phone died. I don't pay much attention, since I mostly use it to keep in touch with Lucie. I'm sort of a caveman in terms of technology."

Vanessa didn't point out that he'd told Lucie to have her call him on that phone when she landed. Which she had. Five times. "Huh. Must be nice to be that carefree." She mentally cringed at the judgment in her voice. Just because she was a little cranky from sitting in the sun while hungry for an hour didn't mean she could abandon all her manners. "So did you have car trouble or something?"

"To be honest, I was surfing and sort of lost track of time."

Well, that answers the surfing question. Glancing at

his wrists, Vanessa noticed he must have sort of lost track of his watch before leaving home with his dead cell phone. All her pleasantries ground to a halt, and the smile on her face morphed from genuine to a tight imitation. Any warm and fuzzies her lady parts had begun harboring for the MMA stud in front of her went poof.

Rule #7: Never take your responsibilities lightly.

What happened to the responsible, shoulder-the-world man Lucie had always described?

"I wish I would've known it was going to be an issue for you to come and get me," she said, trying hard to keep irritation out of her tone. And failing. "I could've just as easily taken a cab."

He put his hands up, palms facing her in resignation. "You're absolutely right. I was a thoughtless jerk."

"I didn't say—"

"And I totally deserve a thorough tongue-lashing," he said with another smile, "but let's do it on the way to my Jeep because I'm double-parked and I'd rather be lectured by an angry woman over a burger and a beer. I'm starving."

Angry? She'd barely even portrayed miffed, much less angry. But he was on the fast track to front row seats if he kept feeding her bullshit and trying to push her around.

Without waiting for her response, Jackson popped up the handle on her suitcase and walked away. A potent cocktail of shock, panic, and indignation lit up her insides. Before he could take two steps with it rolling behind him, she pulled the bag from his grip. He looked at his hand as though stunned she'd taken her luggage back, then glanced up, a brow cocked in question.

"There a problem, princess?"

Princess? She gritted her teeth. Hell, yes, there was a problem. Several, in fact, not the least of which was him acting like he was running her show. Vanessa couldn't remember the last time she'd let anyone control her or her circumstances. And she sure as hell wasn't about to start now.

She'd waited for him out of respect for Lucie, despite wanting to find her own way to the resort. Then when he finally arrived, he thought to whisk her luggage from her, expecting her to fall in line behind him. Then apparently he had plans of stopping for lunch—which actually sounded pretty glorious, but that wasn't the point. He hadn't even bothered to ask if she was hungry. Then, after that, who knew, maybe he wanted to stop by his house and do some laundry before dropping her off at the resort so she could help his sister.

It was clear Jackson was the wrong guy to get involved with on any level. If she had time to get her itch scratched while on vacation, she'd have to find a different scratcher.

Vanessa sighed. Meeting the wrong men seemed to be the case more often than not over the last couple of years. Another one bites the dust, Nessie. But now wasn't the time to wallow in thoughts of never finding her own happily ever after. This week was all about making sure Lucie's fairy tale came true, and clearly her brother wasn't on the same page.

"You know what?" she began with a gracious smile—fake though it was. "You don't need to worry about me. I know Lucie asked you to pick me up, and I'm sorry for your trouble, but it's not necessary. I'll just take a cab."

"And risk the wrath of my baby sister the week of her wedding? No thanks. I'd rather fight a kickboxer without a cup. So come on." This time he slung the strap of her duffel carry-on over his shoulder and turned to walk away.

"Oh my God!" She jammed her hands on her hips,

the incredulity at his arrogance preventing her from doing much else. "You really need to stop taking my things."

He lifted an eyebrow while holding back an amused smirk. Unsuccessfully, she might add. "Not big on chivalry?"

"There's a distinct difference between chivalrous and pushy. You are being pushy."

"Pushy?" He made a face like he'd never heard the word before. "I'm just trying to do what I came here for. I apologized for being late and now—"

"No, you didn't," she blurted out before she could stop herself. Remembering every word of a conversation could sometimes put a damper on social situations, but as a prosecutor in the DA's office it was a valuable asset. And calling dickheads on their "chivalrous" behavior? Priceless.

"Yes, I did."

She sighed. She'd already hopped on the damn train, so she might as well ride it out of the station. "Uh, no, you didn't."

"Yes, I—"

She crossed her arms in front of her and cut him off. "Your exact words were, 'To be honest, I was surfing and sort of lost track of time.'"

"Wow, nothing gets by you, huh? I'll have to remember that," he mumbled. Rubbing a hand over the back of his neck, he actually had the gall to grin at her from under his impossibly long lashes like a lying teenager who knew how to charm his way out of trouble. Un. Effing. Real. "Then I'm definitely sorry I didn't say 'sorry.'"

Vanessa bet there weren't many women who told Jackson Maris "no." Even with the irritation from his high-handedness still riding her, the idea of giving in to him sprouted in the back of her brain. Thankfully, she still had enough sense to squash it before it grew into a Garden of Dreamy Sighs and Head Over Heels. Squash.

"Let's just forget it. I'm going to take a cab to the resort, and you can do . . ." She waved her hands around. "Whatever it is you do, and I'll see you at the rehearsal dinner on Friday."

There. That wasn't so hard. Despite being tired, hungry, and disappointed in her Welcome Wagon, she refused to cave in to the desire to be snippy and rude. Just because she lived by a certain code didn't mean the rest of the world did.

Forcing herself to remain civil for the sake of her friendship with Lucie—and to prove she had complete control over her emotions—she said, "It's been a pleasure meeting you, Jackson," and grabbed the strap to her carry-on, still perched on his shoulder.

His hand covered hers as he leaned in, eclipsing the sun and most of the world around her. When he spoke, his voice dropped an octave and the low vibrations snaked their way through her body, hitting every erogenous zone she didn't even know she had. "You don't sound all that pleased, V." He paused, his gaze flicking to her mouth a moment before offering a sinful smile. "Come with me."

Unbidden images of hot Hawaiian sex with Jackson flashed in her mind at warp speed, messing with the signals from her brain to the rest of her body. Certain parts of her clenched tight with need, while others, like her knees and jaw, slackened with lust.

Either her desperation for some adult one-on-one time was worse than she thought or this guy affected her way more than she could safely handle. Thankfully, both problems had only one solution. Squash, squash, squash!

"Good-bye, Jackson."

Grabbing her bags, she took off in the opposite direction. Luckily, a cab waited only a few yards away. She'd already put her things in the trunk and was reaching for the door handle when he called out after her.

"I'll just meet you in the lobby of the resort, then."

Civility dissolved in the acid now churning in her gut. Did he take some sort of sick pleasure in aggravating the hell out of people, or was he really just that clueless? Unfortunately for him, she assumed the former.

Turning around slowly, she addressed the man now leaning against a large concrete column, hands in his pockets, an easygoing smile gracing his face. "That won't be necessary. I'm quite capable of taking care of myself."

He pushed himself off and sauntered over into her personal space. He smelled like the island itself, of salt water and sun.

"I have no doubt of that, princess," he said. "But there's one little detail you're not aware of."

"And what's that?"

"The celebrity wedding planner Reid hired insists that for any destination wedding, the couple needs to be on location a week beforehand to meet with him and go over all the arrangements."

"I know that. Why do you think I came down this early? I know Lucie's tastes well enough to do this with my eyes closed."

He didn't even acknowledge her statement. "And due to the celebrity clientele at the Mau Loa, absolutely no one other than the guests registered to the room may claim the reservation."

She cocked a hip out to the side and crossed her arms over her chest. "Then why am I down here if I can't check in?"

"You can't check in," he said, "but Lucie can."

She was about to ask him if he was smoking something, for all the sense he made, when the way he cocked his eyebrow in her direction suddenly made everything clear.

And so completely messed up.

"Oh no," she said, hands rose to ward off his message already sinking its fangs into her brain. "Absolutely not."

"Absolutely yes."

"You've got the wrong girl, Maris. That's lying, and I don't lie. I'll simply speak with the manager and explain the situation." She turned and yanked the cab door open.

"That won't work. Look, the Mau Loa is the most exclusive celebrity resort in all of Hawaii. You need at least three forms of ID just to check in. The rich and famous like it because, with the exception of hanging out of a helicopter, it's impenetrable to the paparazzi and crazy fans when all they want is a little time to themselves and maybe a private wedding ceremony."

Her heart beat rapidly, trying to escape the confines of her ribs. "Then I'll stay in another hotel and go to the Mau Loa for the meetings with the planner," she argued weakly.

A grouchy voice came from inside the cab. "Hey, lady, in or out? You're costing me money!"

Jackson ducked in front of the open passenger window. "You want to say that again?"

"Yeah." The driver clearly intended on setting things straight. But as soon as he saw the hulking figure curling his fingers into a fist and shooting him a dare with his eyes, the cabbie's bravado fell dead away. Clearing his throat and shifting in his seat, he finished with, "I meant, take all the time you need."

"Appreciate it."

As Jackson straightened to loom over her again, Vanessa was reminded of the fact that he made a living from using his fists. And though she knew it was a sport and not the drunken beatings she'd grown up with, she had to wonder how much of that contained violence leaked into his personality.

"Sorry, where was I?"

Swallowing hard, she looked around, wanting to avoid the truth in those topaz eyes. She feared that, when everything was said and done, her closing arguments wouldn't be enough to avoid participating in this charade. Thank God she could depend on her sharp tongue to act as her shield. "I'm pretty sure you were about to impart more of your infinite wisdom and explain why I can't stay somewhere else for the week."

"Lucky for you," he said with one corner of his mouth hitched up, "I've decided to waive all infinite wisdom fees today." She rolled her eyes and crossed her arms as he grabbed the top of the door with one hand. "The wedding planner is eccentric and known for dropping clients if he even suspects things aren't on the up and up. If he finds out Lucie and Reid aren't coming until the last minute, he's liable to call it off. No planner, no wedding. And if there's no wedding, Reid'll have my balls, never mind the guilt trip we'll be on with my sister for the next decade or so. Understand what I'm getting at here?"

Feeling deflated, she finally met his gaze and filled in the big, fat blanks. "You and I need to check in as Reid and Lucie in order to secure their wedding."

"Bingo."

Her mind raced, warring between helping her best friend and going against not only her occupational code of ethics but also one of her Rules. They'd been carved in stone and then traced with her blood since the day she made them. They kept her balanced. One could even say they were like her religion. And this wasn't going to be one instance of one lie. This would be a whole week of lies. Of deceit. It didn't matter to whom or for what reason.

Rule #6: Never indulge in the poison of lies. She'd had enough lies from her mom and stepdad growing up to last her five lifetimes. She excused lying about as much as she excused Hitler.

Tamping down her uneasiness over the situation, she focused on assessing it logically. "How do we even pull it off without IDs?"

"I have a connection at the resort who will help with check-in at least, so that part will be taken care of."

"How do we explain why Lucie is staying at the resort while her fiancé stays off grounds?"

A devilish smile curled his lips. "Nice try. We don't. We'll be staying in the same bungalow together."

"With two bedrooms."

"The reservation is already made for a premier one bedroom. There would be no reason for a bride and groom to request two. But no one will know that 'Reid' is sleeping on the couch."

Think, Nessie! "What happens at the end of the week when we're not the ones walking down the aisle?"

"There's another wedding on Saturday that's higher profile. A-list celebrity trumps former UFC light heavyweight champ. According to my connection, the planner needs to attend that one so he, and therefore the resort, won't know that the people who made the decisions aren't the ones actually getting married."

As smooth as he countered her every issue, she wondered if he made a habit of deceiving others. And why did that notion disappoint her so much? "Well, you certainly have all your bases covered," she said tightly. Squaring her shoulders and lifting her chin, she added, "Fine, I'll do it for Lucie. But I'm still taking a cab."

Jackson's face lit up like he'd just been told he won a

harem of Playboy bunnies. "That's fine. We'll have plenty of quality time this week. See you soon, *pupule wahine*."

"Poo-poo-lay wah-hee-nay? What on earth does that mean?"

Winking, he said, "It's a Hawaiian endearment."

"Lovely." She'd meant that to sound sarcastic, but it came out closer to reverent. So what if she thought the native language was pretty? And so what if it had been such a long time since anyone had called her anything other than Nessie or Counselor? She certainly didn't need to hear endearments from the likes of Jackson Maris.

Vanessa climbed in the cab and pulled the door closed, doing her level best to ignore the deep laughter floating through the open window as they pulled away from the curb.

Drawing in a deep, calming breath, she met the cabbie's eyes in the rearview mirror. "Take me to the Mau Loa, please. But first let's hit a drive-through. I'm in no hurry, and I'm starving."

I am such an asshole.

Jackson shoved his hands in his pockets and watched the strangest, most striking woman he'd ever met leave him in a cloud of exhaust fumes. Though he could think of several reasons to look forward to spending time with her this week—full lips, emerald eyes, silky red curls, and a body to make a man sit up and beg, to name a few—it wasn't her appearance that had him revved up.

It was her firecracker personality.

He was used to women with laidback attitudes. Easy to charm, easy to please. Vanessa MacGregor was obviously neither of those. And while he had no intention of giving up, she'd come very close to making him tap out. That intrigued the hell out of him.

But that was no excuse for the B.S. he'd just fed her about needing to check in as their friends.

Walking back to his car, he ran over their conversation in his mind. He hadn't expected his first meeting with his sister's best friend to go down that way. He did feel like a jerk for being so late. It was a testament to the lax way of life he'd adopted over the last decade that he hadn't considered it would be something he couldn't make up for with a little charm and an offer of lunch.

It might have been forgivable—eventually—if he hadn't dropped the little marriage-ruse bomb on top of it.

When Reid called him to explain the situation and ask for his help, Jackson had planned on picking her up, getting her settled into the Mau Loa (the part about him being able to get her past their tight security policies had been true, at least), and then returning to his regularly scheduled program until the wedding at the end of the week. Reid had mentioned how eccentric the planner was, but the plan had never been for her to pose as Lucie. Jackson had kind of made that part up in the heat of the moment.

He'd been blindsided by her crazy Jekyll and Hyde allure. And then she'd rebuffed and dismissed him like a puppy who'd dropped a ball at her feet when she wasn't in the mood to play catch. He was beyond fascinated. He wanted to open her up and see what made her tick. Hence his sudden and inexplicable need to spend as much time as possible with her over the next week. Jax was fairly certain most of his blood had drained from his head to a more southerly area when he'd spouted that bullshit.

Realizing he now had the pleasure of breaking the news of his deception to Vanessa and almost certainly earning himself a kick to the nuts, he got into his Jeep, made his way out of the airport, and reluctantly headed for the resort.

He'd only lived on Oahu for about twelve years, but it felt like a lifetime. His twenty-three years living in Sun Valley, Nevada, was little more than a collection of faded childhood memories. Whether due to the passing of time or his conscious effort to forget a huge chunk of those years, he wasn't sure. Either way, despite missing his sister like crazy, he was happiest on the island. Growing up, he'd always felt like a cog in the wrong wheel.

It wasn't because he hadn't been blessed with a great life. His parents had been wonderful people who'd loved him and his sister with everything they were and made sure they wanted for nothing. He'd had a great childhood.

It was the start of his adulthood when everything had gone to hell—starting with the accident that killed his parents shortly after his graduation.

Then it stayed that way for more than five years. But as soon as he'd been able to get away, he'd packed up and left for Hawaii. It was as far as he could go without leaving the good ole U.S. of A. His destination choice had been more for genealogical reasons than geographical, but the literal distance sometimes helped with the mental distance he'd needed.

Once he settled on Oahu in his modest beachfront cottage with the ocean in front and the mountains in back, he'd joined Team Titan, the best MMA training camp on the island. With his career off on the right foot and some changes in the way he viewed life, he felt free and happy for the first time since before the accident.

Remembering the weeks that followed their deaths,

Jackson's hands tightened on the steering wheel. Deep loss and sadness mixed with anger and betrayal to form a volatile riptide of emotions that threatened to pull him under. Taking a deep breath, he held the car steady with his knee and released his hold with deliberate slowness.

The rare tension in his body was a reminder that nothing good ever came from dwelling on the bad. He contemplated the surfboard riding snug on the top of his Jeep and wished he could head back to the beach to let the waves pound his muscles and memories back into submission. But his usual therapy would have to wait.

Navigating the winding road down the coast, he focused on the warm, salty air whipping around him, letting it center him as the natural elements of the island always did.

A few minutes later he pulled into the elaborate drive of the Mau Loa. Towering palm trees of identical height alternated with elegant streetlamps along the sides of the semicircular road that arced around a massive five-tiered fountain. After parking in the guest lot, Jax headed for the lobby to make sure everything was in order and wait for Vanessa's arrival.

Behind the front desk, a young woman issued keys to a couple and instructed a porter where to deliver their luggage before sending them off with a smile and customary "Aloha."

When she caught sight of Jackson, her smile transformed from the customer-service kind to one of pure joy. She was beautiful and petite with the bronze skin of the natives and dark chocolate eyes that danced over his body. A blue hibiscus flower peeked from the long, black curtain of hair behind her left ear. She whispered something to the other girl working, then came out from behind the counter to greet him.

"Hey, Jilli."

With a lighthearted laugh, she stepped in to him and wrapped her arms around his neck and squeezed him tightly. He returned her affection with a hug around her slim waist. After a few moments, she pulled back on a contented sigh.

"Aloha, Jackie. It's good to see you."

He screwed up his face at the nickname she used specifically because he hated it. Or at least pretended to hate it. "It's good to see you, too, gorgeous. How've you been?"

Jilli laid her best puppy-dog eyes on him. "How've I been since you broke my heart, you mean?"

The woman was so full of it. She was a newlywed and madly in love with her husband, a fighter from another camp on the island. Jax respected him as a fighter and as someone who did right by Jilli. The man treated her like royalty.

"Something tells me your hubby would take personal offense to that, and I happen to like my teeth the way they are."

Chuckling, she gave up the pretense. "Yeah, I suppose you're right. So where's your guest of honor?"

"Thanks again for doing this, Jilli. And assuming she doesn't stop off to hire some thug to take me out, she'll be here soon."

Jilli crossed her arms. "You just met the girl. What could you possibly have done to upset her already?"

"I think the question is what didn't I do?"

A devious grin spread over her face. "Ooh, this sounds good. Come on," she said, slipping out of his embrace to grab his hand and drag him away from the counter. When they were far enough away from possible eavesdroppers, she stopped him. "Okay, tell me what happened."

Jackson barely suppressed a groan as he told her the

story of how he started with the minor infraction of arriving late, moved on to the misdemeanor of being pushy, and ended with the moral felony of lying his ass off for his own selfish reasons.

When he finished, Jilli's expression of pure shock was as effective as a mother's scolding. He crossed his arms over his chest defensively. "I know. I fucked up. I'll apologize and tell her the truth when she gets here, okay?"

"I think that's a very good idea. Just take it easy on her, Champ. She's probably exhausted from the trip." Lighting up, she added, "Hey, you still have some clothes in your locker in the break room. Why don't you change into something a little less surfer boy? It might help her take you more seriously. You know, like the rest of us adults."

"Very funny. Fine, I suppose it won't kill me to play grownup for a while."

Jackson kissed her on the cheek and thanked her yet again for helping him with getting Vanessa past the strict policies that would normally have prevented her from checking in.

"You know I'd do anything for you, Jackie. Now get going," she said, patting his cheek before returning to the lobby.

Grabbing some clothes out of the employee locker he sometimes used, Jax crossed to the small private bathroom. He'd just changed into a pair of cargo shorts when his cell vibrated on the sink. Not even bothering to check caller ID, he shoved the phone between his ear and shoulder as he picked up the white linen shirt.

"Yeah," he barked into the receiver.

"Jax."

"Reid, my man, how's my baby sis? Any better?"

"Unfortunately, not yet. These things can last a few days until her body gets rid of all the bad shit in her system or whatever." Jackson could practically feel the tension coming through the phone from his oldest friend. "Seeing her like this and not being able to help her makes me want to throttle something."

"Yeah, I know that feeling." Jackson remembered the month when Lucie had pneumonia her sophomore year. The constant worry had driven him insane. To help break some of the tension, Jax took a jab at Reid. "Maybe you can pound some clay into submission to get it out of your system."

"Listen, asshole, just because I replaced fighting with sculpting doesn't mean I can't still whoop your ass. Did everything go all right with Vanessa?"

Jax shrugged the shirt on and began buttoning it. "You know how I am with the ladies, Andrews." A statement that answered absolutely nothing.

"Yeah, I do. So how's your ego handling the rejection?"

Okay, that was freaky. Either Vanessa had called and ratted him out to Lucie—which he didn't think she'd do, knowing how sick Lu was—or the woman had a rep as a man-eater a mile long. "I don't know what you're talking about. Things couldn't have gone better."

"You're almost as bad of a liar as Lucie, you know that?"

Jax thought about the lies he'd told not even half an hour ago and muttered, "Tell that to Vanessa."

"What was that?"

"Nothing." Jax leaned back against the bathroom sink and crossed his arms over his chest. "Hey, speaking of which, is she super religious or something?"

"Not that I know of, why?"

"Lying came up in conversation, and she was pretty adamant that she never does it. Like, ever. So if it's not religion, what's her deal?"

"It's one of her lucky seven rules."

Walking back into the break room area, he stopped to throw his discarded clothes in the locker and grab a bottle of water before heading out to the lobby. "Like the Golden Rule?"

"More like her own set of commandments minus the 'thou shalt nots.' According to Lu, she never breaks them."

"Never, huh? Interesting."

His friend's sigh came through the phone, loud and clear. "Listen, Maris, if you know what's good for you, you won't mess around with her. I've seen her in action. Confident men approach her and by the time she's through with them, they're licking their wounds in the corner of the bar. And you're not even close to her type."

He smiled at the image Reid painted. "Well, I was planning on seeing how you like it when I seduce your sister, but seeing as you don't have one, my dating calendar is pretty open this week. Besides, it sounds like fun."

Yeah, like in the way trying to escape the lion enclosure at the zoo with steaks tied around his waist sounded like fun to the normal man. Then again, Jax never claimed to be normal.

"Hey," Reid countered, "you and I both know that once the smoke cleared—and my nose healed—you were glad it was me with Luce and not someone else."

The man had a point there.

"And secondly, I'm not fucking around, Jax. I need you to make sure everything goes smoothly out there. You told me you have a way of getting around the reservation policies, so focus on that. I refuse to tell Lu her dream wedding—the one she deserved to begin with instead of the joke of a ceremony that piece of shit gave her last time—is a no-go. You feel me?"

"Yeah," Jax answered with steel in his voice. "I feel

you." Being reminded of the asshole who screwed his sister over years ago was all he needed to leave the joking behind. "There's no way in hell I'm letting my sister's wedding get canceled."

He wanted to guarantee it wouldn't get canceled. As part owner of the Mau Loa, he had that kind of power, but due to his contract, he couldn't tell Reid or anyone else about his role. Several years ago, as a way of securing his future, Jax became a financial backer of the resort. Since his focus was on his fighting career and he didn't want the notoriety that came with owning high-end resorts in Hawaii, he requested to be a silent partner. Jilli knew only because she'd stumbled upon the contract while cleaning his place when they were dating. He'd sworn her to secrecy, and she hadn't let him down yet.

Jax took up residence against the front desk as he cracked his water open and winked at Jilli. He chugged the ice-cold liquid, letting Reid vent in his ear about all the bodily harm he'd impose on Jax if shit went south, just as Vanessa's cab rounded the semicircular drive and pulled to a stop at the entrance. Though he'd just drank almost the whole bottle, as soon as the leggy redhead stepped from the car, his mouth went bone dry, his adrenaline kicked in, and somewhere he imagined a ring girl walking around holding up a giant card with ROUND 1 painted in bold block letters.

Right then he made the decision to wait until she'd had a chance to settle in and relax before telling her the truth. Maybe he'd take her for a drink and tell her then. Surely she'd be less likely to hate him once she felt the sun on her face, the sand in her toes, and the booze in her veins. Right?

"No worries, man," he assured his friend. "I've got everything under control."

Reid's curse wasn't very encouraging. "Why do I have a bad feeling about this?"

"No idea. Gotta go." Jax hit the end button as he pushed off the counter. "My fiancée's here."

Closing the trunk after extracting her bags, the driver accepted her money and hurriedly returned to his cab without so much as an "Aloha" before peeling away. She coughed from the exhaust and picked up her things to move onto the curb. Weren't the island people supposed to be friendly and accommodating? Although, she supposed after making him wait for her at the airport and then stop at a little café so she could get a quick bite to eat, the guy had a right to be a little agitated. Still, it's not like he hadn't been duly compensated for his time.

What a day. Stranded at the airport, informed she needed to change identities, and stuck with the only surly cabbie in all of Oahu. Not exactly how she imagined her first few hours in one of the most beautiful, carefree places on Earth.

But, she amended, those had been things she couldn't control. What she could control was how she dealt with her current situation and—

"Hello, sweetheart."

—him.

Taking a deep breath, Vanessa turned and regarded the thorn in her side. He'd changed out of his surfer duds into something more appropriate for a man who'd supposedly just flown over from the continental forty-eight. His khaki cargo shorts paired with a lightweight white button-up and sandals said casual-and-understated.

So why the hell was she hearing sexy-and-overdressed?

Vanessa's pulse jumped and goose bumps broke out over her skin despite the balmy weather. Standing as close as he was, he towered over her. The man was simply massive. How in the world did someone so big share the same DNA as her tiny friend?

Getting off to a rocky start with the man didn't make her blind. He was easily one of the most gorgeous men she'd ever seen. Too bad he so obviously broke several of her rules. Hell, if she were being honest, she'd bet he broke almost all of them.

Jackson bent down to pick up her duffel bag, and on the way back up, leaned in to press a warm kiss to her cheek. At the unexpected intimacy, she sucked in a breath and almost pulled away, but his soft words of warning held her in place. "Remember who we are here. If you accuse me of sexual harassment, there's a good chance it'll blow our cover."

His low chuckle both liquefied her insides and made her blood boil. His infectious smile tempted the corners of her mouth to lift up the slightest bit, though she ordered them to hold firm. To save face, she went with it, widening her grin and telling him in the sweetest voice she could muster, "Don't worry about me, darling, I have stellar acting skills in the courtroom. But if I were you, I'd worry about how thick you lay it on, because if you take advantage of this situation, you'll have to worry about what I'll do to your manhood once we're behind closed doors instead."

He raised his left eyebrow, which had a jagged white scar running diagonally through it, giving his good looks a rakish edge. Though she knew her appearance was nothing short of atrocious at this point, his eyes skimmed over her body like she'd been dipped in his favorite candy. Maybe the aloof Prince of Tides wasn't as unaffected by her as he'd like her to think.

"Looking forward to it, princess," he said, smirking in amusement and giving her a wink before walking into the lobby.

What was wrong with this guy? He should be backing down, talking her down, or at the very least, toning it down. One of those downs. That's what any normal male would do when his junk was threatened. Maybe he was into masochism. That thought perked her up. A closet masochist would effectively douse any sparks of desire that may or may not be going off somewhere deep inside her every time he turned those light eyes on her.

Feeling better already, Vanessa grabbed the handle of her suitcase and wheeled it behind her along the tiled entrance of the lobby. Jackson stood at the front desk speaking with an exotically pretty woman who handed him an envelope of paperwork and two key cards with a smile that probably won her customer service awards.

"There's my lovely bride," Jackson announced as he put an arm around her waist and pulled her into his side.

"Bride-to-be, dear," she said with a fake look of happiness frozen on her face. "I'm not officially your bride yet." Then, before she could stop herself, she added, "And anything can happen between now and then."

As the lunatic holding her laughed, the woman behind the counter assessed her in the way women size up their competition. Not that it was obvious, but Vanessa noticed the split-second crack in her Employee of the Month persona before picking up where she'd left off.

"Welcome to the Mau Loa, Miss Miller. It's a pleasure to have you and Mr. Andrews at our resort. If there's anything we can do to make your stay more enjoyable, please don't hesitate to ask."

"Thank you . . ." She glanced at the nametag that claimed her as the reservations manager. "Jillian. I'm sure everything will be fine. In regards to meeting with the wedding coordinator, can you please tell me when my—"

Jackson cleared his throat and gave her waist a squeeze. She barely stopped an eye roll.

"—our first appointment is?"

"Of course. Let me check that for you." After a few moments clacking her nails over the keyboard, she said, "You're scheduled to meet with him at four o'clock this afternoon in the Honu Café."

"Great," Jackson said with a light slap on the counter, as though it signaled the end of their discussion. "Now, Jilli, if you don't mind, it's been a long trip so I'd like to get Lucie to our bungalow so she can freshen up. She normally doesn't look quite so haggard."

The air from Vanessa's lungs slammed out like he'd just punched her between the shoulder blades. Was he serious? Her pulse spiked and her need to fire back clouded her better judgment—and opened her big, fat mouth. "Well, at least I can fix my problem with a shower, darling. You need a tiny blue pill to fix yours."

Jackson barked out a strange combination of choking and laughter, which he tried to bring under control behind his fist. Before she could stop, think, and regret the words she'd just put in her best friend's mouth, she snatched the envelope and keys off the counter. "Why don't you go make friends while I freshen up for you? I'll probably be a while, so I'd take my time if I were you."

Catching the eye of the woman who stood with equal parts shock and delight on her face, Vanessa gave her the best apologetic look she could muster. "I'm so sorry. I'm under a lot of stress right now with the wedding and all, so I'm not quite myself. Thank you so much for your help."

Without a backward glance, Vanessa spun on her wedge sandals and strode in the opposite direction of the entrance, hoping it would lead her toward her bungalow. Stepping into the sunshine, she found a gigantic pool and several hot tubs surrounded by lush palm trees and occupied lounge chairs. A waterfall cascaded down a large rock face on one side, bringing a bit of the island inside the resort parameters.

As she followed one of the paths that led her around the more touristy areas, she peered at the guests through the cover of her sunglasses. Though she couldn't be sure, she swore she saw Reese Witherspoon with her husband in the pool and someone who looked a lot like Alec Baldwin standing by the bar. Lucky for them she was too exhausted to be even remotely starstruck and kept on walking, eager to find her destination.

The Mau Loa wasn't like the other commercial resorts on the island. It didn't have hundreds of rooms in a gigantic hotel-style building. Instead, it housed several dozen private bungalows spread throughout the property. Essentially small homes in the lap of luxury surrounded by paradise. Not too shabby.

It only took her a few minutes to find her bungalow on the outermost boundary, making it one of the more private houses. Relieved, she quickly used her key and entered the white stucco home. The inside looked like something out of a travel magazine. Large, open, and breezy, everything in white or muted blues to match the ocean only a stone's throw away from her front lanai.

The main room consisted of a cozy living area with inviting couches like clouds plucked out of the sky. The wall on the left was made entirely of sliding glass doors that opened onto a small yard, complete with kidney-shaped pool, hot tub, small bar, outdoor shower, and hammock, surrounded by an eight-foot-tall privacy fence. The small but fully stocked kitchen sat off to the right of the living area, separated by a breakfast bar and stools.

Vanessa crossed the room and opened the door on the far wall to find the most romantic bedroom she'd ever seen. A wispy canopy draped the sides of a gigantic four-poster bed and rippled in the sea breeze sweeping in from the open French doors that also led to the private yard.

Just then a porter arrived with her bags. She wasted no time grabbing fresh clothes and hopping in the shower. She couldn't remember the last time hot water felt so good, and the orange honeysuckle scent of all her bathing products relaxed and invigorated her at the same time. After toweling off and slipping into a pair of cotton shorts and a T-shirt, she headed straight for the bed.

"Caviar dreams and champagne wishes," she whispered with a smile before falling back on the cloud they called a mattress . . . and dozed off.

A knock on the door startled her awake. Checking the time on her watch, she relaxed. About thirty minutes had passed, which was a pretty good power nap. She definitely felt more refreshed.

The knock sounded again. If there was a God it'd be a waiter holding one of those yummy blue drinks she'd seen everywhere.

"Coming," she called, hopping from the bed. Yanking the door open, her excitement fizzled. "Oh. It's you."

"Tiny blue pill? So classic." Jackson put a hand against his heart as he stepped over the threshold. "It hurt, but it was classic."

She closed the door behind him a little harder than necessary. "Yeah, well, you won't think it's so classic when the news about our Lucie and her rich and famous fiancé being on the rocks ends up in the tabloids. Which will be all your fault, by the way."

He leaned a shoulder against the wall and crossed his arms over his chest. "How will it be my fault?"

"Because!" She poked him in the chest. "You got me all fired up with your insults. Reid would never have said something like that about Lucie. He worships the ground she walks on. But it's obvious you wouldn't have the first clue as to how to treat a woman, so how we're going to pull this off for an entire week is beyond me. Then again, when the girl from the front blabs about our little production back there, we'll probably be thrown out on our asses, and then we won't have to worry about it."

She started to turn, but he held her arm captive, preventing her from storming off. "First of all, Jilli isn't going to tell anyone anything."

"Oh really. And why is that?"

"Because she's the contact I told you about. She's in on the whole thing."

That little tidbit zipped through her brain, hitting all the necessary compartments needed to read between the lines. Her eyes widened. "So we didn't have to . . ."

"Make such a big production?" he said with a wide smile. She noticed for the first time he had shallow dimples hidden beneath the short beard growth, adding to his panty-melting charm. Why were all the assholes so damn gorgeous? "Yeah, I know, but I figured we should get in the practice. Besides, now we've gotten our first fight out of the way."

"Oh, you have no idea—"

"Secondly," he said, interrupting her would-be rant as he dropped his amusement as easily as removing a mask, "contrary to your belief, I know exactly how to treat a woman. In every aspect."

The charming, good-natured man she'd met had been obliterated by the serious one now standing before her. Vanessa had a feeling that this man—a man who could no doubt grant a lover's every desire or conjure an enemy's every nightmare—was his true self.

Something had stolen the air from the room. Topaz eyes burned into her, heating her body from the inside out and creating warmth between her legs from the suggestion his words lent. Words. Where were her words? She was never speechless. She argued for a living, for shit's sake.

This man is Dangerous. Capital D intended.

Considering she wasn't planning on going toe-to-toe with him in a cage any time soon, the threat of danger wasn't to her physical person—unless earth-shattering orgasms had the potential to land her in a hospital—but to her emotional sanity.

Then, like the wind changing directions after a storm, he released her arm and the intensity and brought back the happy. Just. Like. That. "Now that we have that out of the way, I'd like to take you to an apology lunch."

She had to tell her brain to stop analyzing his peculiar personality switches and fast-forward to his newest attempt at taking control of their situation. Clearing her throat, she smoothed her hands down her shirt and crossed her arms. "I've already eaten."

"Okay, lunch is out. We'll go get a drink on the beach."

Damn, that sounded good. Not to mention there was a tiny part of her that wanted to know what he'd be like in a public setting, now that she knew the whole thing with Jilli was just his twisted way of amusing himself. Bastard.

"Sorry, but I have things to do. But don't let me stop you. You should go enjoy yourself."

He bit the inside of his cheek as his eyes narrowed in contemplation. "Reid said you'd be a tough opponent."

"Reid's a very smart man."

"Come on, give a guy a chance to atone for his sins. You had to deal with a lot of my shit today. Let me make it up to you. We'll have some drinks and start fresh."

She'd definitely earned a drink. Hell, she'd earned several, in her opinion. Maybe if she let him buy the drink, he'd back off the rest of the week and she wouldn't have to constantly avoid the distraction he was so capable of being. "Fine. We'll go for one drink and call it square. Deal?"

He let loose that spectacular smile, accentuating the strong lines of his stubble-covered jaw. "Deal." He clapped his hands together and made for the door. She followed him and then stopped as soon as he walked onto the porch.

"I'll change and meet you at the bar in ten." And with that, she closed the door on his too-handsome-for-his-own-good face.

Brushing her hands off from a job well done, she started to turn away when she heard him yell, "Why don't you go ahead and get changed? I'll meet you at the bar." She could just barely make out the muffled sound of laughter as he walked away.

The Moana Bar sat in the center of the Mau Loa's pristine beach, less than fifty yards from the ocean. An open square bar in the middle of the sand with stools on all four sides. Like most things in Hawaii, it sported a polished wood structure under a thatched roof with strings of lanterns to act as beacons in the night to thirsty guests. Surrounding that, small tables with umbrellas were scattered in the sand for patrons to sit and eat at or people-watch while they sipped their drinks.

The atmosphere was a fusion of native and tourism: the crescendo of the ocean waves rushing toward the shore, the conversations and laughter of the resort's patrons, and the raucous antics of the bartenders entertaining with spinning bottles of liquor like scenes from Cocktail.

Jackson stood at the bar, enjoying the Heineken in his hand and the memory of Vanessa's reaction to the unnecessary act they'd put on for Jilli. A reaction he'd cut short with his declaration of knowing how to treat a woman, and by the look on her face, it had set things spinning in her head she did not want there. Which made it all the more fun.

Of course, that fun was about to come to a screeching halt. Once he plied her with a drink or two, he needed to tell her the truth. They'd talk to the planner, explain the situation, and Vanessa would be free to make the wedding arrangements and be herself for the rest of her stay.

While despising him and avoiding him like the plague.

Jax took a swig of his beer and wanted to kick his own ass. He wouldn't be in this situation if he'd have just shown up on time like he was supposed to. Then again, if he hadn't been late he probably wouldn't have seen the spitfire side of her that intrigued him in the first place, compelling him to spew lies so she couldn't dismiss and avoid him for the entire week. Of course, this was the most asinine thing he'd done since thinking he could still spar when he forgot his cup. Now he'd be damned if he told her the truth and damned if he didn't. Fuck.

With all the noise, there was no way he'd be able to hear Vanessa coming, which made it all the more odd when he felt compelled to look over his shoulder the moment she approached the table area.

Winding her way through the erratic seating arrangement, she swung her hips to avoid chairs in her path. Either that, or to make every man in a fifty-yard radius forget his point mid-sentence.

Emerald scraps of cloth clung to her breasts with nothing but a gold ring nestled in her cleavage to hold the sides together. The purpose of the white netted skirt tied low around her hips was a mystery. Although it hid the general design and cut of her bottoms, it slashed diagonally to the mid-thigh of her left leg, leaving the creamy expanse of her right leg prominently on display.

As she approached the bar, Jackson assessed her over the top of his mirrored shades and let out a soft whistle. "You vacationing or entering the swimsuit competition in the Miss America pageant?"

Sliding onto the stool next to where he stood, she began, "You see, Jackson—"

"My friends call me Jax."

Vanessa pushed her tortoise shell sunglasses up on her head and regarded him with a twinkle in her green eyes. "Ah, like those annoying pointy little things for kids that always seem to be underfoot." She nodded as though all the world's mysteries suddenly made sense. "I so get that."

Damn, he liked her spunk. "I'll just bet you do," he said, giving her a huge smile he didn't have to fake.

"As I was saying, Jackson," she emphasized with a saccharin-sweet grin, "a girl should always look her best. She never knows when she might meet a handsome stranger at a beach bar who can rescue her from her lunch date."

"Drink date."

She waved her hand dismissively. "Semantics."

Gesturing for the bartender, she ordered herself a Blue Hawaiian, or as she called it, "That big blue thingy I keep seeing." How adorably tourist.

"Unfortunately, you can't get rid of me. How would it look if Lucie left Reid to cavort around the island with another man the week of her wedding?" He didn't bother mentioning he planned on leaving her after they shared their drinks and he came clean about his impulsive fibbing streak.

"Sadly, you're right. But next week, while Reid and Lucie are enjoying their honeymoon on a Mediterranean cruise, I'll still be here and incredibly available."

Jax's gut twisted at the images of a sexy Vanessa being fawned over by every man within a square mile. His brain told him it was none of his damn business how she spent her vacation, and logically speaking, he knew it was right. Unfortunately, he'd always been a man who followed his gut.

Her Blue Hawaiian arrived, and she didn't waste any time sampling it. Lifting the large bowled glass, she sipped the electric blue liquid, made a sound of approval that tightened his groin, then licked the sugar on her lips she'd lifted from the rim.

Clearing his throat to disguise a groan, he ordered a second Heineken and then killed his first. By now, the idea of her spending time with random locals was on its way to giving him an ulcer. His other half—the side he fully acknowledged was more caveman than gentleman—was trying to claw his way free.

Tamping down his irrational shit, he thanked the bartender for the new beer and kept things light. "You know, as your personal host, I feel I'd be shirking my responsibilities if I allowed a bunch of jerks to circle you like sharks around chum."

"I'm sorry," she said with a look of disbelief, "did you just refer to me as fish guts?"

"You are a lawyer." Wink. Drink.

She laughed in the same way his buddy Corey did when they got into a good-natured pissing match about who was the better fighter. "Okay, Maris, I'm giving you fair warning." She gestured back and forth between them. "When this is over with, I have every intention of finding some hot Hawaiian hunk to entertain me for a few days. And should you interfere in any way, shape, or form, I'll be forced to hurt you."

Chuckling, he removed his shades, set them on the bar, and leveled her with patronizing amusement. "You hurt me? That's adorable; truly it is." She opened her mouth to fire back, but he didn't give her the chance. "I will say I'm glad you've decided to have fun with a local boy while you're here, though."

Her mouth closed and a small furrow creased her brow. He loved it when strategy worked.

Crossing his forearms on the bar, he slowly leaned toward her. Her exotic citrusy scent filled his lungs, the smell so intoxicating he resented the need to exhale. Trying to ignore the pang of desire, he lowered his voice and layered on the suggestive tone. "I'm local. Think I might be the man for the job?"

Staring up at him, her jaw slackened, opening her mouth a bit. Testing the waters, he sucked his bottom lip between his teeth and let it drag itself free. Her eyes dropped and fixated, darkening with interest.

And Bingo was his name-o.

"I think that's a yes, princess." He allowed himself the satisfaction of a half smile before bringing his beer up for a victory sip.

Snapping out of her temporary trance, she let out an indignant huff. "Please. You have heat stroke if you think I'd even let you apply for the job."

Laughing at her indignation, Jackson pried his eyes from Vanessa's long enough to sign his tab. Points for him. It was a damn hard thing to accomplish. She was so different from the women he'd been around the last decade. Island girls typically had happy-go-lucky, easy-going, go-with-the-flow personalities. But she was full of opposites. Fire and ice. Both the calm and the storm.

And her eyes were the purest shade of green. They weren't brownish green or hazel green. She turned her head in his direction, rewarding him with the very things that mesmerized him, even if it was in the form of a glare. He looked for the telltale, barely visible rim revealing them as counterfeits . . . and found none.

"You don't wear contacts," he stated.

A feathery eyebrow hitched up her forehead. "You say that like you're surprised."

"I am. Usually color like that only comes from cosmetic lenses. I've never seen authentic eyes the shade of yours before." A small sigh accompanied a roll of said beautiful eyes. Amused at her assumption, he added, "That wasn't a line."

"You've been throwing innuendos at me since the airport, Jackson. Why wouldn't I think that was a line?"

He dropped one arm from the counter and turned his entire body toward her. She was taller than most women—he guessed somewhere around five-nine, five-ten—but at six-four he still had a huge advantage. Especially since she was sitting and he wasn't.

Letting his gaze slowly trail over every exposed inch, he made her wait, not saying a word until he'd thoroughly soaked up every detail. Alabaster skin and smooth curves on a willowy frame. Breasts that filled out her bikini top to perfection with tight nipples pushing against . . . and this train of thought was nothing but a hard-on wreck waiting to happen. His cargo shorts were in serious danger of taking on a new shape.

Dragging his eyes back up, he met the emerald pools and told her the God's honest truth. "I don't use lines. I use compliments. And telling a woman something she already knows isn't a compliment. You have to tell her true things she doesn't know."

"Okay," she said, "I'll bite. What would you say to me?"

He tucked a stray curl whipping across her face behind her ear, then slowly trailed his finger down the long column of her throat as his eyes followed. "I'd tell you how I think seeing the curves of your silhouette against a Hawaiian sunset would be absolutely breathtaking."

She reached up and pulled his hand away, but when he met her gaze she must have forgotten her purpose and their hands stayed clasped together between them. He rubbed his thumb over her knuckles just once and spoke again. "I'd tell you you're the most intriguing woman I've ever met, and I'm dying to discover what's underneath that sexy confidence you wear so well."

He lowered their hands and gently released hers. He waited for a verbal backlash, a scoff, anything that would prove he was seeing something that wasn't really there. But she did none of those things. Simply sat there, stone still, her chest the only thing moving as she took in shallow breaths of the ocean air.

He'd affected her.

A burst of adrenaline kicked in from the small victory. Holding back a smile, he broke eye contact to give her a short reprieve, which she used right away to take several big sips of her cocktail while he drank his beer.

"So, V, tell me about yourself."

"Your sister calls me Nessie. Most people do."

"I know your ancestors hail from Scotland, what with that hair and last name and all, but you don't look like an elusive aquatic dinosaur hiding in a loch to me. I'll stick with V."

"Strange," she said in the sarcastic tone he was growing accustomed to from her. "Lucie never mentioned how incredibly annoying you are."

She's back, ladies and gentlemen.

"That's a shame because it's one of my finer qualities." As he'd hoped, the ridiculous comment cracked a
smile over her stoic face. "Back to the original topic,
though: what's your story?"

She fiddled with the bright blue paper umbrella hanging on the rim of her drink. "Nothing exciting. Just a big
city girl who went to college in Nevada and became a
lawyer."

"You any good?"

"They don't call me the Red Viper in the courtroom
for nothing, sweetie."

"I'll just bet they don't."

"So now I spend all my time putting the bad guys
away in big cages." She pinned him with the look he was
beginning to recognize as one that preceded any sort of
dig on his person. "You know, kind of like you."

Bingo. He'd have her figured out in no time. "I'm a
bad guy in a big cage, huh?"

"You are a cage fighter, are you not?"

He smiled. "So what accounts for the 'bad' part?"

She finished her drink, dropped her sunglasses in
place as she stood, and somehow managed to seem as
though she looked down on him and not the other way
around. "That has yet to be seen, Mr. Maris, but I have
no doubt whatsoever that it's the absolute truth. Thanks
for the drink."

The mixed comment of his bad nature and her speaking the truth was flippant at best, but because of his re-
cent deception, it hit home a little too hard. That's why,
as she dismissed him for the fourth time in half as many
hours, hips swaying like palm fronds in the breeze, he
blurted out yet another thing that did absolutely nothing
to correct the situation.

"Come swimming with me."

She didn't even pause in her steps. "Another time maybe."

"Now's as good a time as any, V."

"Later, Jackson," she said with a dismissive wave over her shoulder.

Yeah right. She didn't intend on doing anything with him later.

Yet.

"Would you be interested in a deal, Counselor?"

Vanessa halted mid-retreat and bit the corner of her lip. A deal? Vaguely feeling like a mouse sniffing cheese in a trap, she turned and crossed her arms. Narrowing her eyes, she studied him, trying to figure out his angle, but he was impossible to read. Leaning back, elbows resting on the bar behind him, his face boasted that damn smile that melted her insides while he looked for all the world like he hadn't a care. That was all she had to go on, and it told her absolute jack shit.

"What kind of deal?"

"If you come for a swim with me, I promise to not overact during the times we need to be a couple."

She raised her chin and squared her shoulders. "And if I don't?"

His smile morphed into a wicked grin. "I hope you enjoy public displays of affection."

Desperate to keep her face from breaking into the smile it wanted to let through, she sucked her cheeks in just enough to bite down on them. The worst part was knowing that if it weren't for her damn pride, Jackson would be charming the bikini bottoms off her right about now. Figuratively speaking, of course. She normally wasn't such a sourpuss, but the whole situation—starting with the airport—had rubbed her the wrong way, and she was too stubborn to let it go just yet.

"Whaddaya say, V? Quaint couple or obnoxious newlyweds?"

"You can't be serious." Oh, he was serious all right. As a death sentence. She could read at least that much about him. Trying another tack, she said, "You're not even in your suit."

"Last I checked, the ocean didn't have a dress code." Starting at the top, he began unbuttoning his shirt, exposing several inches of gloriously tanned skin with each flick of his fingers. He kicked off his sandals, shrugged out of his shirt, and dropped it on the stool without ever taking his eyes from her. "Come swimming with me."

Good Lord, he was stunning. Vanessa had dated plenty of guys, and some of them were in impeccable shape, but not one of them held a candle to the man standing in front of her. He looked like a bronzed god, all muscled and toned.

Broad shoulders framed a defined chest with dark, flat nipples she'd like to flick her tongue over. His torso, completely smooth and hair-free, lent complete access to the visual treat that were the hills and valleys of his abs. And those obliques that arrowed in a V to taper down to his—Oh, damn, snap out of it, Nessie.

"I could just thwart your attempts at affection, you know." Holy shit, she couldn't stop! A swim actually sounded amazing. Water had never looked so inviting. But for the life of her, she couldn't accept the invitation without eliminating all the possible outs first.

"You could. But then people would get the impression Reid and Lucie were on the rocks before they even get hitched." He winked. "What else you got?"

Nothing, that's what. A big. Fat. Nothing. And if

something deep inside her started jumping for joy, it was only because she wanted to wade into the Pacific waves. Not because she wanted to have fun with her best friend's older brother.

"Fine, I'll play it your way. I was planning on swimming later anyway, so all I'm doing is moving up my own plans."

Untying the knot at her hip, she removed her sarong and crossed the few feet to where he stood. She tossed it over his head and kept walking past him toward the edge of the water, making sure that her hips swayed like a supermodel on a Paris catwalk. Looking over her shoulder, she saw the very thing she'd hoped for: Jackson, clutching her sarong and staring after her with an awestruck look on his face. She didn't bother hiding her smug satisfaction when she called back, "Now who's not ready for a swim?" and then dismissed him as she waded into the waves lapping at the beach.

The warm water felt heavenly, and the sand squished between her wriggling toes. Her long curls whipped around her face in the salty ocean breeze. Just as she tucked the sides behind her ears, a pair of muscled arms grabbed her from behind and yanked her off her feet. She squealed in protest and tried to squirm free, but her annoying assailant refused to listen to her pleas for release. Probably because she couldn't stop herself from laughing as he splashed into deeper waters.

"Jackson, come on, put me down!"

"Not on your life, MacGregor. You're a cruel woman teasing me like that, and you need to be punished." Then he unceremoniously tossed her into an ebbing wave.

She sank under the surface, but then quickly pushed up from the bottom. As she sprang to her feet, the salty water streamed into her mouth and she spit it out, pushing the hair out of her face and taking in big gulps of air.

It didn't take her long to find the giant of a man standing a couple feet away, laughing his ever-loving ass off.

Narrowing her eyes, she sank back under the water, grabbed his ankles, and yanked them toward her as hard as she could before breaking through the top of the water . . . just in time to see the end of his backward fall. The ensuing splash drenched her again, but it didn't wash away her smile as he resurfaced and used his hands to squeegee his face.

His look of surprise morphed into the evil grin of a predator homing in on his prey. Lowering his arms out to his sides, he flexed his fingers like he was preparing to draw his guns at high noon or ready himself for an epic takedown. Since he wasn't wearing a hip holster with his cargo shorts, she assumed it to be the latter.

She started to back up, one slow step at a time. But every time she stepped back, he stepped forward. "Jackson, I only returned the favor. We're even now." Another step back. Another step forward. "Come on, what's fair is fair, right?" Another step. A quick glance to gauge the distance to the safety of the bar. Damn it. Too far. And he knew it.

Mischief danced in his eyes, and the devil drew up the corners of his lips. The low rumble of his laughter made the tiny hairs on the back of her neck stand on end.

"Jackson?"

"Run, little rabbit," he said. "Run."

Vanessa whispered a curse and spun around to make a break for the beach. An attempt that proved to be as futile as they'd both known it would be.

No sooner had she made it five feet than he growled and swept her up, hoisting her over his shoulder like a sack of potatoes.

"Jackson Maris, you put me down right this instant!"

She watched the beach get farther and farther away

as he plodded through the foaming waves, carrying her into deeper water yet again. "Are you listening to me?" Frustrated that he didn't have the decency to answer her, she did the first thing that came to mind . . . she slapped his ass as hard as she could.

He stilled, his muscles tensing underneath her, making her instantly regret her action. "Did you just spank me?"

"Umm . . ."

With an effortless heft, he rearranged her in one fluid motion until he was cradling her in his arms so he could look her in the face. She kept her arms around his neck, since the chance of him suddenly dropping her was pretty high.

"That's the first time anyone's dared try that," he said, sounding amused.

She didn't doubt it. The image of this big, strong man getting spanked in any capacity was ludicrous enough to make her laugh, but she bit the inside of one cheek to hold it in. "Then you could probably use a little discipline."

"You think so, huh?" She nodded. He looked up at the clear sky as though giving it some thought, then shook his head. "I disagree. However . . ." Bending his head close to hers, he leveled her with a look that warmed her in places it shouldn't. And when he spoke, his words were coated in carnal promises. "I can give you spankings that'll have you begging for more."

Her breath caught in her throat as she lost herself to the picture in her mind. Tingling started from deep in her belly and spread to her extremities. He leaned in, so close they shared the same air. Oh, God, he was going to kiss her, and for the life of her, she couldn't remember why it was a bad idea. Her fingers clenched behind his neck in anticipation.

The moment before their lips touched, he paused and said, "I'd be happy to show you what I mean later. But you'll have to ask me nicely."

Jackson couldn't have shocked her any less if he'd slapped her in the face.

He drew back with that shit-eating grin he wore so well. He'd known exactly what he was doing. She'd bet he never even intended on kissing her. The heat of desire previously curling through her body now burned in her veins, boiling her blood in preparation for battle.

"Oh, you are so—"

Apparently he didn't care because he tossed her back over his shoulder. She squealed from the momentary weightless feeling, followed by an oof when her stomach landed on his shoulder. "Before you get all pompous on me again, princess, you should think about my offer." He ran a finger over the outline of her bikini, making her aware for the first time just how close her backside was to his face. She felt his warm breath against her skin.

"I promise you'll like it, V."

If she hadn't heard the smartass smile behind his offer she would've already plotted the demise of his family jewels. But he didn't have to know they were safe. "You can spank me if I get to shave your balls with a straight razor." Then she added in a mocking tone, "I promise I won't slip, Jax."

His laugh rumbled in his chest. A moment later she found herself flying through the air yet again just before landing butt-first into the sea. This time, though, she'd been prepared and had taken a big breath. Once fully submerged, she turned over and swam underwater away from him until her lungs burned and she had to come up for air.

Spinning around to see how far she'd gone was pointless. Jackson had swum after her. "Okay, I concede," she said, holding her hands up in resignation. "You win. Now will you please stop tossing me on my ass?"

"As long as you concede, yes, I'll stop."

"Good, because I have to go."

"What are you talking about? We were just starting to have fun."

She looked over at him and had to remind herself to keep breathing. The sun hitting the water trailing over his muscles made it look like diamonds dripped from his body. His cargo shorts, heavy with retained water, hung deliciously low on his hips, showing off that incredible V. He really was something to behold.

She gave herself a mental shake and continued walking back to their things at the bar. "Success comes from ninety percent work and ten percent play, and that," she said, pointing to where he'd recently tossed her, "was my ten percent for the day." Adjusting the back of her bottoms to ensure they weren't skewed into a compromising position, she trudged toward the beach.

Aaaaaand Jackson followed. Naturally, she thought. This guy didn't know the meaning of "quit while you're ahead."

"Is that one of your seven rules?"

Her feet glued themselves to where the sand met the sea and her head whipped around. "Excuse me?"

"You know, your rules that you follow or whatever."

"How do you know about those?"

He shrugged a shoulder as he dragged a hand over his dark hair. "I asked Reid what your deal was with lying. He told me you have a list of rules you live by, that's all. Are they supposed to be a secret?"

The question took her aback. "No, not necessarily. But they're personal, so they're not something I go around advertising. And, no, that isn't one of the rules. More like a mantra, I guess."

They picked up their walk again, trudging through the soft white sand toward the bar. She'd hoped claiming her rules as "personal" would prevent further discussion, but she was beginning to see Jackson as a junkyard dog that wouldn't let go once he'd latched onto something.

"So why do you have them?"

She shrugged. "They keep me in line with the way I want to live my life and the kind of people I want to surround myself with."

"Wow. That sounds really . . ." He seemed to be searching for a polite way to say what he really thought. "Careful."

She shook her head and smiled, refusing to let him get under her skin any more.

When she didn't take the bait, he continued. "Where'd you get the idea for something like that anyway?"

It was on the tip of her tongue to tell him she'd gotten it from Gandhi's life teachings or something equally profound . . . but that would be breaking Rule #6.

"It doesn't matter where I got the idea. What matters is that they mean something to me. And they work. You should try coming up with a few of your own. I'd bet you could use a little structure in your life."

"I have plenty of structure when it comes to my training. I don't need it for anything else."

She laughed. "Oh, yes, you do."

Crossing his arms, he braced his legs shoulder-width apart. A stance she now recognized as his challenge-issuing pose. Also, his mega-alpha super-hot pose. "Give me a rule you think I should have."

"How about 'Anything other than early,'" she said, pinning him with a meaningful look, "'is late.'" She waited only a few beats for his next witty remark. When one didn't seem to be forthcoming, she mentally marked it as a win in her column. Shabba! "Now if you'll excuse me, I have an appointment with the wedding coordinator at four o'clock, and although it's not one of my rules, I still refuse to be late."

"We."

"What?"

"We have an appointment with the coordinator."

"Oh, that's not necessary. I can take care of it."

Please let me take care of it. Her emotions were all over the place around him, and she didn't have the first clue as to what to do about it. She needed a few hours to herself. Time to flush all things Jackson from her mind. Time to gird her loins before she needed to act like half of a couple in love.

"I don't doubt your capabilities, V, but I don't think Reid would let Lucie take care of everything herself. After all, as you so aptly pointed out earlier today, Reid is a very attentive man." He took her hand and held it between his, the roughness of his fingers a scintillating whisper of possibilities. "In fact, I doubt he'd ever let Lucie out of his sight."

Yep. Capital D Dangerous.

She tried to clear her throat delicately to disguise her sudden unease. "So, I take it you plan on attending all of the appointments this week?"

Cue shit-eating grin. "Oh, yeah."

She withdrew her hand from his, ignoring the shiver that zipped down her spine as his calluses dragged over her skin, and gave him her best you don't faze me smile. "Fantastic."

With that she walked the rest of the way to the bar, retrieved her things, and headed toward the bungalow without looking to see if he followed. As her feet carried her closer to her room, she fiercely prayed for a miraculous mandatory evacuation of every MMA fighter on the island.

* * *

Jackson stood outside the Honu Café where Vanessa was due to meet the wedding coordinator. Sensing she needed some time to herself earlier, he'd gone home, showered, and changed into a dry pair of cargo shorts and a blue polo. Most days he was either surfing or training, so it wasn't often he wore anything other than board shorts or athletic shorts. And even though he looked identical to every other guy at the resort who wasn't poolside or oceanside, he still felt overdressed.

As a couple exited the café, he asked, "Excuse me, can you tell me what time it is?"

"Certainly," the woman said, checking her slim wristwatch. "It's ten till four."

He offered her a warm smile. "Mahalo." Perfect. He'd made sure he was plenty early to prove to her he wasn't a total slacker. He could be on time to something if he had to be. Hell, he was never late for training.

Leaning back against the wall, he put his hands in his pockets and thought about his afternoon with her. She'd accepted his deal, as he'd known she would, even though she claimed it was only because she wanted to and had nothing to do with his proposition. There was still a lot he didn't know about Vanessa MacGregor, but one thing he knew for sure was that she hated losing control. She needed things to be on her terms at all times.

Unfortunately for her, even though he'd adapted to a much more laid-back way of life, he was still very used to being in control. However, when he consciously thought about it, control wasn't something he needed. Outside of the cage and the bedroom, anyway. But old habits die hard, and raising a younger sister for five years made him accustomed to playing leader to Lucie's follower.

Beyond that, he was used to women playing coy

with him. They liked to think of themselves as hard to get, pulling all the strings and leading the guy along by the short-hairs. And he happily played along. To an extent. Then he flipped the switch and took hold of the reins. Especially during sex. He preferred to have the control. Well, perhaps "preferred" wasn't the right word. It was more how he was hardwired.

But the women he'd been with hadn't posed any sort of challenge. They were like sheep in wolves' clothing. They liked to think they were tough, but when he crooked his finger, the ruse dropped and they followed his lead.

Vanessa was different. She didn't merely pretend; she was a wolf. When he pushed, she pushed back. He never would've thought he'd be attracted to someone so strong-minded, but he couldn't get her out of his head. She was like a ball of fire, ready to explode, and he was a pyromaniac who couldn't bring himself to keep his distance. Time would tell what sort of havoc she would wreak. Until then, he had every intention of enjoying the fireworks.

A wry smile spread over his face as he remembered the way she threw her skirt on him and walked toward the water like she owned the very sand under her feet.

"I thought maybe you'd changed your mind."

He'd been so wrapped up in his thoughts about her that he hadn't even seen her approach. She looked beautiful in a sundress with large red hibiscus flowers splashed across a white background. Casual and graceful. "You mean you were hoping I'd changed my mind."

"That's not what I said."

"You didn't have to," he said, offering an understanding smile. "That's okay, I don't blame you. I didn't make things easy on you today. But I promise to be on my best behavior from now on."

Her eyelashes nearly twined as she scrutinized him. "Why the change of heart?"

"Aren't you going to comment on my punctuality?"

To his surprise she did that thing where she tried to stop herself from smiling by biting on her own cheek. It was quite possibly the most adorable thing he'd ever seen a woman do. At last she huffed a sigh and said, "All right, let's go in. But don't say anything. Just let me handle this, okay?"

He winked at her. "Whatever you say, darling." Fat chance, honey.

Jackson held the door for her and followed her into the air-conditioned restaurant. It was one of the more casual eateries the resort offered, if you considered mahogany tables with fine china and centerpieces made of orchids in crystal vases casual.

"Aloha!" A cute girl at the hostess counter smiled like she'd never been so happy to see two people. "Table for two?"

Vanessa jumped in. "Actually, we're here to meet with the wedding coordinator. Can you point us in the right direction?"

"Ah, yes! He told me you'd be arriving and to seat you right away. He should be here shortly."

"Perfect, thank you."

They followed her to a small table in the back with a RESERVED sign in the center. Taking the sign, the girl handed them menus, but Vanessa politely refused. "We won't be eating now, but I'd love an iced tea, please."

Their hostess eagerly nodded and looked to him. "Heineken, thanks." Another nod and she was off.

"I like your sandals," he said.

"My sandals?"

She turned her head and stuck a foot out to the side to examine them as though she'd forgotten what she wore.

Raising an eyebrow in his direction she asked, "Are you a women's shoe expert in your off hours or something?"

"Hell no. I don't have the first clue about fashion."

Her brows drew together, causing her skin to squinch between them. It must be something she did often, probably while hard at work on cases. "Then what exactly is it you like about my current footwear?"

He paused as the waitress set their drinks in front of them, then said, "I appreciate how the heels accentuate your calves."

She studied him with a bemused smile. "I've never had a man compliment my shoes based on how they make my legs look."

"We've already established you've never been complimented properly. And Vanessa . . ." He leaned forward and stared into her gem-colored eyes until her mirth tapered off and her pulse leapt just under her jaw. "I could compliment you properly all night long."

Sitting back, he raised his beer to his lips without breaking eye contact. Watching her watch him intrigued him, and he thought of all sorts of things he'd like for her to watch him do.

"Hi, hello, bonjour, and aloha!"

Jackson turned his head to see a thin reed of a man making his way to them, wearing a pair of white dress shorts and a Hawaiian shirt. He looked like a fashionable Gilligan without the white hat. The guy had an extra bounce in his step that indicated he was either extremely hyper or literally the happiest guy on the planet. He didn't hesitate to hug Vanessa like they were long-lost friends. When he pulled back, he held one of her hands in both of his and sat across from Jackson.

He pointed to the nametag pinned to his breast pocket. "I know it looks like my name is Robért, but it sounds like someone commanding a grizzly in a canoe. Row, bear!" He giggled at a joke he'd no doubt told to thousands of tourists. "Row-bear, get it? My mother's French, but I was born here, which explains both the strange pronunciation and my lack of a French accent."

Vanessa echoed the man's giggle. If it were strictly for Robért's benefit, she was very convincing. Jackson, on the other hand, dragged a hand over his mouth to wipe the amusement from his face at the guy's over-the-circus-top personality.

"Anyhoo," Robért continued, "enough about me. It is so nice to finally meet the both of you. We're going to be the best of friends this week as I make all your dreams come true. We have so much to do before you walk down the aisle, so let's get crack-a-lackin.'"

As Robért chatted on about options for favors, flowers, and other things, Jackson sat and listened. Not to the actual details but to the overabundance of words Robért liked to emphasize. It gave his half of the conversation almost a melodic cadence and certainly made for an entertaining time as a spectator to the whole thing.

As Vanessa started talking about her—or rather, Lucie's—vision for the wedding, Jax took the opportunity to study her. The way she smiled at the flamboyant coordinator almost stole his breath. It was wide, brilliant . . . sincere. She hadn't smiled like that with him, but God did he want her to.

He scooted his chair closer to hers and felt her tense up, but if the coordinator noticed, he didn't let on. Without forethought, he draped his arm over the back of her chair, tipping his body closer to hers. When he used his free hand to tuck her hair behind her ear so he could get a better look at her profile, she jerked back slightly.

Probably realizing she'd reacted out of character for

her role as Lucie, she let out a nervous laugh. "Sorry. I guess I was so wrapped up in our conversation that you startled me."

"No need to explain, honey." Jax moved his arm from the chair to wrap around her. Her bare shoulder fit perfectly in the palm of his hand. Impulsively, he pulled her in and planted a soft kiss at her temple. "You've been jumpy lately from the stress of the wedding."

Through a tight smile, she said, "I suppose you're right."

"Of course I'm right. But, hey," he said, using a finger on her chin to guide her eyes to his, "we're here now, and you have Robért to help you with everything. So I want you to take some deep breaths and try to relax."

Jax wasn't trying to help "Lucie" relax but Vanessa. Her role in the deception had her wound tight. He inhaled long and slow through his nose and was relieved when she followed suit. They exhaled together and some of the deer-in-headlights look vanished from those pretty green eyes. He gave her a reassuring smile and a slight squeeze on her shoulder.

"That's my girl," he said softly. It was only after she smiled wanly and broke eye contact that Jackson realized he'd said that sincerely, not even considering his role as Reid. And he didn't know what to make of that.

An eruption of enthusiastic clapping from the jovial wedding coordinator interrupted any musings on the puzzle. "Oh, you two are ab-so-lute-ly love-ly! This is why I love my job. There's nothing else in the world as precious as new love."

"There certainly isn't, Rob," he answered with a grin.

At the end of the meeting, Robért told them he needed a moment with the hostess to schedule their appetizer-tasting appointment for later that week and Vanessa claimed she needed some air. Ever the doting "husband,"

Jax followed her out into the sultry late-afternoon heat. As soon as the glass door shut behind them, she let out a huge breath and rolled her head around, trying to work out the tightness in her neck and shoulders.

Since they were still in plain view of Robért, Jackson took the opportunity to move behind her and place his hands on her shoulders. Using his thumbs, he rubbed firm circles between her shoulder blades. Letting her head drop to her chest, she melted under his touch, but not for the reasons he'd like.

"Oh, God, that feels so good."

"Why so tense, my pupule wahine?"

She shot him a glare from the side. "Don't try and butter me up with pet names. You know exactly why. Go back on your deals often, Maris?"

"Never."

"Really? Then what do you call all that unnecessary affection you were laying on me in there?"

Drawing her back against his chest, he moved his thumbs to the base of her neck. "Affection is never unnecessary, V."

"Ooh, yeah, right there," she groaned.

Damn, what he wouldn't give to hear her say that under different, less clothed, circumstances.

"It's not like I hauled off and kissed you passionately in front of the guy. Besides," he argued as he turned her to face him, "that's not what's really bothering you." Her stubborn chin raised an inch, but she didn't contest his observation. "What do your rules say about lying, V?"

For a while, he thought she wouldn't answer him. That maybe he'd asked for too much. But then she surprised him. "Never indulge in the poison of lies."

Poison. A person had to have experienced the consequences of some pretty awful lies to consider them poison. And here he was, making her a party in the very thing . . . He gut twisted. Jax wanted to ask her more, to understand, but over the top of her head he noticed Robért exiting the café.

"Okay, we're all set to go. Here's my business card, and I jotted down the date and time for the hors d'oeuvres tasting on the back. If you ever need anything, don't hesitate to call and I'll be here in a jiffy. Sound good?"

Vanessa smiled and said that it did, while Jax held out his hand. Gripping Robért's in a less-than-manly shake, he put on his best Happy Groom show. "Thanks so much, Robért. You've already been a huge help, and I know you're going to make my fiancée's dream wedding come true."

"Oh, please, no need to thank me, Mr. Andrews. Honestly, I can't tell you how excited I am to work on this account. It's so refreshing to work for a couple who is so obviously in love. So many are here just for the glitz and glamour." He looked around briefly to make sure no one was within earshot, then lowered his voice. "I'll take clients like you over those arrogant A-listers any day of the week."

"I understand you have one of those this Saturday."

"Blech. Don't remind me. They only arrived yesterday and already the bride has changed her colors six times and the groom demanded we make Italian food for their Hawaiian wedding. Italian!"

Vanessa looked properly horrified for the man. "Oh my gosh, I can't even imagine. I bet they cause problems right up through the end of the reception."

"Sweetie, you have no idea."

Jax slid his arm around Vanessa's waist. "That's a shame. Lucie and I would have loved to have you as a guest on our big day."

Slapping his chest, Robért gasped, making Jackson think they had a cardiac arrest on their hands. "Oh, that is just the sweetest thing! No one ever asks me to attend. They always just expect it because I'm the coordinator." Waving his hands in front of his face, he blinked back the moisture gathering in his eyes. After a long, awkward few seconds, Robért finally composed himself. "You know what? Screw that other wedding. I'm coming to yours!"

Now it was Jax's turn to have a heart attack, and next to him he felt Vanessa's knees give out. If he hadn't been holding her around her waist, she'd be kissing the paved sidewalk right now. Instantly, they started protesting in the nicest ways possible.

They couldn't expect him to abandon his other clients.

They didn't want him to lose his job.

It really wasn't going to be anything all that spectacular.

The other wedding would look great for his résumé.

But nothing could sway Robért the Sentimental. He had an excuse for everything they'd thrown at him, including informing them that he'd bring in his coordinator friend who "owed him big time" to work the other wedding on Saturday for him.

When there was nothing to do to avoid looking suspicious but pretend to be ecstatic at his change of plans, they said their good-byes and stood in the shade of the café's awning until Robért rounded the corner with an extra bounce in his step. If that were possible.

Without a word, Vanessa extracted herself from his side, spun on her heel, and stalked in the direction of the bungalow.

Fucking hell. Shit had definitely just hit the fan.

He watched her for a few seconds, contemplating his next move, then jogged to catch up with her. "V, come on. Maybe it's not as bad as we think. I'm sure we can figure something out."

Vanessa didn't stop, and her distraught feelings seemed to be growing with every step. "You know, despite the fact that I hated being deceitful, we were doing fine in our roles as Reid and Lucie. He never once questioned our behavior and the plans were off to a great start. Now, because you felt the need to play Prince Charming to the wedding coordinator, he'll be with us every step of the way, including the rehearsal dinner and the wedding!"

"Wow, that's uncanny. You sound just like him." They rounded the corner to the path that led to their home away from home. "The overemphasizing thing sounds more natural when he does it, though."

"You always have something to say about everything, you know that?" She stopped short at the front door and shoved her key in the lock. "Which is precisely the reason I told you to keep your big mouth shut and let me do all the talking!"

He followed her inside and closed the door a little harder than necessary. Now he was getting worked up, too. "Yeah, well, I don't appreciate being told to stay quiet like some yippy dog. I'm not a sidekick, and I'm sure as hell not a mute."

Tossing the keys on the console table by the door, she spun around and poked him in the chest. "No, you're definitely not a mute. Believe me, there's no chance of me ever forgetting that. You haven't shut up since the moment I laid eyes on you. But let me tell you something, Maris," she said, stepping in closer and glaring at him like he was her lifelong nemesis. "You have to know when to talk and when to shut your trap. And as far as I can tell, you have no concept of the latter."

She had no idea the envelope she was pushing. "You're

challenging me, V. Are you sure you wanna go down this road?"

"Ha! You bet your ass I do. In fact, let's play the Quiet Game. The one who makes the first sound loses. How about that?"

"I think that's the best thing you've said all day."

"Good!"

"Fine. Just say when."

"When!"

Vanessa turned, no doubt to stomp off in a huff to ignore him in the silence she thought she'd created, but Jackson wasn't letting her go anywhere. Grabbing her arm, he spun her back to him and caught her in a tight embrace a split second before he crushed his mouth to hers. She froze, her body stringing wire-tight. But then he nipped her bottom lip and all hell broke loose.

She plunged her fingers into his hair and pressed her body closer to his as she opened her mouth to invite him in. Delving inside, he licked over her tongue again and again. His hands splayed across her back and kept her tight to him as his cock grew hard and begged for the extra pressure. The moment he ground it into her, she moaned in the back of her throat. Technically that was a sound, which claimed him as the victor, but it wasn't enough. Her accusations wounded his pride, and he'd prove to her he knew exactly when words weren't necessary. And on top of that, he was going to win her stupid game, because if he didn't, he knew she'd lord it over him. He expected no less from her.

Breaking from her lips, he moved his kisses to her jawline and down her neck. At the bottom where it met her shoulder, he nipped her again before making his way back up. He made a note that every time he used his teeth, her body jerked like electricity shot through her veins. Seems the Red Viper likes the sting of a bite. What luck. So do I.

Jackson spun them around and pushed her back into the wall, pinning her there with his hips to let his hands roam. He cupped a breast and gave a gentle squeeze as he scraped his teeth over the tight cord in her neck.

And that's when it happened. She moaned his name.

He wanted her until he couldn't think from it. But if anything was going to happen between them, she needed to want him, too. And she wasn't there yet.

Though it killed him, he kept to the game. He stilled all movements and whispered in her ear, "I win," then crossed the room, entered the bathroom, and shut the door behind him.

Day 2: Monday

Vanessa sat on the couch, laptop on the coffee table, coffee on the end table. Almost noon and still no sign of Jackson. Which was fine with her. She'd never been more pissed off at a man in all her life. First, he screwed everything up with Robért, and then he had the nerve to not finish what he started.

Shit, what was she saying? She should be grateful he'd had the sense to stop. If she took all of her rules, broke them in a thousand pieces, and molded them into a man, she'd get Jackson. There was no way she was getting involved with him. Right? She nibbled on her lip. Maybe a list of pros and cons would—She shook her head to empty it of that idea. Squash!

After he'd gotten her all worked up the night before and then dumped her for what she hoped had been a shower so cold his balls got frostbite, she'd gone to dinner and then for a walk on the beach to clear her mind. By the time she returned, she felt more levelheaded about the situation. She was a professional and somehow she'd figure out how to get them out of the mess they were in. Until then, she'd play along so Lucie didn't lose her dream wedding. She refused to fail her friend.

Vanessa had steeled herself and prepared for another confrontation as she'd walked into her bungalow, but a quick look around the room had shown it empty. It wasn't until she checked the small private yard that she found Jackson, in nothing but a pair of boxer briefs, sleeping in the hammock.

Relief and disappointment had washed over her, which then added confusion to the mix. Why would she be disappointed he was sleeping? It wasn't like she'd looked forward to dealing with him after what happened. When she hadn't been able to answer her own question, she took advantage of studying him for as long as she liked without social repercussions.

One arm was bent over his head and his other hand rested on his stomach. His face was turned to the side, giving her a beautiful view of his profile. Straight nose, high cheekbones, and a hard square jaw. She imagined a jaw like that could take more than its fair share of punches before affecting it much. His beard was notice-able now, having grown all day. The moonlight slid over his bare chest, tempting her to reach out and feel if it was as smooth as it looked.

Her gaze drifted lower. She tried using the Jedi mind trick to move his hand from his stomach, but it didn't work. Shocker. With most of his washboard abs covered, she realized his hand was sexy in its own right. Strong with long fingers and sprinkled with a few white scars. Only hours earlier that hand had squeezed her breast and the mere memory of it had the butterflies kicking up dust in her belly.

A trail of dark hair beneath his belly button gained her attention. He didn't seem to be an overly hairy man, but he still had a light path that led to the—Whoa. Her eyes settled on the maroon pair of underwear. Or rather, what was inside the underwear. She told herself to look away. This bordered on inappropriate and could arguably be violating the man on some subconscious level. And still she stared.

Lying in a hammock, sleeping as peacefully as could be, was a giant of a mostly naked man who was undeniably, and quite impressively . . . hard.

The tight material of his boxer briefs didn't allow it the full northerly direction it wanted, but it didn't let that hinder it. At some point her mouth gaped. She clamped it shut again with a snap of her teeth. Then she spun on her heel and raced to the bedroom.

She took a long shower and then hopped into bed, but every time she closed her eyes she saw Jackson's hard-on on the inside of her lids. After an hour of lying there, she'd resorted to popping a Benadryl for a pleasant eight-hour coma. By the time she'd awakened, Jackson was gone so she met Robért to go over centerpieces and linens by herself.

Vanessa looked up from her laptop when she heard a key in the door. Jackson walked in with a brilliant smile, freshly shaven and showered, it seemed, in a yellow pair of board shorts—she wondered how many pairs of those he had—and a T-shirt that said, LET'S DO STUFF TO-NIGHT THAT MAKES TOMORROW AWKWARD.

"Good morning, beautiful. Sleep well?"

The cheerful attitude threw her for a loop, but only briefly. She offered a small smile in return—she wasn't sure what his game was yet, but she'd be damned if she let him be the only "bigger person"—and said, "Yes, I did, thank you. Of course, I had the most comfortable bed in the world, whereas you slept all night in a hammock. How was that?"

He set the large duffel he'd brought in on the floor and sat beside her. "Are you kidding? Sleeping in a hammock that sways in the breeze underneath the stars? I loved it."

She picked up her coffee mug and mumbled, "You clearly loved something."

"What was that?"

"Nothing. So what time did you leave this morning? Where did you go?"

"Am I being examined on the stand, Counselor?"

"Just making conversation. Believe me, if I were examining you on the witness stand, you'd know it by the fear clawing your gut."

"Only the guilty have claw marks in their guts. What makes you think I'd ever be guilty of something?"

She shrugged a shoulder. "You're a man. That's already a huge strike against you, since men find it almost impossible to behave like decent human beings for very long. Eventually you all screw up big."

"Ouch. That's a huge generalization, don't you think?"

"Yes, I do. Unfortunately, I haven't been proven wrong yet."

"So you're telling me I'm guilty until proven innocent. Is that it?"

She stood from the couch and crossed to the small kitchen to refill her coffee. "Haven't you ever heard the expression, 'Expect the worst and hope for the best'?"

"Yeah, but that's for things like planning parties. You hope for great weather but still set up a tent in case it rains. It's generally not used in relation to people. That's downright cynical."

"True. But the best prediction of the future is looking at the past."

She hadn't heard him cross the room, but suddenly he appeared at her side, standing so close his body heat penetrated her thin cami. When he spoke, his voice was soft, concerned. "How many men have hurt you, V?"

"Men I've had relationships with?" He inclined his head in the affirmative. Clutching her coffee mug in front of her like a shield of armor, she turned to him and told him the absolute truth. "None."

Jackson watched Vanessa walk back to the couch and settle in with her laptop again. Something was off about her answer. She was so jaded when it came to men and relationships, and yet no one had hurt her in the past? It didn't make any sense. She was a puzzle with missing pieces, and he wanted to find them.

"How long do you plan on working today?"

She looked up briefly, then continued jotting notes on a yellow legal pad on her knee. "I don't know, probably for a while yet."

"Have you been doing that all morning?"

"Yes, I have. What were you doing all morning?"

He smiled and leaned his hips back on the counter. "Afraid I'd run off with the maid, darling?"

She looked up, gave him an exaggerated smile, and batted her eyes innocently. "I'd hoped."

He slapped a hand over his heart. "Wife, you wound me."

"I'm not your wife yet, sugarbug, and once I can figure it out, I won't be your fiancée for much longer, either."

"Well," he said, rubbing his hands together, "then I'd better make the best of it until then. You've got exactly a half hour left to toil on those boring-ass files before I whisk you away from here."

"Since when did fiancé become interchangeable with master? I'm not going anywhere until I'm damn good and ready."

He walked over, cupped her chin in his hand, and kissed her firmly on the mouth. "Then get damn good and ready in exactly half an hour." Then he left the bungalow and a stunned redhead behind.

It took him only about twenty minutes to get the things he needed for their afternoon. He'd hunted down Robért, who had only been too happy to help him put a picnic basket together with food from one of the restaurants and some bottles of water. Since he had a few extra minutes, he stopped at the beach bar and enjoyed the view of the crystal blue ocean and chatted with the bartender.

Thirty minutes past the time he'd left, he walked up the path to the bungalow with basket in hand, fully expecting to find Vanessa in the same spot he'd left her. But to his surprise she was sitting in one of the Adirondack chairs on the front lanai, arms crossed and a stern look on her face.

"You didn't tell me how to prepare."

"Uh . . . what?"

"I have no idea what we're doing or where we're going. How am I supposed to know what to wear or if I need to bring anything? If we're going sightseeing then I'll want to wear shorts and a cute top and comfortable shoes for extended walking. If we're going swimming somewhere then I'll want to wear a suit and flip-flops. If we're going to lunch in one of the restaurants at the resort I have to dress up a little, which is neither of the outfits I mentioned previously. And that doesn't even cover my makeup and hair."

Jackson stood still, not wanting to make any sudden movements and scare the animal into an attack frenzy. "Holy shit, are all women like this? If you told me to be ready in a half hour I would've made sure I wasn't indecently exposed, then pulled a sixer of beer out of the fridge for the trip."

She threw her hands up and let them fall to slap her thighs in frustration. "Why am I not surprised?"

That's when it hit him; this wasn't anger. It was distress because she didn't have control over the situation. She stopped working, so she obviously wanted to enjoy an afternoon out of the house, but given the circumstances, she didn't know how.

Setting the basket on the steps, he walked over to her and brought her up by her hands. "I'm sorry. I didn't realize you needed more information. Next time I'll make sure you at least have an idea of how to prepare for any surprises I make for you. Deal?"

"Next time?" Her face softened and the sparks quelled in her green eyes. "You plan on giving me more surprises?"

He hadn't really thought about what he said, but now he took a few moments to evaluate it. "Yeah, I think I will. I don't have anything in mind at the moment, but something tells me I'm going to like keeping you on your toes."

She bit the corner of her lip and lowered her eyes. "Jackson, about last night . . ."

With a finger he lifted her face, forcing her to meet his gaze. "What about it?"

"I acted like you'd done something on purpose to make this week difficult for us, which is ridiculous. I'm sorry I yelled at you."

The idea wasn't ridiculous at all. A pang of guilt struck him right in the chest, but though his head told him to tell her the truth right then and there, something else told him to hold on to this time with her just a little while longer.

He tried for an easy smile and said, "I didn't exactly take the high road with the stunt I pulled to win your game. So we'll call it even, okay?"

"True," she said, returning his smile. "So, what am I wearing?"

"A thong and stilettos."

Her jaw dropped.

"What?" he asked with a look of innocence. "You didn't mean in my fantasies?"

She laughed and shoved him away.

"Beachwear," he finally answered. "And you can put a suit on underneath in case you want to lay out or jump in the ocean. If you want to read or nap in the sun, then I'll entertain myself with a little surfing. The goal is to relax and enjoy Mother Nature."

"That sounds great. I'll be ready in just a few minutes."

Jackson retrieved the basket and waited while she changed. They drove to one of his favorite spots, a secluded beach only the locals knew about, so it wasn't clogged with tourists. He parked his Jeep and took the picnic basket and other supplies to a nice spot next to a high cliff. He spread two blankets next to each other, one in the sun and one in the shade of the cliff, so she could get out of the sun if she needed to. With her fair complexion, he was afraid she'd get a tan like a lobster.

"Jax, this is . . . absolutely the most beautiful place I've ever seen."

He liked the fact she used his nickname and hoped it meant she was starting to like him, if only a little. Standing behind her, he tentatively laid his hands on her hips, unsure of how she'd react. Just because he fought a hard-on every time she looked his way didn't mean she wanted any affection from him. When she relaxed against his chest on a sigh, he felt a high rush through him like when he knew he'd won the first round of a match. Feeling bolder, he circled his arms around her and rested his chin on the top of her head as he tried to view the scape through her eyes.

Cotton-ball clouds lined a powder blue sky and met the royal blue ocean in a flawless horizon. As the eye traveled in toward the shore, royal turned to cerulean, which turned to aqua, and each with several shades in between until the clear water finally met the white beach. To the right, black cliffs covered in a myriad of foliage stretched up into the sky and out into the ocean, tying everything together in a magnificent package of paradise.

"Yeah. It's in my top three favorite spots."

"Will you show me the other two before I leave?"

The question took him by surprise. This was in second place. The third one wasn't so much picturesque as it was his favorite hangout spot with friends, so he could for sure take her there.

But his absolute favorite spot was very private to him. Though he wasn't the only one who knew about it, his "neighbors" rarely hiked that far up the mountain to enjoy it. He thought of it as his own slice of heaven, a place to think and reflect. A place he'd never shown anyone before.

He pictured taking Vanessa, seeing her there in his place, and surprisingly it didn't bother him like he thought it would. In fact, now that the idea was in his head, he kind of wanted her there. Besides, soon she'd be gone, so it wasn't like he had to worry about her randomly intruding on his privacy in the future.

Remembering he hadn't yet answered her, he said, "Definitely."

"Good," she said, stepping away from him. "Now, what's in the basket? Because I'm starved."

They sat next to each other on the sun-drenched blanket. Vanessa licked the strawberry juice from her fingers and moaned in pure foodie bliss. Jackson had somehow wrangled one of the resort chefs into packing a veritable feast, and she'd eaten until she passed "stuffed" about three times over.

As he drank some water and watched shore birds play in the surf, she took the time to study his tattoo stretching across his shoulder and bicep. She'd never been one of those girls enamored with ink, but she found the images in Jackson's rather beautiful in a masculine way.

Waves inside a black band wrapped around his bicep. From that, ocean waves arced up and over his shoulder with other more geometric-looking waves. Everything was in stark black with the exception of four cherry blossoms with red petals and yellow centers. Two of them were in the middle of the design and the other two were riding the crest of a giant swell.

"Does your tattoo have a meaning behind it?"

He looked at his arm, then up at her. "Sort of. I wanted something to represent the culture here and show my love for the ocean and how much it's become a part of me since I moved to the island. Also, Maori tattoos are believed to have protective qualities, so putting the waves on me is supposed to keep me safe when I surf. But the flowers are really the only things that have any true symbolism."

"Which is what?" Too pushy. "Sorry, you don't have to answer that."

"It's okay. Cherry blossoms were my mom's favorite flower. The two inside the main part of the tattoo represent Lucie and me, still trying to make our way through life." He lowered his head, clearly focusing on the two flowers riding the wave at the top of his shoulder. "These represent our parents . . . swept away from us by powerful things we couldn't control."

Vanessa's heart broke. She couldn't imagine losing parents who loved you. It must have been so hard for him and Lucie. Probably still was. "I'm sorry, Jackson. It's a beautiful tattoo."

"Thanks." He gave her a warm smile. "Did you get enough to eat?"

"Oh my God, are you kidding? I feel like I could give birth to a Vegas buffet right now. That was so good. Did you have to charm the pants off a hostess to sneak all that out for you?"

Leaning back on one hand with his other arm propped on his bent leg, he raised his left eyebrow, the one with the sexy scar running through it.

"Is that what you think of me? That I'm just some play-boy who gets what he wants by sleeping with women?"

"I don't know. Are you?" Please say yes so I can hate you and be done with this insane attraction.

"I'm not sure," he said with a teasing smirk. "I've forgotten all the other women since I've met you."

She laughed and shook her head. "You're so full of shit your eyes should be brown."

"Okay, that might be a bit of a stretch." The wide smile slowly faded. Topaz eyes enslaved her with a sudden seriousness she hadn't expected, and her fading laughter died in her throat.

The intensity of his gaze, and what it meant, unnerved her. "What?"

The hand not supporting his weight lifted to the side of her face. He kept his touch so light she wondered how hands meant to destroy could be so incredibly gentle.

"There is something I haven't been able to forget," he said, his voice gruff.

Vanessa swallowed hard as his thumb caressed over her cheekbone, the rough pad causing tingles in its wake. "And what's that?"

His eyes abandoned hers to settle on her mouth, and his thumb followed and traced the fullness of her lower lip. "The way you responded to my kisses last night. And how badly I want to kiss you again."

He pulled lightly in the center until her mouth parted and ran his thumb along the edge of her bottom teeth. The tip of her tongue met the tip of his thumb as she licked, hesitantly at first, then more boldly. The hint of the sweet pineapple he'd eaten earlier made her mouth water and the simulated invasion made her sex ache.

Their bodies leaned toward each other of their own volition, and now they were halfway to an embrace. Even sitting, he towered over her. Not many men were much taller than her, but Jackson was large enough to make her feel almost dainty.

His breathing became ragged as he watched her tongue swirl around his thumb. Then she closed her lips and sucked. He groaned and a wash of heady power gave her the idea to get back at him for the stunt he pulled on her last night.

Her breasts felt heavy in the bikini she wore beneath her tank. She wondered if his body was just as affected but didn't take her eyes from his face. Finally, to prove he didn't completely run the show, she opened her mouth, tilted her head back to get the angle she needed, and bit the pad of his thumb. Hard.

She'd expected him to jerk his thumb away and curse. She'd planned on laughing at his shock and then exact her revenge by leaving him hungry for more. But she thought wrong. Instead of cursing, he growled in pleasure.

"If we weren't on a public beach right now, I'd show you exactly how much that turned me on. For now you have a reprieve. Later . . . you won't."

"And if I don't want you to show me anything?"

Leaning in the rest of the way, Jax sipped at her lips once, twice, three times, and then captured them in a slow and sensual kiss that made her feel cherished and wanted. When at last he pulled away, he grinned and said, "Then I'll just have to change your mind."

Ordering herself to pull it together, Vanessa hoped she didn't appear as breathless as she felt. "You're not off to a bad start."

"Glad to hear it. Now I'm going to go surf off this raging hard-on while you relax."

She couldn't help but laugh. "Good luck with that."

"I'll need it. It'll probably throw off my balance." He winked. She rolled her eyes. "Be good while I'm away, bride-to-be."

"We're not at the resort, Jax."

"I know," he said with another wink before grabbing his board and running into the waves.

She watched as he lay on his board and paddled out to where the waves gathered their strength. She'd never thought much about surfing one way or the other, but when she saw Jackson dive under a smaller wave to get to the bigger one behind it, she found herself in complete awe.

The muscles in his back and shoulders bunched and moved with every rotation of his arms. Just as he reached the wave, he hopped onto the board as easily as if it were on stationary ground, not a rolling swell that changed shape as it flowed toward the shore. His feet seemed glued in place as he alternated between crouching and standing.

His board sliced through the wave, zigging and zagging as he pushed it in different directions. Then the wave curled over him and anxiety nearly choked her with worry . . . until she saw him through the watery window, strong and upright. The nose of his board edged out from behind the shimmering curtain, and then she could see him, water spraying in his face, his hand stretching out to trail his fingers through the side of the tunnel the wave had created. Finally the wave ebbed and Jackson dove off into the water.

Then he resurfaced and started the whole thing over again.

Surfing had officially become her favorite spectator sport.

Vanessa sighed. What was she going to do with him? He was the definition of dichotomy, that was for sure. For all intents and purposes, he seemed to be exactly as he appeared: a talented fighter with the carefree life of a surfer. But something didn't add up. His actions didn't reconcile with the responsible man she'd heard about all those years from Lucie. Was it a simple case of idolization on her friend's part? Or was Jackson hiding the real him? And if so, why?

There were definitely some mysteries about the mega-hot MMA star Jackson Maris. The lawyer in her craved the truth. The woman in her wanted to know the man. Unfortunately, the woman in her wanted to know him a little too well.

She was by no means an inexperienced lover. Being comfortable in her sexuality had been one of the few bandwagons she rode on with the feminists. But it had been a loooooooong time since she'd let herself have enough time for anything other than work. Besides that, her dating pool had dwindled down to more like a dating puddle, and even that was drying up. There just weren't any guys she met that felt like they were worth the effort.

But Jackson . . . She had a feeling he would be worth the effort and then some. Vanessa chewed on her lip and moved ideas around in her head as she watched him conquer yet another wave.

The butterflies in her stomach began a slight fluttering of their wings.

A talk would need to happen prior to make sure they were on the same page with things. After that, there'd be nothing stopping her from getting horizontal Hawaiian-style with Jackson.

Now that she'd decided to give it the green light, the fluttering escalated to a frenzied flight. Anticipation of finally giving in to the desire she felt for Jackson spread through her, settling heavily in her core.

She took a deep breath of salty air and let it out with a smile. She already felt more relaxed. And even though she'd gotten a decent amount of sleep the night before thanks to her allergy pill solution, she still felt a little worn out. Maybe she'd take a power nap while he surfed. Stretching out on the shaded blanket, she yawned and closed her eyes.

She could still feel Jackson's kiss on her lips as she drifted off to sleep.

The sun and late afternoon breeze had already dried Jackson's body and suit as he lay on his side watching Vanessa nap. He'd come in from surfing about a half hour ago and hadn't wanted to wake her. She looked so peaceful, so soft. She was a tough woman and always had a strength about her, like a wary alley cat, ready to fight anyone at a moment's notice should she need to.

But when she slept, her features relaxed, her muscles sank into the sand beneath her, and wisps of curls danced around her face. Her auburn eyelashes, long and slightly curled, lay like fans above fine cheekbones, and her breaths came light and even through parted red lips.

The memory of her taste was its own aphrodisiac. One small sample and instead of quenching his thirst, it only served to addict him more.

As he lay there watching her, he wondered what she was like in her own element back home. He'd heard a couple of stories from college when they'd go out and Vanessa would convince his normally straitlaced sister to do something crazy, which didn't quite match up with the woman he'd seen in the last thirty-six hours. He wondered if she'd calmed down after college or maybe was different because of the circumstances they were in.

As Lucie's best friend, how much did she know about him? Did girls typically talk in depth about their families? He assumed they did. As far as he knew, girls talked nonstop about everything. But even still, Lucie would've only talked about the superficial stuff. Funny stories from their childhood, like when he and Reid ruined Lucie's tea party when their G.I. Joes took her Barbies as POWs. (Hey, it wasn't his fault. Snake Eyes was a highly trained government assassin who had reason to believe Ken was a secret agent working for the Russians.)

But all of that was just fluff. Lucie couldn't tell Vanessa the most important thing about him, because even his baby sister didn't know his secret. How could he tell her that their family—which they'd always thought was so perfect—wasn't so perfect after all?

When his parents died in the car accident, Jackson's life had been turned upside down. He'd just barely graduated high school and was set to go to Vegas with Reid so they could both pursue their careers in MMA. Instead, he found himself fighting to be the legal guardian of his thirteen-year-old sister. And soon after that, he found the paperwork tucked away in his parents' lock box at the bank. Paperwork that shattered his reality.

After the initial shock wore off, Jackson had put it far back in his mind while he raised Lucie the best he could. Really, she'd made it pretty easy on him. She was a great kid, never got in any trouble, always got straight A's, and didn't date. But it still didn't detract from the stress of being responsible for her during the most crucial years of her adolescence and having to learn real quick how to be an adult with a job and bills.

That's why, when he got to Hawaii, he made the decision to live as simply as possible, only buying what he could purchase outright with cash and being responsible for no one but himself. And he'd been living quite happily that way ever since.

Vanessa stirred beside him, rubbing her nose with her fingers and twitching it like a bunny. He smiled and reached up to tuck the curl that had caused the tickle behind her ear. To his surprise, her face turned in to his touch, and she whispered his name. A feeling he couldn't describe ran through him, knowing he was in her dreams. He didn't have long to revel in the idea, however, because almost as soon as she said it, her eyes fluttered open.

"How long have I been out?"

"I'd say a couple of hours."

She sat up like the blanket had scorched her. "Oh my God, I can't believe I was out that long. I mean, I thought I'd take, like, a thirty-minute power nap or something."

"What's the big deal? So you took an afternoon nap on a beautiful beach. It's certainly not a crime, V."

"I realize that," she snapped. "I'm just . . . not used to wasting so much of my day."

"I'm gonna go ahead and state the obvious here. You're a workaholic who doesn't know how to unwind, even on vacation."

"Technically, this isn't supposed to be my vacation. I wasn't supposed to be here until Friday, remember? Next week is my vacation. I still have work that needs to be done. I'm simply working remotely from a tropical island."

"Yikes, that sounds like zero fun."

She stood up and started putting her clothes on and

gathering the picnic items. "Yes, well, not all of us can have jobs that allow us to be carefree surfers."

He stood, too, and picked up his board. He didn't think she'd be one of the people who made assumptions about a fighter's life like it wasn't a real job. "Just because I'm not in a training camp right now doesn't mean that when it's time for me to work I slack off and it's all sunshine and roses."

"Come on, Jackson. Your career consists of eating healthy and working out. Most people do that on top of everything else in their life."

"Really. That's all it is, huh?"

"Don't get me wrong. I'm sure your workouts are tough; I'm just saying that for someone who's as in shape and used to it as you are, you would have a fairly easy time doing it. It'd be like cross-examining a witness for me."

"I'm flattered by your faith in my abilities, but it doesn't matter how in shape I am or how many times I do a camp. Every workout feels just as hard as my first day training. They're like that by design."

The slight arch in her brow as she packed up their things was about as subtle as one of Lucie's snorts. He felt like she'd just insulted his work ethic, which didn't make any damn sense. Jackson was always the first person to joke about how easy and carefree his life was. If his life had shampoo-bottle instructions they'd be: fight, surf, relax, repeat. So why was it suddenly so important to him to prove to her that he wasn't just some lazy half-asser going through the motions?

"Tell you what," he said as they shook out the blankets and folded them, "I'm going into the gym tomorrow morning. Why don't you come with and see for yourself? That way, Counselor, you can make your ruling once you have all the evidence."

"Hmm," she began, making a face like she was really mulling it over. "You make a good case, but I thought you weren't doing a camp right now."

"I'm not, but that doesn't mean I never train." When Vanessa bent down to grab the picnic basket and her purse, he added, "Gotta stay in shape for the ladies, you know."

That had her head snapping up as she straightened, and a competitive spark lit her green eyes for a split second before she could douse it. Gesturing to his waist, she said, "You call those love handles staying in shape?"

"What?" Shit, he knew he'd had too many burgers this last week. Holding his arms out, Jax glared at his sides . . . and found nothing.

A peel of laughter came from a doubled-over Vanessa. "Oh my God, that was too easy! You're worse than a girl!"

"A girl?" he said, raising his voice and enjoying the fake melodrama. She nodded emphatically with a hand muffling her giggles. "I'll show you who's the girl."

As soon as he took a menacing step in her direction, she squealed his name in protest, dropped the folded blankets, and took off at a dead run over the white sand.

And he was more than happy to chase her.

"I want to propose something to you."

Jackson looked up from where he was waxing his board by their private pool. As soon as they'd gotten back from the beach, they'd ordered in room service for dinner, and then she'd worked while he went for an evening run. Since she was still engrossed in her files after his shower, he settled himself by the pool and started waxing his board, listening to the waves hit the sand and the sounds of distant music and laughter coming from the beach bar on the other side of the resort.

"Have a seat," he said, gesturing to the spot next to him. She was wearing a pair of cut-off sweatpants that barely covered her ass and a tank top. Proper island loungewear. Also proper make-his-cock-stand-up-and-say-aloha wear. Christ. Trying to take his mind off his dick, he refocused on his task at hand.

Once seated with the lower half of her legs dangling in the pool, she tucked her hands under her thighs and let out a deep breath.

"Hmm," he mused with a small grin. "Sounds serious. I'm not as clear on the law as you, but can you divorce me before we're even married?"

"I'll get back to you on that," she answered wryly. "Is that pineapple I smell?"

He held up the bar. "Sex wax. Not to be confused with wax you can actually use during sex."

"Have you used wax during sex?"

He cocked an eyebrow. "Are you asking if I've ever tried wax play?"

She hesitated . . . then nodded.

"Not yet." Images of dripping wax on her creamy skin assaulted him. "But something tells me I wouldn't mind experimenting with lots of new things with the right person."

"Oh," she said, her voice taking on a husky tone that warmed his balls. Subject change was in order if he didn't want to maul her without provocation in the next thirty seconds. Which, sadly, was debatable.

"So are you going to tell me what's on your mind?" He glanced down at her breasts and saw her hardened nipples straining against her tank. No bra. Fuck! She was trying to kill him. "Or would you rather I guess?" he offered, his voice dropping in pitch as well.

"Uh, well," she started before clearing her throat. "I came to Hawaii with the intention of letting loose, so to speak. You know, maybe finding a guy I could shake things up with. But, since you've put me in this crazy predicament where we're pretending to be our engaged friends, I can't very well go around flirting and carrying on with anyone I happen to meet."

"Uh-huh." He liked where this was going.

"So since I have no other choice, you understand, I propose you be the one I . . . let loose with," she finished lamely.

"In plain English, V."

"Oh, for shit's sake, you know what I'm saying. I want a vacation fling."

"Which means what exactly?" He understood her proposal, but he wanted to hear her say the words. He leaned in closer until their breath mingled. "Say it," he ordered softly.

She took a deep breath and bravely looked him in the eyes. "I want to have sex with you."

"There. Was that so hard?" He smiled. "Speaking of hard . . ." He grabbed her hand and showed her exactly what he thought of her proposal.

"Jesus," she gasped.

Even with the material of his shorts as a buffer, the feel of her palm against his hardening cock sent shockwaves through his veins. "I accept your proposal."

She yanked her hand back and scooted a few inches away from him as though she needed room to breathe. Exactly the opposite of what he expected her to do.

"We can't start until tomorrow, though."

And that was exactly the opposite of what he expected her to say.

"Come again?"

"Rule #5: Never let a fling last more than three days. Today is Monday. If we start tomorrow, that gives us through Thursday night, which is perfect because Lucie and Reid are due to arrive on Friday in time for the rehearsal dinner."

Jackson couldn't believe she was putting a time limit on a fling like it was a goddamned parking meter. "You can't be serious. Do you do this with every guy?" Suddenly the idea of her having three-day flings with random men made him want to go several rounds with a punching bag. Or better yet, the random men.

"Well, I don't discuss the rule with them. I just always end things before it gets more serious than that. But since we're in the unique position we are, I feel I need to be upfront with you about my expectations."

"So you've never had relationships or dated anyone longer than three days?"

"Of course I have, but we're not talking relationships; we're talking flings. The two are very different."

He rubbed a hand over the stubble on his jaw as he mulled things over. Vanessa MacGregor was a strange creature. He couldn't figure out why she had so many crazy rules and felt she needed to follow them like her own personal bible. Personally, he thought her rules were absurd, but if he wanted to be with her—and he really, really did—he supposed there were worse things than following a few rules. Presuming none of them was off-the-wall crazy.

He narrowed his eyes a little and asked, "If I agree to this, what other rules are going to be involved? I don't want something sprung on me somewhere in day two. You don't have any rules that involve me dressing up in women's clothing, do you?"

"Not even one of my thongs?"

His eyes widened until she cracked a smile. "Careful, princess. By my count, you're already owed two punishments. You wouldn't want to double that, now would you?"

Her face lost some of its amusement and flushed a little, making him wonder if it was from worry . . . or excitement.

Clearing her throat, she reached into her back pocket and unfolded a sheet of paper that looked a lot like— Holy shit. "Is that a contract?"

"Of course not! But I didn't want to forget anything so I wrote down all the—"

"Rules?" he asked with a wry raise of an eyebrow.

She leveled him with a confident stare and her chin lifted a hint more. "Yes. Rules."

He loved that she didn't back down when he tested her resolve. Some women would have given up at the first sign he wasn't thrilled. But not Vanessa. She was totally at peace with her crazy, and for some reason it turned his crank that much harder. Sounded like he'd be doing a lot of things to humor his eccentric pretend-bride-to-be.

Setting his board off to the side, he crossed his arms over his chest and said, "Okay, let's hear it."

"The deal is that we enter into a sexual relationship for the period of three consecutive days starting Tuesday, which is tomorrow, and after that we'll revert back to a platonic friendship. However, because we have mutual friends, it's almost certain that we'll see each other in the future. So we also have to agree not to revisit any part of our sexual relationship during those times."

"So we can't sleep together just for old times' sake? Why the hell not?"

"Because three days is three days, Jackson. Anything more than that and we run the risk of developing feelings for each other, and that's not what either of us wants."

"Uh-huh. And why is that again?"

She looked away from him, finding a sudden interest

in the way she dog-eared the corner of the paper. "You're not right for me."

Ouch. That stung more than he'd have thought. "Because of your rules?"

She nodded but didn't elaborate. He made a decision then and there that his goal for the next few days would be to figure out that list of rules and make her break as many of them as possible. She was strung too damn tight, and he was taking it upon himself to chill her the fuck out.

"What else did you write down?"

She shrugged one slim shoulder. "Just that during our fling neither of us messes around with anyone else, which is not only common courtesy but also to protect Reid's and Lucie's reputations." Then she cut him a look from the corner of her eye. "That includes flirting, so you might want to steer clear of Jillian."

Jackson worked to keep a straight face and bit back the laughter roiling in his chest. He didn't doubt her main concern was for Lucie, but he'd bet his favorite board that hints of jealousy also fueled that last comment. V had nothing to fear from an old flame, but he didn't see any reason to point it out. After all, it wasn't like it mattered for a few days of mutual fun.

Stroking his jaw, he pretended to mull over her terms. He, of course, thought the strict time frame and ban on future dalliances were ridiculous, but he refused to believe those were firm rules. Even a Red Viper had the potential to be charmed.

"All right," he said at last. "I agree to your terms for as long as you do, on one condition."

"Which is what?"

"You give me control."

She shook her head like he'd just told her to assassinate the president. "Rule #2."

He checked the sigh of frustration before it escaped. Patience. "What is it?" She sucked the center of her lip between her teeth, and if she didn't speak soon, she'd break the skin. "V, if we're going to make this work, I need to know what I'm dealing with. What is it?"

"Never relinquish control."

Boom. That rule alone explained a hell of a lot about why she had conniptions any time he tried holding the reins. He tried to imagine what had happened in her past that would make her so adamant about something like that. Nothing he came up with could be categorized as minor, and a fierce protectiveness welled up inside him. But he also wanted to help her let some of whatever was haunting her go, and the only way for her to do that would be to face her fear and give it to him.

"V," he said gently, "I only want control in the bedroom, so to speak. Outside of that, you can boss me around all you want."

"No."

Gently. Firmly. "Yes."

"I can't," she said weakly.

"You can. All I'm asking is you let me take the lead. I'll never ask you to do anything you don't want. The minute you tell me to stop, I stop. But I promise that whatever I do to you, the last thing you'll want is for me to stop." Jax leaned in, nuzzling the curve of her neck with his nose, letting his stubble gently abrade her skin as he lifted his face to whisper in her ear. "Give me control, V."

She shuddered so hard he swore he felt it ripple through him as well. "I . . ." A shaky breath fanned over his cheek. "I promise I'll try, okay? Deal?"

Jax felt like he'd just had his hand raised in a decision fight. He knew, for her, even conceding to try was a huge step. "Deal." Sliding into the water, he placed himself between her legs with his hands on the concrete beside her hips, boxing her in.

"You agreed we wouldn't start until tomorrow."

He leaned in, his face next to hers, his mouth at her ear. "I have no intentions of touching you. But touching isn't the only way to turn you on. For instance, you got me hard last night and all you did . . . ," he said, pulling back to meet her eyes meaningfully, "was stare at me."

Vanessa inhaled sharply, and her back stiffened. "I thought you were sleeping."

"I was. But then I felt those intense eyes burning into me. I felt branded everywhere they touched, and it made me so fucking horny, it's a miracle I didn't jump out of that hammock and attack you."

It took a lot to make her blush normally, but now she felt as though her cheeks matched her hair. "I can't believe you didn't say anything."

"How about I make up for it now by saying a whole lot of things?"

"Like what?" She swallowed thickly. His proximity was too close for comfort if she had any hope of sticking to her own damn rule.

"Like how I plan on attacking that sweet mouth of yours as soon as I'm allowed." He moved until his lips lined up with hers, so close she swore she could feel them on hers, and yet there was still space between them. "And how my hands are itching to touch your smooth skin, knead your breasts, cup that sweet ass of yours as I haul you against me."

Why were her breaths so damn loud? She sounded on the verge of having an asthma attack. And her heart pounded so hard she mistook it for the distant beat of the music. Her skin tingled with sensations in the areas as he mentioned them, like his words gave life to action,

Before she realized what happened, she found herself leaning back on her hands as Jackson angled himself over her, still standing in the pool, still not touching her. But now his face hovered over her chest.

"I can't wait to suck on these." His hot breath seeped through the cotton weave of her top. She felt her nipples tighten, almost painfully, as they strained toward him, begging to be taken. "I've tried to imagine what your nipples look like. I bet with your fair skin they're a pretty shade of light pink."

The deep vibrations from his voice skimmed over her body. "And I bet they'll turn cherry red after I suck them deep into my mouth and flick them with my tongue, maybe give them a nibble."

From somewhere in the back of her throat, a moan escaped at the thought of his white teeth clamping on the hard nubs.

"Ah," he said, looking up at her from chest level, "again I get a reaction with biting. I think you and I are going to be quite compatible in bed, baby."

As he moved farther down her body, her eyes stayed riveted to his. A nuclear blast could go off next door and she wouldn't even blink. Jackson stared at her thighs pointedly, then flicked his gaze back to her.

"Wider."

"What?"

"Your legs. Wider."

She hesitated, unsure if she could handle more of the same where he seemed intent to go. He held his ground, waiting her out. Almost as though he knew it was only a matter of time. Well, she could hold her own against a guy like him. She didn't bend to anyone's will just because he commanded her. She only agreed to give up control during their fling, and even then, only during sex.

His eyebrow raised, the scar slashing up at a sharper angle. "Afraid you'll be tempted to break your own rules, MacGregor?"

Damn it. The man threw down challenges like there was no tomorrow. But that didn't mean she had to keep rising to the bait . . . did it? She was about to answer herself with an emphatic "no" when a smirk crept over his face. There was no way she was letting him think he affected her as much as he did. Arching her own brow, she slowly pulled her legs apart as far as they'd go.

He didn't even spare a second to gloat over what he surely considered a win. It was as if his cocky attitude had only been a facade needed to get what he wanted, and as soon as he had it, the mask slipped away to reveal the intense man underneath still intent on making her squirm with his verbal seduction.

Sinking into the water up to his shoulders, his face now loomed at ground level, squarely in front of her sex. She bit her lip and prayed he'd stop torturing her soon.

"Christ, Vanessa . . ." Her name sounded strangled, like his throat had gone tight. She watched his face for signs of his thoughts. His eyes focused on the apex of her thighs, his nostrils flared briefly, and the muscles in his jaw jumped every few seconds. He looked as if he was trying to maintain control. "You're so wet it's soaking through your shorts."

"It's been a long time for me." Her voice sounded breathy and unstable. Almost unrecognizable from her usual tone of conviction. "A kangaroo could make me horny at this point. It has nothing to do with you."

"Uh-huh," he said sarcastically. He leaned in until the vibrations from his deep voice almost sent her over the edge. "Say the word, baby, and I'll take care of that for you."

"N-no."

"Come on. It's not breaking a rule, it's just bending it a little."

"It won't kill us to show some restraint. We can handle this. We're adults." She sounded about as convinced of her words as she would claiming she believed in Santa Claus.

"Hell, yes, we're adults. That's my point," he said sharply, standing up again. He cursed under his breath and slapped the pavement next to her, making her flinch. "We should be able to do what we want, when we want. We're not kids with curfews and bedtimes."

His clear disdain pulled her the rest of the way from her lust-induced stupor. She scooted back and pushed to her feet. "Look, whether you think this is stupid or not isn't the point. The point is that it's important to me. So if I come with too much baggage for you, that's fine. I have no issues with making use of my vibrator. It satisfies my needs just fine."

In one fluid motion, he used his hands on the side of the pool to launch himself out of the water. He towered over her, dripping water and oozing anger and sex. "The day a vibrator satisfies my lover more than me is the day I make myself a eunuch."

He crossed to where his towel sat in a heap in one of the Adirondack chairs and ran it over his body in short, hurried strokes before pausing at the doors to the bedroom. "Enjoy your last few hours of being in control, V. Because after that . . . you're mine."

Jackson took the longest, coldest shower of his life and even jerked off under the icy water, and he was still hard just thinking of sinking into the woman who lay in that monster-sized bed all alone, mere feet from him. He was going insane with waiting. The fact she slept peacefully right now told him she expected things to start when they woke up.

She expected wrong.

Looking over at the clock on the wall, he smiled to himself. In five minutes it'd be midnight. Officially Tuesday, and he wasn't about to waste any time before starting their three-day excursion into the wild and kinky.

As the minutes ticked down, he went over his plan in his mind, thought of what he wanted to do first, what he wanted to do after that. It was almost too hard to decide. He wanted to do everything with her all at once. The first time wasn't going to be a lingering and slow experience. They were both too wound up for that.

He climbed onto the bed next to her. Only the sheet draped her body, since, even with the AC, it was still on the warm side of comfortable. Carefully, he pulled the sheet down her body until she was exposed to him.

He scooted behind her, gently adjusting her body to conform to his. She moved in her sleep, resting her head on the inside of his arm and tucking her back more firmly into his chest. His free hand swept up her bare thigh to the top of her hip. The cutoffs weren't much of a barrier and they moved aside as he cupped a smooth, round cheek and gave it a light squeeze. She made a small sound and arched her lower back, pressing her ass against his cock that was trying desperately to bust through his boxer briefs.

Burying his nose into her neck, he inhaled her scent deeply into his lungs as he snaked his hand to the front of her body and up her tank top to find a ripe breast that fit perfectly in the cage of his fingers. She responded instantly, her shoulders pressing back as she tried to press into his touch.

"That's it, baby," he said as he rolled the hard nub

between his thumb and forefinger. "Come alive for me. Let me make you feel good."

Jackson couldn't believe how much he wanted to sink himself between her thighs. He'd been horny thousands of times in his life, but that word seemed so lacking compared to how he felt around her. It was more like a deep, gnawing hunger he needed to feed. And according to her rules, the clock on the wall said it was dinnertime, so he'd be damned if he was waiting any longer.

Abandoning her breast, he tucked his fingers between her legs, staying over her shorts for now, and rubbed them back and forth a few times. She moaned and her hips began to rock with him, riding his fingers in small movements.

Suddenly she gasped and her body went rigid. He quickly banded his arm around her waist and held tight as he spoke softly next to her ear. "Shhhh, V, it's okay. It's just me." He felt her relax once again, but she wasn't yet back to her state of sexual abandon like when she'd been asleep.

"Do you always accost women in their sleep, Maris?"

He chuckled. Her question lacked the bite she was probably going for. Instead, it came out breathless and a little relieved.

"Only the ones who make me agree as to when and how long I get them for. It's past midnight, which means it's Tuesday. Which also means you're mine for the next three days, and I intend to collect as much and as often as possible."

"Yeah, well—Oh, God!"

Jackson hadn't waited to hear her rebuttal. He'd moved his fingers back to where they'd been before she'd awakened. Slipping his fingers under her shorts, he continued rubbing her through the silk of her panties. "You're wet already. Your body responds to me, V. It knows what it wants."

She moaned and arched into his touch. "Feels like I can say the same to you. So stop teasing me and give us what we both want."

Even half asleep, the woman couldn't help giving orders. He was tempted to remind her of her promise but thought better of it. He didn't want to argue about who promised what now. He'd do that later, after they got this first one out of the way. Or maybe the first few. The way he felt, he could spend himself over and over in her and still be ready for more.

Jax yanked her tank up and over her head, then grabbed her shorts and panties and tugged them down until they became lost in the sea of linens at their feet. Immediately following was his godforsaken underwear threatening to give him another circumcision if he didn't get them off. Breathing a sigh of relief, he resumed his position at her back and nestled his erection in the soft groove of her ass.

The skin-to-skin contact he'd been anticipating for hours—hell, probably days—was almost enough to set him off right then and there. He held still, not trusting himself to move without losing what little control he had over his body. But then she rubbed herself against his cock, and he lost the thread.

Snatching one of the condoms he'd placed on the nightstand, he quickly sheathed himself so he wouldn't forget later in the heat of the moment. Responsibility taken care of, Jax grabbed her and rolled partly on his back with her half draped on top of him. He reached down and pulled her leg over his, spreading her open. His arm underneath her wrapped around to play with a breast while his other hand returned to the sweet spot between her legs.

He growled his approval when he touched perfectly smooth skin. "I knew you'd be a Brazilian-style girl."

Turning his head an inch, he lightly bit the shell of her ear as his fingers stroked between her slick folds. "God-damn, you're so wet, baby." Whenever he neared her opening, she lifted her hips, trying to force his entry, but he refused her that pleasure for the moment.

"Tomorrow, my lips, my tongue, and my teeth are going to spend an eternity worshipping this beautiful pussy. But tonight . . ." Jax finally eased a finger deep inside, then dragged it out slowly before repeating the process. Her cry of ecstasy reverberated in his ears like a starting bell, and he had to hold himself back from taking her too fast. "Tonight I'm going to give you what you need." *What we both need.*

He added a second finger, slowly working her open enough to take him. The last thing he wanted was to cause her any sort of discomfort. All his blood may have drained from his brain to his dick, but he wasn't so far gone that his main concern was his pleasure over hers. She felt so damn tight he wondered how he'd ever fit. But he would. He'd make sure of it. Because at this point, the idea of not burying himself in her was unthinkable.

"What is it I need?" Her breathy question belied the restraint she tried to exude.

"Sex," he growled. He increased the pace and used the heel of his hand to put pressure on her clit. "Rough, primal, fuck-me-baby sex."

"Yes! Oh, God, Jackson, I need that. Now, do it now." The words tumbled from her lips, her dam of reserve well and truly broken by the force of his plain speech.

"Easy," he whispered. "I have to make sure you're ready for me. Then I promise, nothing will prevent me from burying my cock so deeply, you'll feel me there for days."

She begged with a whimper and a thrust of her hips. He answered, "Almost," and inserted a third finger into her soaked pussy. A fine sheen of sweat coated their bodies, the damp curls framing her face plastered themselves to her cheeks and his. Everything in him screamed to take her, to mark her, to make her his. And he couldn't hold back any longer.

Removing his fingers, Jax palmed the back of her knee and hoisted her farther up his body until the head of his cock slid into place.

Her hands braceleted his wrists, her nails digging into his skin as though bracing herself. "Now?" she asked.

"Now."

In one smooth motion, he buried himself balls deep in her hot channel. When he hit the very back wall, a jolt of concentrated pleasure shot through his body unlike anything he'd ever felt. Vanessa cried out, her back bowing so hard only her shoulders and ass still rested on him. He bent his top leg to hold hers up and keep her open so he could use both arms to hold her, both hands to touch her.

Slowly he withdrew, her swollen sex trying to suck him back in. When less than an inch remained, he held her tightly and plunged back in, her name a beautiful prayer on his lips.

"Faster," she bit out. "Jackson, go faster. You're killing me."

"Believe me, it's killing me, too."

She turned her head and fused her sugar lips to his. He bypassed the foreplay kisses and went straight to fucking her mouth with his tongue as he continued the slow, controlled strokes with his hips.

Time stood still as he reveled in her taste, her smell, her absolute abandon. After what could have been hours later, rather than minutes, they broke apart to catch their breath. Again she told him to go faster, harder.

"Baby, I want you so badly," he said as he fondled her

heavy breasts, "I'm afraid if I go any faster I'll blow like it's my first time."

"I'm so close I'll probably go with you. Please, Jax!"

"Ah, fuck. Hearing you beg is going to be damn addicting." Banding his arms around her body, he said, "Hold on." And with that he flipped the switch from slow-and-steady to fast-and-faster.

In and out, he pistoned his hips, filling her completely on every stroke. Sweat dripped from his brow over his temples. The slapping sounds of flesh against flesh filled the room. He could feel the juices from her pussy coating his balls as they drew up tighter to his body. White-hot heat pooled at the base of his spine, growing more and more with every passing second.

Vanessa wasn't much of a talker during sex, but she made plenty of noise. A chorus of moans, heavy breathing, mewls, and whimpers became his new favorite playlist.

Taking things up a notch, Jax moved his hands. One captured a breast and tweaked the hard bud of her nipple, the other snaked down to run circles over her clit. Now they raced headlong toward the finish line. Gritting his teeth until his jaw felt ready to snap, he made sure he didn't cross it first.

"Omigod, yes," she cried on a gasp. "I'm gonna come, Jax. So. Close!"

He loved that she used his name. That he knew she wasn't imagining anyone else. "Do it, Vanessa. I'm right there with you."

A strangled cry escaped her lips as her sex quivered and convulsed around his cock. And with a few more strokes, he tumbled after her, filling the condom as her body milked him dry.

He wasn't sure how long they lay there in a sweaty heap, but eventually he maneuvered her to the side so he could go take care of cleanup in the bathroom. He returned to the bed with a warm washcloth to find Vanessa passed out cold and snoring softly. Jackson supposed that meant an all-night sex fest was out of the question.

Chuckling to himself, he cleaned her as carefully and quickly as possible. Then he chucked the rag back in the general direction of the bathroom and slid in behind her before lifting the covers over them. He kissed the back of her shoulder and tried to get some sleep himself.

DAY 3: TUESDAY

"Rise and shine, V."

Vanessa felt the warm rays of the sun stream across her face, causing her to squinch her eyes tight and moan into her pillow.

"Come on. I gotta get to the gym, and you're coming with me today, remember?"

Remember? She couldn't remember anything past the feel of his arms around her and the way he felt deep inside her. Even now her breasts tingled with the memory of his touch.

"Give me ten more minutes," she muffled into her pillow.

His shadow fell over her face as he moved in front of her, his voice rumbling through her body and landing deep in her belly. "I usually prefer to go much longer, but considering our tight schedule, I'd be more than happy to give you a ten-minute wakeup call."

Her eyes flew open to see Jackson's wicked smile as he began to untie his white athletic pants. Holy mother of God. As much as she was tempted to let him make good on his promise—or maybe it was supposed to be a threat—she wanted to get her bearings with him before their next encounter. She wasn't used to being caught off-guard, and considering how last night went down, off-guard was a major understatement.

When his thumbs hooked into his waistband and began tugging the material down, she bolted upright in bed and held a hand out to hopefully prevent any further exposure that would change her mind. "I'm up! I'm up. Just . . . uh . . ." She tried to think, but her brain felt steeped in a fog worse than a London morning. "Let me get some coffee in me, and we can go."

"I already made it for you." With a triumphant smile, he righted his pants and hauled her out of the bed by her waist. "It's in a travel mug over on the counter."

It was then she noticed she was standing stark naked in front of him in the garish light of day. Gasping, she yanked the sheet from the bed and clutched it to her chest. He chuckled and stepped waaaaay into her personal space. Unfortunately, if she backed up, she'd only succeed in falling back onto the bed, so she lifted her chin and stood her ground.

"What's so funny?"

He placed those large hands on her hips. Since she hadn't wrapped the sheet around her, his long fingers reached past where the material draped her frame, branding her skin with their rough heat and memories from the night. "The fact that you feel the need to cover up when hours ago I had free rein to do whatever I wished to this very naked body."

"Yeah, well, there's a huge difference between seeing something by moonlight and seeing it in sunlight. So if you don't mind . . ."

Storm clouds rolled over his features. "I sure as hell

do mind," he growled. "I can't believe a woman as strong and beautiful as you has body image issues. Now I know you're crazy."

She scoffed. "Every woman has body image issues, Jax. It doesn't matter if you're an average girl or Kate Moss."

"Then I'm going to make you the first woman in the world to lose those issues." Wrapping his arms tightly around her, he dipped her back slightly as his mouth took hers in a fevered kiss, damn near making her forget her name, much less her nitpicky self-image complaints. When he finally broke away, they were both a little out of breath. "But not now. Now we're going to the gym, so get your cute ass in gear." He pushed her toward the bathroom with a slap on her ass that made her jump and squeal in surprise.

She stuck her tongue out at him over her shoulder as she crossed the room, making sure her hips swayed, hoping it tortured him on some primal level. He more than deserved it for the stunt he pulled last night. Not that she was complaining. Him waking her up had been hot as hell. But now she knew she had to be careful, or Jax would end up taking a lot more from her than just her control.

Jackson ran a hand through his hair and let out the breath he'd been holding since he saw the red mark of his hand on that pale ass walking away from him. Fuck, he was in trouble. She was feisty as hell when she had her wits about her. It surprised him to find it was just as fun being on the receiving end of that arrogant attitude as it was to rid her of it with some well-placed kisses.

He wished he could say he'd slept as well as she had, but the small taste of her had only made him want her more. Most of the night was spent rocking in the hammock and convincing himself to leave her be for the remainder of the night instead of starting a sex marathon to rival the days of the Romans.

By the time the sun peeked over the horizon signaling the time for his morning run, he'd probably only gotten a couple hours of restless sleep. Now his eyes felt scratchy, and he hadn't mustered the energy to shave, so he was sporting a day's worth of stubble.

He wasn't sure what the rest of the day would bring, but one thing was for sure. He needed to get some alone time with Miss MacGregor as soon as humanly possible.

She showered and dressed in record time and a half hour later, they arrived at the gym just as his other teammates were trickling in. He introduced her to his coach, Frank, and explained that she was a guest of his and would be sitting in as a spectator for the workout.

The guys gravitated to her like a Playboy bunny in a monastery. Frank brought out his "nicer than those damn metal things" leather office chair, and she had her pick of the Powerade Zero flavor rainbow from the guys who always brought coolers full of the things.

As he stretched on the mats, Jax looked on with amusement as she laughed at their antics and they dubbed her team mascot for the day. He couldn't blame them for their good-natured flirting. Even with her hair in a ponytail and her simple outfit of khaki shorts and teal halter top, she made a damn pretty picture. Add in her outgoing personality and infectious smile, and there wasn't one of his teammates who wasn't smitten with her.

If they'd been anywhere else and random guys were paying her the same attention, Jax had a feeling he'd be a lot less amused. But his boys knew she was there with him, and regardless if he and Vanessa were openly dating or just friends, they wouldn't break Guy Code by seriously hitting on her.

Soon Frank broke up the group and harassed the

guys into starting their warm-ups. They did a bunch of jump-roping and jumping jacks, then dove headlong into suicide sprints. The entire camp of men worked their asses off, giving their coach one hundred and ten percent of their effort, and sweating enough to soak through their clothes five times over.

They took a five-minute break to rehydrate before they split into groups. Jax was in the group to hit the cardio circuit first. After that he'd move on to agility, strength, grappling, striking, and sparring. Leaning on the wall across the gym where he'd stashed his gear, he chugged his Powerade while trying to figure out why every cell in his body urged him to go to Vanessa and spend the few minutes of break he had left with her.

For that reason alone, he stayed right where he was. Enjoying her company and being eager to get her beneath him for some more fun between the sheets was one thing. But the need to take whatever opportunity he had just to be on the receiving end of that smile was a foreign feeling he wasn't sure what to make of. So he'd prove to himself he didn't in fact need it. That he was fine right where he was.

The double doors leading to the parking lot swung open and a lean kid barely old enough to drink legally sauntered through with a heavy gym bag slung over his shoulder, pushing his mirror-black sunglasses onto his head.

Coach glanced at the clock on the wall then glared at the kid sharply enough to cut right through him. "Akana! Who in the hell gave you permission to walk into camp whenever you damn well please?"

Chewing on gum like a cow with cud, Danny Akana offered an apology about as sincere as a lion to a zebra before his first bite. "Sorry, Coach. Overslept. Won't happen again."

"See that it doesn't," Frank said with a finger jabbing the air in the kid's direction. "Or next time you'll be scrubbing everyone's jocks after practice."

Akana held both palms out in a sign of concession, but as soon as Frank turned his back, the punk made a jerking-off motion with his hand.

The kid was the son of one of Frank's oldest friends, which explained Frank's leniency with him. If any of the other guys had pulled that shit, they'd be punished physically until they puked, passed out, or both. Jackson didn't know Akana well, as the kid had only been with the gym for a couple of weeks, but he knew enough to know that he didn't like him. He was cocky and disrespectful, and Jax couldn't wait for the day when someone knocked him down a peg or two. Or out.

"One more minute, fellas!"

Jax drained the rest of his drink, then crossed to the water fountain a few feet from Vanessa to fill the bottle before heading to the treadmill. She'd kicked the flip-flops from her pedicured feet and brought a foot up to rest on the chair with her arms wrapped around her bent leg. She looked like a pixie princess in casualwear perched on her leather throne while overseeing her subjects.

He grinned as he studied her profile from the corner of his eye. A pixie. That's definitely what she reminded him of with her wild hair, pale skin, and graceful willowy frame. Even her facial features gave her an elfin look. Her pert nose turned up ever so slightly at the end, her lips were full but not overly wide, and her ears had the slightest of rounded points at the top.

But her personality was anything but delicate, and anyone who got in her way learned real quick the age-old lesson of never judging a book by its cover.

Just as he turned to head to the treadmill, Jax caught a sight that held him in place. Akana had approached

Vanessa and was now flirting with her. But it wasn't the harmless kind. He was actually making a play for her.

Jackson's muscles clamped down on his bones. Unable to stop himself, he strode over, prepared to send Akana off with a threatening glare every man understood meant back the fuck off.

"The kid bothering you, V?"

She glanced up at him with a smile and said, "Not at all. Danny here was kind enough to offer me his services. He said he could show me how the local boys do it around here," she said with enough sarcastic innuendo to choke a donkey. Or embarrass the hell out of a dude who'd obviously been a little crude with his come-ons.

Jax glanced at Akana, gauging his reaction. "Awfully neighborly of him."

V nodded. "Wasn't it, though? Unfortunately, I was just about to inform him that I don't do anything with boys, local or otherwise, and I already have a man for the job."

Well, color him shocked as hell. The kid's jaw shifted back and forth, no doubt grinding his molars into a fine dust, and his face looked a little too flushed, considering he hadn't done even a single jumping jack.

"You heard the lady, junior. Job's taken," Jax said. "Now go start your block training before Coach has you scrubbing my jock with your toothbrush."

Akana didn't say anything with his mouth, but his eyes said a whole lot of fuck you. Jax just raised an eyebrow in a silent challenge, daring the kid to start something, but soon he spun around and stalked off in the opposite direction.

"Nice work," he told her with a wink. "You doing okay?"

"Are you kidding?" she said as she stood and stretched. "If I'd have known watching sweaty men with gladiator bodies could be so entertaining, I'd have done this years ago. Next time, I'm bringing popcorn."

He chuckled and stepped in to her. He couldn't help himself. The hand not holding his water settled in the dip of her lower back as he bent his head to her ear, using the pretense of needing to whisper so he had an excuse to feel her skin and inhale her citrusy scent. "We can leave whenever you want. Say the word and I'll pack my gear."

"Aw," she said with a pout in her voice. "Are you tired already? 'Cause that's okay if you are. You shouldn't feel like any less of a man for it."

His head fell back on his shoulders as he let out a quick oh no she didn't laugh. Then he sobered and gave her his warning with his lips brushing her cheek. "That's the start of your punishments for later, woman."

Making a sound like she'd just bit into a Godiva truffle, she took a step back and gave him a saucy wink. "You might just wanna keep a running tab for those, stud." Then she smacked his ass before walking away and loudly informing the entire gym they'd be "eating their junk for lunch" if they stepped foot in the locker room within the next five minutes.

A dozen men froze in place, suddenly wary of their pretty mascot and no doubt afraid for their "junk." Realizing her casually tossed threat turned out to be quite the showstopper, she laughed, the tinkling sound echoing on the tile walls as the door closed slowly behind her.

Every other man in the room may want to turn tail and run from a bold and sassy woman like Vanessa, but Jackson had the exact opposite reaction. He wanted to tackle her to the nearest surface, strip her naked, and make her scream his name.

And he would, too. Maybe not now and maybe not in the next few hours. But soon.

He felt his boxer briefs shrinking and huffed a sigh of frustration as he headed to the cardio area. "Wonderful," he muttered. "Now I have to do a ten-mile run with a hard-on."

Fucking hell.

He was in so much trouble.

Vanessa felt like a complete ass.

As Jax worked through his training routine, her jaw worked at not gaping in awe. She wanted to kick herself for not paying better attention when Lucie had talked about her brother's and Reid's fights over the years. She hated being ignorant in any situation, and at the moment, she felt like the biggest ignoramus on the planet.

He'd already done so much in the first couple of hours: sprints with bungees attached to him, swinging a sledgehammer onto a gigantic tractor tire, and flipping said monstrous tire end over end for what seemed like an eternity.

With each exercise, his muscles flexed and rippled as he isolated them in different motions. They reminded her of the waves rolling and undulating toward the shores. His body was a beautiful machine and though he poured with sweat and his chest heaved with labored breaths, he never once slowed down or even complained when given a task. Instead, it seemed as if he pushed himself harder with each new session.

She'd found the grappling exercises fascinating. Two men trying to best each other with nothing but wrestling moves and submission holds. It wasn't about strength but quick reactions and the ability to outmaneuver your opponent while watching for the moment he left himself open for that split second, allowing you to strike.

Jax had bested his training partner almost every time,

and she heard some of the other guys talking about how his Brazilian jiu-jitsu was his greatest strength.

Now she watched him wrap each hand with over seven feet of three-inch-wide black fabric. Round and round he crisscrossed the wrap over his wrist and palm, making sure to weave them between his fingers and cover his knuckles at the top. Once he secured the Velcro ends and tested his handiwork by flexing and fisting his hands a few times, he grabbed his gloves and walked over to a large punching bag hanging from the ceiling.

For the next half hour, he pounded his fists into the bag. Sometimes he'd perform high kicks or spinning kicks—she didn't know the technical terms for any of them—in combination with his punches. His hair was soaked and plastered to the edges of his face and his white sleeveless shirt could've won him first place in a wet T-shirt contest. Rawr.

"Maris!"

Jax looked across the room where Frank stood inside the cage. "Coach?"

"Come on in here and spar with Danny, will ya?"

An evil grin cocked up one side of Jax's mouth. "My pleasure."

Vanessa didn't know the deal with him and "the kid," as Jax called him earlier, but her Spidey Sense told her there wasn't a lot of love lost between the two. She wondered how it worked when guys who didn't particularly like each other had to fight nice.

"Well," she said to herself, "we're about to find out." Dang it, she thought, settling back in her cozy chair. She really did wish she had popcorn.

Jackson stripped off his shirt, jogged up the few steps into the large octagonal cage, took his mouth guard from where it was tucked in his waistband—ew—and shoved it past his lips over his top teeth. Danny, like the rest of the guys she'd seen sparring in the cage, wore a padded helmet. Jackson donned no such thing.

"Hey," she called out. "Where's your headgear, Maris?"

He looked over his shoulder at her like a teenager upset with his mom for embarrassing him in front of his friends. "I'll be fine, dear." His endearment was laced with sarcasm. She narrowed her eyes at him and crossed her arms over her chest. She didn't appreciate his tone, but fine. She got it. He was a big boy and could take care of himself.

She hoped Danny clocked him a good one.

A hulk of a guy—Corey, if she remembered correctly—squatted next to her, shooting a stream of water into his mouth and swallowing. "Don't worry about Jax," he told her with an easy smile. "Akana's just a rookie. He doesn't stand a chance hurting Jax in a sparring exercise. He's just in there to defend and make the kid work."

"Oh yeah? Then why does Danny look like he wants to exact a pound of Jackson's flesh?"

Corey chuckled. "Probably because the entire gym witnessed you shooting him down, and it was pretty damn obvious who you shot him down for."

Vanessa rolled her eyes and sighed. "Why are boys such cavemen?"

"Can't help it," he said, standing again. "It's in our DNA." With that said, he walked toward the cage and yelled, "That's it, Maris, keep him on his toes!"

For the next twenty minutes or so, Vanessa watched in awe as time and time again Jackson blocked most of Danny's strikes and thwarted almost all of the kid's takedowns. The few punches Danny managed to connect only made Jackson offer a wide, plastic-filled smile as he bounced on the balls of his feet and gave him the universal sign of bring it on with his fingers.

When they ended up on the ground it didn't take more than a minute for Jackson to work his way out of Danny's hold and reverse the situation, landing Jax on top in the power position.

Corey was right. Jackson could definitely hold his own and then some. But what concerned Vanessa was the look in Danny's eyes. With every passing minute, the frustration and anger grew more and more obvious, but a glance around the room showed she seemed to be the only one who noticed.

She wasn't sure what it meant for the two men duking it out in the cage, but nothing good ever came from that kind of a look. She'd seen it over and over again on her stepfather and it had never led to anything remotely good.

Taking a deep breath, she tried to relax, telling herself Jackson knew what he was doing.

At the moment, Danny had Jackson under him in what she'd learned was called full-guard, when the guy on top was between both legs of the guy on the bottom. The guy on top had the goal of trying to gain more power through half-guard—where he straddled one of the other guy's legs—or full mount, which meant he managed to completely bypass both of his opponent's legs and sit on the guy's hips. All while raining down punches to the head and body.

Unfortunately for Danny, Jackson was just too good. Even with Frank coaching Danny, barking out ways to get around Jackson's moves and gain the upper hand, Akana never even managed to get to a half-guard position.

Vanessa's hands clasped together in a viselike grip in her lap as she watched Jackson sweep Danny's legs to one side as he pushed up with his hips, rolling them over until Jax was now on top in a full mount.

Danny immediately spun under Jax to try and push himself up to a standing position.

Frank's face turned red as he shouted, "No, Akana, you never give up your back! Turn around and get him into your guard!"

But it was too late for Frank's order. Jackson already had one strong forearm wedged against the front of the kid's neck and proceeded to pull his clenched fist toward him with his other hand. Danny's face flooded with darkening shades of red. It wouldn't be long before Danny passed out.

This particular scenario had happened once before already, and Danny was supposed to either get out of it or tap out so Jackson would release the hold and they could stand up and start over. But this time Danny wasn't tapping, and it wasn't possible to get out of it; Jackson's arm was in too tight for an escape.

Jackson turned his head to the side and spit out his mouth guard. "Come on, kid, tap and we'll call it a day."

But Danny didn't answer and he didn't tap as his face grew redder than a tomato. Jackson looked to Frank with a questioning brow and received a single nod in response. Jackson released his hold immediately, and Danny took in big choking gulps of air.

Slapping him on the back, Jax said, "Way to show heart and not give up, kid. I'm impressed. Better luck next time."

Standing up, Jax turned to her, breathing heavily and dripping sweat as he approached the black mesh of the cage. He hooked his fingers through the holes and smiled. "You ready to get out of here, gorgeous?"

She stood and crossed to the octagon, keeping eye contact until she had to tip her head back. "I'm not afraid to admit when I'm wrong. You've proven yourself several times over. So get cleaned up and we can head back to Mau Loa. The day is young and we have things to do."

Technically those "things" were cake tasting and reviewing the menus for Friday and Saturday, but she let her eyes tell him she meant much naughtier things than that.

Smart man caught on instantly, if the way his pupils swallowed the amber irises was any indication.

"Don't have to tell me twice. I'll be right there."

Before he had the opportunity to turn around, Vanessa caught sight of Danny getting to his feet in the center of the ring. He muttered something to himself, but with all the noise of the weights clanging and the guys yelling to one another back and forth, she couldn't hear what he said. But his wild look said plenty.

Her eyes flew open wide. She shouted Jackson's name. But the warning came too late.

Everything slowed as though someone had paused the world and now clicked through time frame by frame. Danny cocked his hand back and struck at Jackson like a cobra uncoiling.

Jackson turned around in time to see the fist slicing through the air. He reacted by weaving to the left, but it wasn't fast enough to avoid Danny's right hand. What looked to be a jab intended for Jackson's nose ended up as a glancing hit to his cheek. The impact spun him back to the fence, but he was quick to right himself to keep the threat in his sights.

With Jackson's back now to her, Vanessa moved over several feet, her fingers clutching the fence, to get a better look at his face. Her stomach turned inside out. A gash below his right eye wept crimson blood and spilled over his jaw and onto his chest.

Jackson pushed off the cage and narrowed his eyes

on the man who sucker punched him and now had the gall to get in Jax's face. Vanessa didn't know a lot of the technical aspects of fighting, but anyone with a lick of common sense knew that a guy getting up in another guy's grill was a non-verbal invitation for a good old-fashioned brawl. Exactly the thing she wanted to avoid witnessing.

"Jackson, come on, let's go."

Her shaky voice showed her as weak, frightened. Things she'd fought hard to never show anyone again since the day she left home. But she didn't care. She couldn't. All that mattered was getting Jackson out of there before . . . Before what, Nessie? Before things get violent? The man's a fighter. He's probably violent by nature . . . just like Carl.

Oh, God, please no. Not Jackson.

Vanessa's palms grew clammy, and her skin turned cold. She wanted to plead with him again, but the tightness in her throat had trapped her vocal cords. Jax angled his head and used his shoulder to wipe the blood from his face. Instead of helping the situation, it only smeared it around his stubbled jaw and shoulder like a preschooler's finger-paint project.

Locking eyes with Danny, he ground out, "That make you feel like a man, kid?"

Danny's jaw worked and his nostrils flared as though Jackson's words smelled just as bad as they cut. "Nah," he said. "But I'll tell you what will."

Vanessa held her breath as she watched Danny lean in to speak next to Jackson's ear. Danny's lips barely moved and he was too quiet for her to know what he said. Though he held perfectly still, every muscle in Jax's body gripped his bones that much harder and his hands curled into tight fists as the kid pulled away with a satisfied smirk on his face. As he backed up, Danny went so far as to laugh, confident that whatever he'd said to Jackson had gotten the better of him.

A deadly look—the look she hated more than anything and had the power to stir up the dust in her memory and a sickness in her gut—sparked to life in Jackson's eyes. Normally warm and inviting like a good whiskey on a cold night, his eyes now made her cringe and want to crawl inside herself.

Fighting as a sport was one thing, but fighting out of anger was another entirely, and something she couldn't abide. Somehow she found her voice for a last-ditch effort at saving her perception of this man who had her turned inside out in only a few days. "Jackson, no, don't do it! Please!"

Either he couldn't hear her through the blood roaring in his ears or he chose to ignore her because a second later he threw a punch so fierce Danny's eyes rolled back into his head, and he crumpled to the mat, a boneless version of his former self.

The coach, who'd left the cage after the sparring match ended, now charged back in, putting himself between a still-furious Jackson and the unconscious man. Corey and another fighter grabbed Jax by the arms and dragged him out of the cage, talking him down from the rage that still held him in its clutches.

As the world sped back up into real time around her, Vanessa spun toward the exit and walked as fast as she could until she at last punched through the double doors.

The heat of the early afternoon pressed in on her like a weight, bearing down on her chest and shoulders until her legs shook and she finally sought relief on the grass off to the side of the entrance.

She schooled herself to take deep, meditative breaths and regain control of her body. Soon she felt back to herself, but she still wasn't about to go back into the gym. The guys probably thought she couldn't handle a little blood, which couldn't be further from the truth. It hadn't been the blood that upset her but what came after it.

When she moved out of her mother's house, Vanessa swore she would never involve herself with anyone who settled things with his fists. And even though this thing with Jackson was only a fling, it still bothered her to know he'd reacted the way he did.

Which rankled her even more. Why did it matter how he handled himself in a confrontational situation? It wasn't like she was sizing him up for a potential relationship. She just wanted to bang his brains out for a few days—three, to be exact—and then go on her merry little way. It didn't matter to her how many guys he knocked out outside of the cage. Right? Right.

The sound of the doors opening behind her had her glancing over her shoulder. Jackson strode toward her in his long, easy gait, so uncharacteristic of the intense man from minutes before. When he reached her, he lowered to his haunches, elbows resting on his knees and hands dangling between his legs.

"Hey," he said. "You okay?"

Though he still wore the hand wraps, his gloves were gone and his face and body were cleaned of any blood. Only his slightly swollen cheek and the two butterfly bandages holding the incised flesh together showed any sign that he'd been struck.

She almost reached out to touch it, to test its severity or offer him comfort. But she stopped the impulse by grabbing a fistful of grass and shredding it to pieces instead.

She lifted her chin. "Of course I'm okay. Why wouldn't I be?"

He canted his head and studied her for a moment. "I

don't know. You left pretty quickly after I KOed Akana in there."

"What did he say to you?"

Jax's eyes hardened and the muscle in his jaw ticked. "Nothing worth repeating."

An insult, then. Whether to her or him, it didn't really matter. She nodded and looked down at the blade of grass she'd rent in two.

"V, I'm sorry. Once my head cleared, I realized you'd tried to stop me."

She didn't say anything at first, but when it seemed he was waiting on some sort of explanation, she said, "And?"

"And although I know a lot of women hate violence in general . . ." He paused to run a hand over the back of his neck before exhaling and wincing up at her from under his lashes. "I'm kind of thinking maybe I broke a rule."

That took her aback. Either he suspected that everything he did or said broke one of her Rules, or he was tuning in to her in a way that allowed him to differentiate between trivial reactions and meaningful ones.

She sincerely hoped it was the former, for her sanity's sake. Or my heart's sake.

"Have I, V?" he asked more gently.

She sighed and looked away from those intense eyes of gold and focused on the safe vibrant pink hibiscus flowers lining the parking lot. "I know you think I'm crazy—that my Rules are crazy—but I have them for a reason. And yes, you broke one."

"I don't think you're crazy." He paused, then added, "A little high-strung, maybe."

She whipped her head around, ready to retaliate, but his crooked grin told her he was merely trying to get a rise out of her. It should piss her off—or at the very least annoy her—but that little hitch in the corner of his mouth was like a Vanessa MacGregor bomb diffuser.

"So what are the reasons you have the rules?"

Oh, hell no. Talk about opening a can of worms. Except this was more like a can of snakes. Of the poisonous variety. "No offense, but I rarely tell people I even have them. Why I have them is definitely not a topic open for discussion."

He seemed to think on that for a while. If she had to hazard a guess, she'd say he was probably weighing his options for arguing the point. At last he conceded. "Then tell me which one I broke."

"Rule #4: Never date a man who chooses fists over words." He raised a questioning brow. "Believe me, the irony of you fighting for a living isn't lost on me. Obviously the rule doesn't apply to fights involved in your career, but that's not what that was in there."

He inclined his head. "Agreed."

"But then again," she said, meeting his gaze again, "since we've agreed we won't be dating—now or ever—I guess you technically didn't break anything."

Vanessa stood and brushed the grass from her shorts. "Go hit the showers so we're not late meeting Robért. I'll wait for you in the car."

The Mahina Lounge was empty except for the bustling wait staff snapping crisp linens, placing pristine china and silverware, and arranging the freshly cut hibiscus centerpieces onto the dining tables of various sizes. Jackson sat at one of the four-tops in the back, close to the kitchen, waiting for Robért to emerge.

He didn't like the idea of choosing his sister's wedding cake for her, but there wasn't anything they could do about it. This whole mixed-up-identity situation was sprouting legs and soon it'd be running out of control if they couldn't figure a way to rein it in.

Looking across the room, Jax studied Vanessa as she spoke to Lucie on the phone. *Trying to get an idea of what she wants,* he guessed. V stood with her back to him. Yet another sign she was shutting him out since the incident at the gym. On the ride back to the Mau Loa she'd been quiet and stiff in her seat. With back straight and hands folded in her lap, she looked every bit the professional attorney sitting in court, as opposed to the carefree girl who'd sang to the radio as her bare feet tapped out the beat on his dash earlier that morning.

Fucking Akana. Jax wasn't sorry he'd decked the kid—he deserved it for the shit he'd said just low enough for Jackson to hear—but after seeing Vanessa's reaction, he was sorry he'd done it in front of her. When he'd turned around to see her leaving the gym, his stomach had dropped. He tried running after her, but Corey had strong-armed him into a chair so Frank could butterfly his cheek. Once all the blood was cleaned off him he went in search of her, and seeing the look on her face— one that looked a lot like disappointment—had almost stopped him in his tracks.

He couldn't remember the last time someone had been disappointed in him other than himself. He'd forgotten how much letting someone down burned like acid in the center of his chest.

Vanessa was turning out to be a puzzle he couldn't solve. If he'd read her right, then for her to be disappointed in him would mean she cared for him on some level. At least a little more than one generally cares for her best friend's brother whom she barely knew. But that didn't add up with the calculating woman who made him agree to formal stipulations regarding their sexual relationship.

For probably the fiftieth time since he met her, he wondered what prompted her to make the rules in the first place. He couldn't shake the feeling that she was more than just a woman scorned by a few ex-boyfriends.

His phone vibrated in his pocket. He grabbed it, glanced at the caller ID, and answered. "What's the word, man? How's Lucie?"

"She was feeling better until Vanessa spilled about your little role-playing fiasco down there." Shit. Reid sounded like he wanted to use him as a punching bag. "What the hell is going on, Jax?"

"Look, this isn't exactly anything I planned, all right? It started out as something I said just to get under her skin. Or maybe it wasn't, I don't know. I meant to tell her the truth, but then the planner got involved and it all went to hell."

"So what happens when we show up at the end of the week? Because I'm sure as hell not pretending to be you while you get hitched to Vanessa."

"Whoa! Chill out, okay? The only people getting hitched this weekend are you and my sister." Jax glanced over to where it looked like Vanessa was finishing up her phone call. There were a lot of hand gestures that, if Lucie could see them, would probably reassure her Vanessa had everything under control. Now he had to convince his best friend of the same thing. Whether Jackson believed it or not.

Scratch that. He had to believe it. Because one way or another, he wasn't going to let anyone—including a pissed-off not-quite-French wedding coordinator—stop his baby sister from having the wedding of her dreams.

Across the room, V ended her call and started walking toward him just as Robért pushed through the swinging doors of the kitchen with a rolling cart. "Don't worry, I'll handle everything. You just get my sister healthy so she can travel and marry your punk ass. Gotta go."

"Jackso—"

Jax tapped the end button and put his phone away just before Vanessa sat in the chair to his right. She kept her attention on Robért setting out a silver tray of mini cakes and small bowls of filling.

He hated that she refused to look at him. Hated that he'd upset her.

Without thinking about it, he gently lifted her hand and pressed his lips to the delicate skin above her knuckles. He didn't hear it, but rather saw the breath catch in her throat as her eyes flicked to his. Within their depths he saw the barest glimmer of desire beneath the uncertainty.

"Oh, look how sweet!" Robért exclaimed. "I swear, you are just the loveliest couple. You still act like new lovers. So refreshing!"

Vanessa snatched her hand back and gave the man a nervous smile. "So, what do you have for us, Robért? I'm anxious to figure out the cake."

"Of course, of course! Let's get down to the hard work of cake tasting, shall we? Then you two can go back to the room and work off those extra calories, if you know what I mean."

Jax peeked over at Vanessa, who turned bright red and took a sip of her ice water as Robért busied himself with presenting the first cake.

"O-kay, here we go. The first cake is a vanilla cream. It's light with a delicate vanilla flavor, the most popular cake we have, and of course can be paired with any of our specialty fillings. Popular choices are pineapple curd, guava buttercream, and white chocolate cream cheese. Go ahead, dig in."

They each sliced off a piece with the edge of their forks. Being a glutton for punishment, Jax watched as Vanessa placed the cake in her mouth and slid the utensil back out. Torrid images—the sort he definitely didn't need right now—flooded his mind. Giving his dick a command to heel, he focused on tasting the cake he'd put in his own mouth. It was just as Robért described.

"Well?"

Jax looked over at their host and lifted an eyebrow in question.

"What do you think? You can't taste the cake and not say anything. You need to tell me if you like it, if you don't like it . . ."

"Oh," Jax said, clearing his throat before taking a sip of his water. "I like it a lot, but it's a little on the plain side. Don't you think, babe?"

Vanessa didn't look at him when she responded. "I agree. I like it, but I think she—uh, I want something a little less common."

Robért clasped his hands to his chest and said, "I couldn't agree more. Next cake!"

He took another sample from the tray and placed it before them.

"Now, this is a chocolate butter cake. It's used in our chocolate decadence and mocha macadamia cakes."

Vanessa was busy taking another drink of her water when Jax cut a small piece of the cake onto his fork. Instead of taking it himself, he turned it to her and waited expectantly. Her eyes flicked to the cake. Then up at him. Back to the cake.

Whether she was uncomfortable with acting like a couple in front of Robért or it was something else, he wasn't sure. But he didn't back down. He hated that she'd shut him out. He missed seeing the sparkle in her eyes when she looked at him. So if he had to force her to acknowledge him, then that's what he'd do.

Finally, she leaned forward and took the offered cake as she held his gaze. Absolutely stunning. As she pulled back, he again watched as her lips dragged on the metal tines, and he swore the temperature in the room kicked up at least a dozen degrees. Holy hell.

"Mmm. That's really good," she said. "What kind of fillings would be used for this?"

"Ah!" Robért placed two of the small bowls next to the plate of cake. Pointing to the first bowl, he said, "The chocolate macadamia is filled with chocolate ganache, coffee buttercream, and crushed macadamia nut brittle. Very unordinary. And the chocolate decadence is paired with a classic combo of chocolate ganache and rich raspberry."

This time she made sure she was on point with dipping her own spoon in the creamy ganache so Jax didn't have the opportunity to feed her again. For posterity's sake, he did the same and tasted the filling, but he couldn't have told Robért if it tasted like coconuts or dirt. His focus was on Vanessa.

When she pulled her spoon out of her mouth, a bit of frosting remained on the corner of her lower lip. Reaching out, he used his thumb to clean it off. Again, she seemed to stop breathing for a second. But this time when their eyes met, the desire that had been pushed to the back now shined through.

It took everything Jax had to not tell Robért to pick the damn cake himself and haul her off to their room.

They tasted a few other combinations and ultimately decided on a light coconut cake with haupia coconut custard filling and Italian buttercream icing. Even if Jax hadn't known Lucie had an affinity for coconut, he'd have known Vanessa made the choice based on Lucie's likes and not her own. Based on subtle hints he'd picked up on, he was pretty sure that not only was the chocolate decadence her favorite, but that fruit with chocolate in general was something she enjoyed. He made a mental note.

"Thank you so much, Robért," Vanessa said as she stood. "Please tell the chef they were all wonderful. I appreciate it very much."

"It was our pleasure, believe me. Now go have some fun and I'll see you soon!"

Jax rose as well, waited for their hug and double air-kiss to be over, shook Robért's hand, then started to escort V out of the restaurant.

"Oh, my goodness, I almost forgot!" They turned around to see a distressed Robért following after them. "I'm afraid I have some bad news."

Vanessa gave Jax a concerned look. "What is it?"

"I heard from my friend this morning and he can't cover the other wedding for me. Something about a last minute vow renewal he got roped into. I'm so sorry, can you forgive me? I wanted to be there so badly."

Palpable relief relaxed Vanessa's shoulders as she released a long exhale. Thankfully, to Robért it would just appear as disappointment. "Please don't give it another thought, Robért. We completely understand, don't we, Reid?"

Cue terrible acting. "Oh, yeah," Jax added. "Completely. Man's gotta do what a man's gotta do, right?" Don't ask him what the hell that was supposed to mean. It was all he could come up with on short notice.

The other two people in the conversation stared him blankly for a few seconds before simultaneously deciding to ignore him and move on with their emotional back and forth. Eventually they wrapped things up and they gave leaving another shot.

They'd no sooner hit the path outside when her cell rang. Sounded like a client, and based on her half of the conversation, she was gearing up for a long night of work.

Shoving his hands in his pockets, he followed after her and smiled to himself. There was no way he'd let her ignore him the rest of the night. Time to formulate a plan.

Vanessa stared at the file in her lap and chewed on the end of her pen. It had been a bad habit growing up. All of her pens and pencils looked like rats had gnawed on them. Once she became an attorney, she'd managed to break herself of it. The last thing she wanted was for the opposing counsel to see her chewing on her writing utensils and thinking she was nervous or incompetent.

But here she was, a half hour into working, and the top of her pen looked like a beaver attacked it. Damn it.

The bathroom door opened. She discreetly peered up through her lashes . . . and then wished she hadn't.

Jackson emerged, crossing the open bedroom doorway with nothing but a towel . . . that was currently drying his hair. Vanessa clenched her teeth to prevent her mouth from hanging open at the glistening, Olympian body he'd just paraded openly. She heard the sound of a dresser drawer opening, then closing, and then cursed herself for praying he'd dress in the bathroom.

Whistling the chorus from the Pussycat Dolls's "Don't Cha," he strode back into the bathroom carrying—thank you, baby Jesus—a pair of jersey shorts and a wifebeater.

As soon as the door closed, she groaned in frustration. She couldn't concentrate with him around. He was a distraction and a nuisance. A really hot nuisance who almost never wore a shirt. How the hell was she supposed to focus with him strutting around half naked all the damn time like some Hawaiian god?

If he knew she'd been staring, he hadn't shown it, but then again, what reason would he have to go back into the bathroom naked? The tramp probably knew she'd been watching the whole time.

She'd done her best to stay emotionally distanced from him since they left the gym. The fact that she'd been so upset over him attacking Danny didn't sit well with her. To disapprove of how he handled something was one thing. But it was another thing entirely to feel like her insides were turning out at the possibility of him hiding violent tendencies. It should not have affected her that much.

Which could only mean one thing: she'd let herself get emotionally invested with one Jackson Maris.

Vanessa thought back to the cake tasting. Jackson had actually been tender with her. The softness of his lips on her hand made the room around her fade to black as she stared into the golden light of his eyes. When he fed her the cake from his fork, it seemed more intimate, more sensual, than the act warranted. And when he wiped the frosting from her lip, she'd wished he'd removed it with a kiss.

But how did she know he hadn't been doing all of those things for Robért's benefit? Even worse, what if his tenderness had truly been sincere? The former made her want to kick his ass. The latter made her want to kiss him until they both forgot to breathe. Which then made her want to kick her own ass for getting the least bit sentimental when it came to that man.

"I'm a hot mess," she muttered to herself. And if there was one thing Vanessa Ann MacGregor hated, it was being a hot mess. On the outside or the inside. That's why her Rules worked so well for her. It kept everything in her life the way she needed it to be.

So what are you going to do about it, Nessie?

There was only one thing she could think of to untangle herself. She had to avoid having sex with Jackson the rest of the week. Not that she'd tell him outright, of course. But women got out of having sex every day. They had headaches or cramps or they were too tired . . . She'd never used excuses before, but surely it couldn't be that hard to convince a man you weren't up for the occasion, so to speak.

Just then a knock sounded on the door.

"I'll get it." Jackson entered the room, giving her equal relief and disappointment, and answered the door. A few moments later he sat next to her on the couch and set a tray on the coffee table that held a bottle of Patrón, two shot glasses, a saltshaker, and a bowl of lime wedges.

"What's all that?" she asked with a point of her disfigured pen.

"Has it been so long since you've had fun that you forgot what it looks like?"

"For your information, I have fun all the time. I'll have you know I'm Queen Fun back home. Ask your sister."

"Instead of calling my poor sick sister to verify your story, why don't you just put your money where your mouth is?"

"I have work to do, Jackson."

"You've been working for the last several hours, including straight through dinner. It's way past closing time, V," he said, cracking open the bottle with a mischievous smile.

She tried to hold it back, but at least half of the smile crept on her face anyway.

He stopped and studied her. "What?" he asked.

"We're about to find out if you pass the Bonus Rule."

"Which is . . ."

"Never date a man who can't out-drink you in tequila."

He smiled widely and leaned in. "You're going down, MacGregor."

Vanessa quickly weighed the pros and cons of participating in what boiled down to a pissing match involving alcohol with the man she'd recently decided was off-limits. In the Pros column: a break from work, good tequila, and taking Mr. Arrogance down a peg or two by drinking him under the table. In the Cons column: strong probability of getting drunk, thereby skewing her good judgment, and Mr. Arrogance taking her downtown to Shag Town. And that would be bad.

On the other hand, it'd be drunken sex, and drunken sex was never about emotions or touchy-feely crap. It was crazy, awkward moves performed by inept, half-dressed individuals who ended up with bruises from falling into lamps and who almost never had anything more than a bare recollection of the night's events. Therefore, even if worse came to worst, it still wouldn't interfere with the new keep-her-distance rule. Perfect, she thought, smiling to herself.

Moving her files off to the side, Vanessa situated herself sideways on the couch to face her opponent. "We'll see who goes down, Maris. Pour."

Jackson uncorked the bottle, poured the tequila in the shot glasses, then picked one up and waited for her to do the same.

Without hesitation, she raised her glass, said, "Salut," and tossed it back.

"No salt or lime chaser?"

"I don't need that stuff, but don't let that stop you.

Some people can't handle the bite of tequila. I promise I won't judge."

An evil grin curled the edges of his lips. "I didn't order the extra stuff for me, princess." After throwing the clear liquid down his throat, he added, "At least not for that."

And with that cryptic statement hanging between them, Jackson took her glass and poured them each another round.

"What do you say we make things a little more interesting?"

Vanessa raised a brow as she poured them both their next shot. "That depends on what you mean by interesting."

"A harmless get-to-know-you game."

"A drinking game?" She actually looked excited about the prospect for a whole two seconds. Then she narrowed her eyes, nearly twining those long sable lashes. "Does it involve losing articles of clothing?"

He held up his right hand, "I swear the loser is not required to remove any of his or her clothing." Said the spider to the fly.

Her shoulders relaxed and she leaned in slightly. "Okay, how do we play?"

"I'll make a statement about myself. It can be true or completely fabricated. You then have to guess which and say 'true' or 'bullshit.' If you're right, you get to pick a place on your body that I do a shot from. If you're wrong, I get to pick the spot. Then we switch roles."

Vanessa opened her mouth but nothing came out. She closed it. Tried again. Finally, she shook her head. "I've played a lot of drinking games in my day, but I've never heard of anything like this. Dare I ask what it's called?"

Jax grinned. "Bullshit Body Shots. Reid and I made it up with our girlfriends in high school."

"I have no doubt," she said wryly.

"C'mon, V. You're a lawyer, and according to you, a damn good one. You should be able to smell my bullshit from a mile away. Unless of course you're not as good as you claim."

Yeah, he was baiting her. Again. He seemed to be making it a habit with her. And even though she clearly recognized them for what they were, she couldn't resist accepting his challenges. A trait he loved about her.

Finally, with a roll of her eyes, she said, "Go ahead and start."

Game on. He'd start them off easy. "I was all-conference in wrestling my senior year in high school."

"True. Your sister told me that forever ago."

He figured as much, but he wanted her comfortable. And unsuspecting. "Where am I doing the shot?"

She made a show of thinking it over, then held out the inside of her wrist. He knew she'd go with somewhere safe. Or at least what she thought would be safe.

Grabbing the saltshaker in one hand and her wrist in the other, he kept eye contact with her as he brought his face slowly closer to his target. He licked a languid path across the soft skin, feeling her strong pulse speed up against his tongue. Vanessa's pupils grew larger as he added a dash of salt, then licked it off in the same manner as before. He threw back his shot, enjoying the burn as it slid down his throat.

When she tried to pull her hand back—most likely assuming that was the end of its use—he held firm. "Ah-ah-ah. I still need this."

"For what?"

He didn't answer her with words but took one of the lime wedges and lightly squeezed it—enough for several drops to land and stream over the edges of her wrist—

and then finished the process with an open-mouthed kiss to suck off the remaining juice. Then he released her.

"That's not . . ." Her voice broke slightly and she cleared her throat to try again. "That's not how body shots are done."

"They are in this game. Your turn, Viper."

Reminding her of her tough-girl persona did the trick. She composed herself, donned her game face, and took her turn. "I grew up in a really shitty neighborhood in Queens, New York."

"Bullshit. You don't have the accent."

"Wrong, and your assumption is the reason I worked to strip the accent out of me. I didn't like that people could identify where I grew up and pass judgment on me simply for how I sounded."

He wasn't surprised to hear she'd actively worked to improve something about herself she saw as a fault. Vanessa seemed intent she and everything else in her life was above par. More than ever he suspected something in her past was what drove her to be so strict about how her future should be. The question was, what?

"Good for you, V, I think that's great. It also means you get to choose where you'd like to do your shot."

The thought of Vanessa licking him anywhere had his blood draining to a central area of his body. She indicated his neck and didn't hesitate to go through the ritual. Every stroke of her tongue licked flames up the side of his throat, consuming him a little at a time. He swore he almost cracked his jaw from clenching it to keep from turning his head and attacking her mouth.

When she finished, he gave her a half smile that he hoped said, That was about as much of a turn-on as shopping for car insurance, but thanks for trying. The slight widening of her eyes revealed a hint of incredulity at his lack of reaction, but he played it off like he was oblivious. Oblivious. Yeah, right.

Jax felt more like he was wired to notice every minute detail about her. From the shape of her eyes to the freckle on the back of her left knee. From the way her green irises could throw sparks when pissed to languid pools when relaxed.

Oblivious was the last thing he was when it came to this woman. And for the life of him, he didn't know why.

"Are we done or are you going to take another turn?" she asked.

He grinned. "Anxious to have my mouth on you again?"

"In your dreams, surfer boy."

He dropped the joking manner and stared directly into her eyes. "Actually, I'd appreciate it if you'd stay out of my dreams. Lusting after you during my waking hours is about all I can handle right now."

Her mouth opened as if to respond, but nothing came out. For a long moment they were silent, just stared at each other, until she lowered her gaze and tucked a side of her hair behind her ear. Finally, he broke the silence by taking his turn in the game.

"I'm deathly afraid of spiders. True or bullshit?"

She studied him carefully and then rendered her verdict. "Bullshit."

"Wrong."

"Really?"

"Reid and Lucie are the only people who know my weakness, so I expect you'll take that intel to your grave, MacGregor."

She made a production of crossing her heart and holding her right hand up. "I swear. I won't tell anyone you're afraid of itty-bitty bugs."

The little wench thought his phobia was amusing, eh? He'd show her amusing.

"My turn to drink." Grabbing the hem of her tank in his hands, he started lifting it up her stomach. He didn't make it much past her belly button before she grabbed his wrists and held tight. He looked up at her with a questioning arch of his brow.

"I thought you said there wouldn't be any removal of clothing."

"No, I said the loser wouldn't be required to remove any clothing. However, the winner can remove anything that gets in the way of him doing a shot in the location of his choosing."

"Holy shit," she said with wide eyes. "You lawyer loopholed me."

He winked. "Don't take it too hard. I took advantage of your arrogance."

"My arrogance?"

"Settle down, princess." Jax rotated his hands up, breaking free of her hold. "Your arrogance is one of the things I like most about you."

When she opened her mouth to protest, he laid a finger against her lips. "Shh. Rules are rules, after all."

She slitted her eyes, but there was no hiding the humor dancing behind her lashes. Sure she wouldn't argue anymore, he pulled her shirt over her head, discarding it somewhere on the floor behind him. A fancy black bra covered with sea green lace encased her breasts. They swelled over the tops of the cups that barely covered her nipples. It was quite possibly the most glorious piece of lingerie he'd ever seen.

"Sweet Jesus. Is that a matching set?" He zeroed in on her shorts, praying for X-ray vision.

"You'll have to win another round to find out." She gave him a satisfied smile. "Rules are rules, after all."

"Touché," he said, answering with a smile of his own. Too bad he was about to wipe that smirk right off her face.

Wrapping his hands around the sides of her ribs, Jax lifted her enough to set her back against the armrest of the couch. The look in her eyes told him she couldn't decide if she wanted to chastise him for man-handling her or let go of her need to control and see where it led.

He shifted over, keeping one of her legs behind him and pulling the other over his lap, until his hip pressed against her. Placing a hand on the center of her chest, he lightly pushed until her body yielded, allowing her shoulders and head to rest over the cushioned arm with her long curls spilling over the edge.

Seeing Vanessa in a vulnerable position like this was enough to damn near shatter his resolve. She was in an unfamiliar role, offering herself up to him without knowing for certain what he had planned. Shallow breaths caused her breasts to rise and fall, tempting him to abandon the game, tear off her bra, and devour the soft mounds until his lips were numb. And that was just the beginning of what he had planned for her. All in good time.

Leaning over her, he licked a path along the top swell of her breast. The way her supple flesh gave way to the gentle pressure of his tongue made his balls tighten, and when she tipped her pelvis slightly, rubbing herself against his hip, his cock jumped in anticipation.

Jax knew if he didn't finish the shot within the next few seconds, he'd lose all self-control. Salt, lick, shot, lime, and lick again. Having finished without giving in to his baser needs, he gave himself a mental pat on the back before supporting her head and lifting her back to a sitting position.

Her eyes weren't quite as sharp as usual and she didn't come back with a sarcastic remark. In fact, she wasn't saying anything. Merely staring up at him, her lower lip creased in the center like she'd been biting down on it.

"Your turn," he said, his voice rough.

Vanessa blinked hard, and he could almost see her coming back to herself. The dazed look was replaced with her cool, confident air. Clearing her throat, she gave a little toss of her hair and arched her brow at his still-close proximity. But he wasn't letting her distance herself more than she already had.

"Problem, princess?"

"Of course not." With a sly smile, she bent her front leg and tucked her foot between his legs. Jax clenched his jaw and forced himself not to react, even as lightning bolted from his balls all the way up his spine and back again. Instead, he casually held her leg against his chest as though he hadn't a care in the world and listened as she took her turn.

"In college I got really drunk one night with my RA, and we ended up having the stereotypical and experimental girl-on-girl action. But it was just that once."

"As much as I'd love the images floating around in my head right now to hold some truth, I'm going to say bullshit."

She let out a noise that said she wasn't happy with his answer. "What makes you think it's a lie?"

He shrugged. "I probably would've believed it had you said it happened with my sister. It makes more sense because you're best friends, and there's that level of trust there. You're too structured and in control to have drunken, spontaneous flings."

The initial aggravation of losing seemed to dissipate under the interested arch of a single eyebrow. "You've been paying attention; I'm impressed. So where do you want to do it?"

His mind raced through a dozen possibilities—the couch, the kitchen table, the shower, the bathroom counter, the—Hold up. "Where do I want to do what?"

She gave him a saucy smile that said she was more than happy to rain on his fantasy parade. "Where do you want me to do my shot?"

"Ah." Yanking his shirt over his head, he tossed it to the side, and holding her gaze, tapped the area between his pecs before stretching his arms along the back of the couch.

She paused for a moment and stared him down. She was thinking about something, willing her brain to fire on all cylinders despite the Patron in her blood mucking things up. He saw the determination in her eyes the moment she made up her mind. All that was left to do was wait for the verdict.

Reaching over, she gathered the necessary items, placing her shot glass in his left hand, the saltshaker in his right, and her wedge of lime between his teeth. Then, in one smooth motion she rose up to her knees on the couch and swung a leg over his hips like she was mounting a horse. He'd thought he had the upper hand, but as he stared into her fiery green eyes, stretched out beneath her, holding things she gave him, he felt more like a submissive.

And at the moment, he couldn't give a good goddamn.

Pressing herself to him, she slowly sank down, rubbing the crotch of those thin cotton shorts of hers over the ridges of his abdomen until firmly seated over his stiff cock. The double layer of clothing did nothing to prevent the heat of her sex from searing him through the material. He bit back a groan and forced his hips to remain still. Not an easy task when his dick wanted to play Heat-Seeking Missile and the hottest thing for miles was in the deepest recess of a redheaded beauty, mere fractions of an inch away.

Placing her palms on either side of his chest, Vanessa leaned over and licked a slow, languid path between his pecs up to the hollow of his throat. The softest of moans escaped like a purr from a cat savoring the last drop of cream in her bowl.

She raised her head, giving him a wicked smile as she took the shaker from his hand. A dash of salt and she was at it again, the coarse grains scratching his flesh before sticking to her tongue. Jackson barely contained another moan. He didn't want her knowing just how much she affected him. Not yet.

His recently freed hand abandoned the back of the couch for the supple curve of her ass. She didn't bother trying to get him to take back the salt, instead reaching behind her to place it on the table.

A moment later she retrieved her shot. As soon as his hand was empty it filled itself in the same manner as the other, all ten fingers digging into her ass, pulling her down on his hard cock. To her credit, she remained in control, the only sign she'd felt anything at all was a small hitch in her breath. It was enough.

Lifting the small glass to her lips, she slowly tipped her head back, gradually displaying her graceful neck as the liquid emptied into her mouth. Once she'd placed the glass behind her, she plucked the lime from his mouth and squeezed it over the center of his chest. The cold, sticky juice streamed between his pecs, through the valley of his abs, and pooled in his navel briefly before spilling over and soaking into the waistband of his shorts.

Vanessa scooted off his lap before he had the chance to protest, but as soon as she knelt between his legs, he quickly forgave her the infraction. He held his breath, his heart pounding in his ears, as she lowered her head to lap the juice from his skin. She trailed her tongue up the line of dark hair, laved the recess of his belly button, and continued through the valley of his abs and between his pecs.

The higher she went, the closer her body pressed to his, her breasts caressing his balls and the length of his cock on their ascent. Unable to handle any more torture, he grabbed her by the upper arms and hauled her the rest of the way until she once again straddled his lap.

The restraint he used to keep himself in check made his throat tight and his voice little more than a rasp. "You went rogue on me, babe. I pointed to my chest."

She shrugged a slim shoulder. "Creative license. Do you object?"

"Not even a little." He rocked his hips up once, making her gasp. "Did I taste good?"

"Like a margarita during happy hour after winning a long case."

"Wow," he said, rubbing the stubble on his jaw up her neck as he spoke in her ear. "That does sound pretty good."

"I should try another sample, though. To make sure the evidence is conclusive. But this time, I'll choose the location."

He wanted to tell her she could sample him as much as she liked. Hell, he'd even give her suggestions for where to start. But he wasn't going to rush this. Not tonight. Not again. Just as she leaned in to kiss him, he stopped her with a finger to her chin and said, "Then you'll have to win that right."

Eyebrow cocked, she leaned back to study him as though expecting him to retract his dumbass statement at any moment. A part of him—namely the part that was hard enough to nail railroad spikes—waited for the same thing.

He ignored them both.

"My turn." He pretended to be thinking of a statement, hoping she'd take it as him trying to think up a lie as opposed to thinking up a truth. "Got one. I lost my virginity to my high school girlfriend's older sister when she was home from college."

"A college girl slumming with her little sister's boyfriend? No way. Bullshit."

He couldn't stop the shit-eating grin from plastering itself on his face. "Wrong."

"What? Are you serious?"

Jax had to wonder if her incredulity was due to the truth of the statement or the fact that she was actually wrong. Probably a little of both. Or a lot of both.

He held his right hand up. "Swear to God. Junior year. I'd just started dating Aimee Anders. I showed up at her house that Saturday to hang out, but she was late in getting back from a volleyball tournament. Her older sister, Jean, a sophomore at UNLV, was home for the holidays and told me I could wait for Aimee with her. One minute we're watching TV, the next minute Jean was on my lap tutoring me on the finer points of higher learning."

"Unreal." Vanessa shook her head and added, "You realize that makes you a total dog, right?"

"Technically, yes, but Aimee and I were only dating to make her ex jealous. We were strictly friends, which absolves me of any wrongdoing."

"Yeah, I'm afraid the jury's still out on that one, Mr. Maris."

Without warning, Jax grabbed her and tossed her on her back. Her wild hair spread out around her head and the smile she gave him was as bright as the full moon on a clear night. He pinned her down with his weight, pressing his hard length against her sex. She gasped and arched into him instinctively. He forced himself to hold still, despite his body's insistence he roll his hips over her to find release in whatever manner possible.

"My turn again."

"And where, pray tell, do you plan on doing it this time?"

"Talk is cheap, Counselor. I'm a man of action." He captured her wrists and placed them above her head on the arm of the couch. "Be good and keep those there for me."

"And if I don't?"

"Move 'em and find out." He nipped her earlobe, then whispered, "I'm kind of hoping you do."

Without waiting for her to respond, he rose up to his knees, tucked his fingers into the elastic waistband of her shorts, and pulled them down. As he drew them over her hips, his mouth dried up and his eyes glued to her panties. Tossing the shorts over his shoulder, he studied the small triangle of sea green lace over black satin until he knew he could draw every detail from memory if needed. Only then did he allow himself to look at her body in its entirety.

"So damn gorgeous."

He planted his hands on either side of her hips and slowly lowered himself. He hovered over the juncture where thigh met pelvis, keeping her bound with anticipation. Her eyes transfixed to his mouth and the rise and fall of her chest became faster and faster. The black of her pupils swallowed the green of her irises, her front teeth captured her lower lip . . . and still he held. She wanted his mouth on her just as badly as he did. But he wasn't moving another millimeter until she asked.

Later, he'd make her beg.

Seconds ticked by, the pair of them locked in an un-spoken match of wills. He felt the heat coming off her and he smelled her arousal. Finally, she succumbed to the need and rolled her hips up.

Good girl.

He gladly licked the line all the way up to her hip-bone. A little salt and he was at it again, this time add-ing pressure and causing her to whimper, her body to shudder.

He took his shot, not even pausing to register the burn before squeezing a lime wedge along the lace edge of her panties. Not one to waste anything, he quickly dipped down and licked the stream that had spilled over between her legs. She moaned in the back of her throat as he moved to kiss off the liquid that had pooled at the top.

"Enough," he growled as he moved up her body. "No more games. I'm taking what I want. What we both want."

Vanessa could already tell her earlier thought process had been way off the mark. Drunken sex with Jackson Maris wasn't going to be any less intense than sober sex. Probably because neither of them was drunk. Buzzed, yes. Wasted . . . not even a little.

It didn't matter that they'd both just had enough shots to put most people on their asses. She should've guessed a man like Jax wouldn't have suggested something he couldn't win. The man could seriously hold his liquor, and it just so happened tequila was the only thing she could drink her weight in and still be coherent. Had he picked something else, she'd have passed out a half hour ago in an unattractive heap after making a total ass of herself.

But instead, she'd played a game with a dragon and

ended up pinned beneath his massive body as he prepared to breathe fire. Golden eyes framed in dark lashes held her captive. With the instinct of a moth, she cupped his face and kissed his lips, sacrificing her better judgment to the hypnotizing flames.

Jackson accepted her kiss, then pushed her back into the cushion as he took over. His tongue was a sweet invasion, exploring and tasting between nibbles on her lips that made her feel like the most delectable of desserts.

Slipping one arm under her head, he snaked his other hand behind her back. With the flick of his fingers, he released her bra and tore it from her. Her breasts, which had always been very sensitive, felt heavy and full and charged with electricity. The moment his bare chest pressed into hers, her nipples tightened painfully, pleading for the attention they'd been denied the night before.

As though reading her mind, he broke the kiss and plumped her right breast with his large hand. His calluses dragged over her skin, causing delicious vibrations that had her arching farther into his palm. She never knew a man's hands could create such sensations. She'd always dated white-collar men. Not because she preferred them, but because those were the men in her circle. Their hands were smooth and unremarkable. Not like Jackson's. If she had any musical talent whatsoever, she'd write an entire album dedicated to the man's hands alone.

She peered down to see one of the most erotic sights. The top of his head hovered over her chest, his dark hair slightly mussed. All his attention focused on the breast he held. He swiped the rough pad of his thumb over her distended bud, sending the white-hot electricity on a one-way trip to her core. Her breath hissed through her teeth as the shock took hold in its new home.

He looked up, a knowing glint in his gaze as he slowly lowered his head and enveloped her nipple in the glorious heat of his mouth. She cried out and fisted her fingers into his short hair so hard she knew it had to hurt, but he didn't seem to mind. In fact, his pupils dilated and he opened wide to take as much of her into his mouth as he could. His tongue swirled and flicked on the inside, building frissons of pleasure that exploded when he scraped his teeth over the hard tip.

Needing the same attention for her other breast, she held it in offering with one hand while trying to push his head over. He did release the one he'd worked over, leaving it cherry red and glistening wet, but didn't follow her lead as she'd hoped. Instead, he paused just before descending on her aching breast, then switched directions and kissed his way down her body.

She groaned, both frustrated and aggravated he'd ignored what she wanted to follow his own agenda. Once he moved low enough where she was no longer pinned by his body, she scooted up to a sitting position. The surprise on his face was only there for a split second, but it was enough to calm the slight need to jump out of her skin.

She pushed him back into a sitting position and straddled his lap, grinding herself on the erection straining under his shorts. Now it was his turn to groan as his head dropped to the back of the couch. Unable to resist, she licked up the column of his throat and sucked on the spot just behind his ear. His fingers burrowed beneath her panties and dug into the flesh of her ass. Returning the favor, he brought his mouth to her neck and trailed wet kisses up to her jaw. But she wanted more.

Leaning back, she again palmed her left breast. "Kiss me here," she said.

He circled two of his fingers around her nipple, making

it pull tighter as the pent-up tingling followed the path of his touch and made her needier with each passing second. He made sure to stay at the edges of her areola, teasing her mercilessly. She clenched her jaw and held still, telling herself the torture would be worth it when he finally gave her the release.

"Are you sure?"

"Yes."

"Right now?"

"God, yes, now."

When she thought she couldn't take it another moment, he stopped, looked her in the eyes, and said, "Ask me nicely."

Record scratch. "What?"

"You heard me." He dragged the rough pads of his fingers over the under swell, igniting every nerve ending in the vicinity. "Ask me nicely to suck on your beautiful breast."

His demand rankled. A lot. "You want me to beg. I don't beg anyone for anything."

He cocked his eyebrow, the jagged scar raising its own doubt in her direction. "I believe you agreed to give me control during sex."

A bolt of panic sent the hairs on the back of her neck up. "That doesn't mean I'll beg for what I want."

"Is that so?"

She lifted her chin and tried to ignore the screaming needs of her body. She'd walk away from him and spend the night with a battery-operated substitute if she had to.

"Yes, that's so."

"Challenge accepted."

"What—"

Before she had time to register anything, he picked her up, spun around, and deposited her on the couch where he'd sat moments before. Kneeling on the floor between her legs, he pulled her hips forward to the edge of the cushion. Too shocked to do anything else, she watched as his hands pushed her knees out as far as they'd go before sliding up the inside of her thighs.

When his thumbs grazed the edges of her panties they slid over the silk, one pressing over the sensitive spot at the top, the other sliding over the path already wet with desire. Up and down, up and down his thumb stroked, each time adding a little more pressure.

Her sex pulsed with the need to be filled, aching from denial. When at last he pulled her panties off, she released a shaky exhale and tried to control herself. He was trying to get her to crack, but if the state of his cock was any indication, he wouldn't be able to hold out for much longer. She just had to ride it out and wait for the typical male screw it reaction. No pun intended.

"Starfish, huh?"

She glanced down at the coral-colored tattoo the size of a quarter that could only be seen if she was fully naked. Most of the time she forgot it was even there. "Sea star."

"Whatever."

"Not whate—"

"Hey, Red, lecture me later, okay? Right now I need to look at you." He laid his hands over her breasts and trailed them down her body slowly until he reached the smooth skin of her mound.

"Christ, V, you're gorgeous." Pulling her swollen folds apart, he stared like under a spell. Butterflies took wing in her belly, and she felt new wetness where he pierced her with his eyes. "Pretty in pink," he whispered, using a finger to spread the warmth over her outer lips.

Finally, he licked a wide path from bottom to top, adding a flick of his tongue over her clit that had her hips rocketing off the cushion. Jax wrapped his arms under her thighs and brought his hands around at the juncture of her pelvis to hold her down. Then he dove in to perform the most illicit acts with his tongue ever attempted by any human. That was probably conjecture on her part, but it sure as hell felt like fact.

He was not a man who did anything without intent, and oral sex was no exception. There were no random patterns or juvenile ideas of tracing out the alphabet. Every lick, every flick, every thrust of his tongue had a purpose more lascivious than the last.

Her hands gravitated to her breasts, heavy and tight, and she plucked her nipples, adding pangs of pleasure that shot back and forth as he continued to make love to her with his mouth. Her hips tried to rock against him, but he easily pinned her with his strength. Whimpers escaped her lips, blood roared in her ears as her pulse skyrocketed out of control, and her breaths came fast and hard.

There was no denying it any longer. Jackson Maris was pure evil.

As though supporting her argument, he inserted two thick fingers and started thrusting as he focused his tongue on her clit. Sweat trickled between her breasts. The storm of desire deep in her center swirled faster and faster, threatening to explode in a thunderous clap.

He actually looked like he did this for his pleasure, not hers. When he used his fingers to explore and tease, his eyes never strayed, as though her sex was the most beautiful thing he'd ever seen. And when he closed his mouth over her, his lids drifted shut like the world's richest chocolate truffle was melting on his tongue. On top of the dizzying sensations he gave her, watching him was almost enough to make her come.

"Oh yes," she moaned. "I'm so close."

"I know, baby."

"Make me come."

He slowed his movements, bringing her down a level. The exact opposite of what she wanted. She groaned in frustration.

"You don't get to call the shots, princess. You need to ask me nicely."

Vanessa sucked her lower lip between her teeth and clamped down. Her body vibrated, both from the frenzy he'd whipped inside her and resisting what he demanded of her.

"Understand, Vanessa, that I never take my release before my lover. However," he continued, his gaze boring into her, "I also have the resolve to keep you on the edge like this for hours. It won't matter how blue my balls get or how badly I want to feel your pussy squeezing my cock. I won't give in until you give me what I want."

Shivers raced over her skin, leaving goose bumps in their wake, despite the sheen of sweat proving she was anything but cold.

"Now," he rasped as he dragged the pad of his thumb in circles around her clit, "I want you to ask me for what you want. Ask me to let you come, V."

His words coated her like honey as hers coated his fingers. No lover had ever spoken to her like that. It was hard to believe he could talk like that. Normally he was all charm and killer smile.

This side of Jackson was the complete opposite. His tone brooked no arguments, and there wasn't anything about the way he looked that led her to believe he was joking. On the contrary, she knew he meant every word.

And it turned her on. Way more than it should.

He flicked her clit with his thumb and she almost blacked out. Could you die from orgasm deprivation? She'd bet the answer was yes, but she had no desire to find out.

"Please, Jackson," she said, not only pleading with her words but in the way her back arched toward the ceiling and her fingers dug into her breasts. "Please let me come."

The muscles in his jaw leaped with a slight flare of his nostrils. "My pleasure."

An instant later he filled her up with three fingers, turning them up to stroke the sinful spot at the top with every retreat. The pleasure flared deep in her center. He'd kept her primed so long it took less than thirty seconds before she crested the swell. Her breaths turned to pants, her hands clawed at his strong shoulders, needing to ground herself as her body threatened to fly apart.

Her eyes had squeezed shut and she couldn't hear much over her own sounds, but she thought she heard him growl a "fucking beautiful" right before placing his mouth on her clit and sucking it in pulses that finally and blessedly gave her sweet release.

Jackson kissed his way up her body. With each sensual touch of his lips, she came back to herself a little more. By the time he reached her neck, she was fully aware again and somehow just as hungry for him as when they started.

Grabbing him by his head, she brought his mouth up and lifted her head to attack it. He met her urgency, moaning as she boldly licked his lips then bit down on the plump center. They fused together in a molten kiss, their tongues warring against each other. She tasted her sweet tang and the reminder of how her essence came to be there released another wave of warmth between her legs.

Jackson started to pull away from her, but she followed him, not wanting to release him from the kiss. He smiled against her lips, obviously enjoying her desperation to keep their connection. It should've tripped her defenses, prompting her to wrap herself in indifference and show him just how unaffected she was. But it didn't. He'd triggered something in her, uncovered a hunger she hadn't known she had. And now she no longer cared if he knew just how much she wanted him.

Once she sat all the way up, he held her shoulders to prevent her from following him as he stood. She looked up at him, mesmerized by his dominating presence and his sculpted physique. Being a fighter definitely gave him muscles she wasn't used to from the businessmen she usually dated.

He took out a condom from his back pocket and tossed it carelessly next to her on the couch. "Take my shorts off, V," he ordered gruffly.

She'd do as he said and take them off. But he hadn't specified how to take them off. Vanessa schooled her features to hold back the smirk that itched to flaunt her thoughts, then she placed her hands on his pecs. Moving them down his body, she reveled in the way her fingers undulated over the ripples of his abs and the deep V of his obliques slashing to the center of his body and her ultimate destination.

He arched his scarred eyebrow as she skirted her hands past the elastic of his shorts. No doubt he'd expected her to catch the waistband and do as he'd instructed. And she would. Eventually.

They continued down either side of his straining cock, her thumbs just barely brushing the sides. He sucked a sharp inhale through his teeth and narrowed his eyes at her. It hadn't been a huge reaction, but even that little bit of control gave her a heady rush. He hadn't stopped her yet, but she could see the warning on the tip of his tongue.

Using her teeth, she pulled his shorts down a couple inches on both sides, then pulled the center out and down, dragging the material over his erection and causing a delicious moan to escape his chest. Once they fell to the floor and he kicked them to the side, she was left staring eye-level at an impressive display of virility.

Their quick yet explosive session the night before had been all about feeling, not seeing. But now she looked her fill. She'd known by the feel of him that he wasn't a small man in any sense of the word, but she was surprised at just how not small he was. As she touched him, she discreetly gauged his size with her fingers. From root to tip, he spanned the length of her thumb and forefinger, and when she gripped him, her fingers barely touched. Well, hello there, big boy.

"I fit once already, V. I can do it again."

She'd been so lost in her own thoughts, his comment startled her. Glancing up at him, she huffed, "I know that."

He slid one of his hands into the hair at her nape and gave her a crooked and way-too-knowing smile. "Just wanted to make sure. You looked like maybe you were worried."

This man saw way too much with her. Good thing she knew how to distract him. Starting at the base, she kept her tongue loose so it hugged the underside of his cock and licked a slow, wet path all the way to the smooth cap at the top. His fingers contracted, fisting her hair, and his hips bucked.

She smiled, letting her satisfaction show on her face. "I may be smaller than you, but I can take anything you give me."

"I'm so holding you to that."

He let loose an animalistic growl, picked her up, and switched their positions so she once again straddled him on the couch. She wrapped her arms around his neck and pressed her body against his, obliterating the space between them. Following suit, Jackson's arms banded around her waist as he finally latched onto the breast that had started the whole series of events.

The feel of him drawing her deep into his mouth sent showers of sparks riding her skin and heating her blood. Her body bowed, her head dropping back until the ends of her hair tickled the base of her spine. He leaned over, their bodies melding from hips to ribs as he worshipped both of her breasts with his lips, his tongue, his teeth.

Unable to hold back any longer, she rocked her pelvis to cradle his cock between the slick folds of her sex. He groaned. She moaned. And they both reached for the condom next to them at the same time.

"Reading my mind, V?"

"I doubt it's your mind I'm reading, Maris," she said, scooting back a few inches.

"Probably right about that."

He tore the wrapper, but she took the latex ring from him before he had a chance to do anything. Despite her body's urges, she moved slowly, using both hands to encircle his thick shaft and roll it down to the base. Jackson sucked in a breath when she let her thumbs graze his tight sac underneath.

Then he loosed his caged beast.

Strong fingers dug into the flesh of her ass as he lifted her up and positioned the head of his cock at her swollen entrance. Between her tightness from already climaxing and his sheer size, Vanessa had a split second of panic that he'd never fit.

"Yes, I will," he rasped. "If it's the last thing I do, I'm burying myself in this sweet pussy." Oh, God, had she said that aloud? "Ease yourself down, baby. You can take me."

Jax reached between them and rubbed over her clit. She gasped as more wetness trailed down the inside of her thighs. It didn't matter if she believed him or not anymore. There was no way anything could take the place of holding him inside her. She needed it like she needed air. He'd been right the night before when he said no vibrator would ever be able to pleasure her more than him. Hell, she had a suspicion no other man would be able to, either. But for her sanity's sake, she couldn't let herself go down that road. Not now. Not ever.

She spread her knees a little at a time, slowly impaling herself. Down a couple of inches, then back up. Down an inch or so more, then back up. As he stretched her more and more, her insides tightened and her breaths shortened. Finally, she grabbed onto his shoulders for purchase and took him in to the hilt.

Pressing his forehead to her sternum he ground out, "Ah, fuck. Hold still, baby. Gimme a sec."

But holding still was the very last thing she wanted. She wanted to move. Needed to move. So she did.

Vanessa circled her hips once before pushing up, almost completely unseating herself. Jax made a sound like he'd just gotten kicked in the gut. His eyes snapped up to warn her. A warning she couldn't heed.

She began to move, up and down, back and forth, combinations of the four that she wasn't even sure were legit moves, but they felt so good with him she let instinct take over.

Suddenly, she heard a loud smack! a split second before she felt the sting on her left ass cheek. She gasped over a squeal and jerked up hard from the shock. But he'd apparently been ready for that and held her in place to prevent an escape.

"What in holy hell was that for?" she demanded, leaning back all of the three inches he allowed her and trying to ignore how the pain melted into a warm heat between her legs.

"What, that?" A wicked gleam appeared in his eye as his hand now rubbed the sore area in a soothing manner. "That was the first of several punishments I owe you, princess."

She thought back to the several instances he'd warned her of punishments. Shit, how many were there? She couldn't remember. But she'd bet her lingerie collection he remembered every one of them in detail. What she did remember was that her mouth, or sarcastic comments, had always been the trigger. Which was why she couldn't for the life of her figure out why she wasn't careful to temper the sarcastic tone in her response.

"So what, now you want to break out the whips and floggers, is that it?"

His hands roved over her back, her sides, her breasts. The roughness of his fingers and palms ignited her skin and reminded her body of where they left off seconds ago. As if it needed reminding.

"No, I'm not into the hardcore stuff. Besides," he said with a quick nip on her clavicle. "All I need to make your ass red and your pussy wet are my voice and my hands."

And with that she received a crack on the other side, causing an identical reaction to the first.

Vanessa mentally counted to ten while her insides stopped vibrating, then prayed her voice didn't sound just as shaky. "I don't like it."

She lied.

He licked the shell of her ear. "You lie."

She did.

"Now move, V," he ordered with a squeeze of his hands. "Ride me and I'll show you just how good a punishment can feel."

With a shudder racing down her spine, she let her lids drift shut and she began to move once again. Her mind dulled, her conscious thoughts fading fast in the wake of her body's more potent visceral demands.

Vanessa had never felt so torn during sex before. Jackson made her feel lost and found all at once. Lost to the intense desire he incited within her. Found, as though there was no other place she belonged more than in his arms. And both feelings scared the ever-loving hell out of her.

It would be so easy to ignore the facts and blame it on the alcohol. But even with the booze-induced carnage surrounding them as evidence, she couldn't make that argument stick. No, this . . . whatever it was, made no sense on any logical plane of existence. It just wasn't possible to have such strong, passionate feelings for a man she barely even liked. A man who made her want to throttle him as soon as kiss him.

Kiss him. Excellent idea.

Grabbing the sides of his face, she attacked his mouth, plunging her tongue past his lips to lick and twirl and drink in the taste of salt, lime, and Patron. This was a true body shot, and one for which she'd gladly suffer any mental hangovers she might incur.

He met her urgency ounce for ounce and then poured a hell of a lot more on for good measure. The kiss became a devouring. Their hands groped and clawed and tugged. It was fast and hard and utterly amazing. The tingling vibrations gathered in her center, pulsing their way up in quick succession like her climax was gasping for breath.

Somewhere in the physical din, she knew Jax continued to slap her ass every ten seconds or so, but she couldn't separate the sensual stings from the rest of the pleasure coursing through her. Every taste, every touch had woven together to create one exquisite sensation.

"Fuck, you feel so good on my cock, baby." Jax let

his head fall back on the couch. The tendons in his neck stood out and the muscles jumped above his jaw. "So. Fucking. Good."

She wanted to let him know how amazing it felt to be stretched and filled by him, but words failed her. All she could do was ride the massive wave hurtling her toward her release merely seconds away . . .

"V."

What? Great. Now her voice had failed her, too.

"Vanessa," he said, this time with a little more force. "I'm not giving you permission to come yet."

The blurred edges of her vision came into sharp relief as her eyes widened. He couldn't be serious.

"Prove to me how strong you are," he continued as he plunged his fingers into her hair and held her face close to his. "Not by taking what you want, but by holding yourself back from the very thing you want the most."

Her movements had decreased to shallow pulses, leaving the majority of her empty and aching. She swallowed hard, trying to create moisture where a desert had taken up residence. "Jax, please . . ."

"I'm not asking you to beg this time, baby." His thumb caressed the edge of her lower lip. "You're in the position to do what you want; I won't stop you. But I want you to feel what it's like to own your submission. To choose it."

"And if I don't?"

Disappointment flashed in his hazelnut eyes, and then it was gone as though it never was. In a firm tone he answered, "Then I'll take back my condition from last night. We'll finish out our fling without the control stipulation."

Clever man. Before, she'd told herself she agreed to his condition because she wanted the fling, even knowing it was merely a convenient veil to hide her taboo curiosity behind.

But now he'd given her the option to choose how they proceeded from this point on, forcing her to admit her desire to submit to his will . . . or choke on her pride and miss the opportunity to explore a side of her she'd never known existed until him.

"Okay," she whispered.

He gripped her hips hard, his fingers sinking into the meat of her ass, and held her still. "Okay what, Vanessa? What does that mean?"

Taking a deep breath, she clasped her hands behind her back. She wasn't sure what protocol was in this situation, but it seemed like the right gesture to support her words. "I want to give myself"—she dropped her gaze to his chest, the deference seeming both a betrayal to herself as well as an awakening—"and my orgasms over to you."

A quiet growl rippled from his chest and over hers, puckering her nipples. He must have noticed, too, because he brought his hands up to cup her curves and swipe his thumbs over the sensitive nubs, causing her to jolt.

"I can't lie, V. Those were the sexiest words I've ever heard. And the way you look right now—hands behind your back, pressing these beautiful breasts toward me, lips red and swollen, eyes downcast and ready for instruction." He gave her nipples a light pinch, causing her to jerk from the bolt of sheer pleasure. "It's the sexiest damn thing I've ever seen. You just might be my undoing."

Before she could ask him what he meant by that, he thrust up in one smooth motion, burying himself balls deep before ordering her to finish what she'd started. She wasted no time, easily finding her rhythm and the angle that allowed him to hit that glorious spot inside. When her hands came up to his arms, he circled her wrists and held them behind her again as she rode him to the edge of her climax.

"Jax?" she whimpered.

"Not yet," he rasped.

She ground her teeth together as sweat ran in rivulets from her temples and between her breasts. Holding herself on the sharp precipice of an orgasm was a sweet anguish she'd never be able to describe. How could something so torturous feel so totally amazing? Maybe this was like the sexual version of the Stockholm Syndrome, and Vanessa would find herself needing and loving the pleasure/pain only he could give her.

A minute longer and she'd die, no doubt in her mind. Thankfully, Jax must have felt the same way, because he spoke the words that released her at last. "Now, baby," he said against her neck. "Let go with me now."

And so she did, praying he'd hold onto her tight enough to prevent the cracks he'd made from breaking her wall into a million pieces.

Swaying gently in the hammock with Vanessa tucked under his arm, the soothing sounds of the ocean waves in the distance and the stars shining overhead, Jackson felt more at peace than he remembered being in the last decade.

Oh, he'd been content. Happy, even. But underneath all that had always been a sense of unease with himself. The mystery of who his real parents were—of who he was—had weighed on him since the day he found those papers and learned he'd been living a lie.

But something about Vanessa quieted the fray of unanswered questions inside him. The way she curled into him with her leg intertwined in his and her hand resting over his heart was surprisingly comforting. Not at all stifling like usual after he'd been with a woman. Not that he was the type to cut and run right after sex, but he liked his space in bed and wasn't much for cuddling in the afterglow.

However, tonight he'd gathered her up in his arms, grabbed the sheet from the bed, and settled them into the hammock with the bed sheet around them just enough to cover their nakedness.

Jax kissed the top of her head and continued stroking her arm with his fingers as he thought of his newest revelations about his faux fiancée.

The sex had been mind-blowing, to say the least. He'd had a taste of her last night, but it hadn't prepared him for what she'd be like completely unbridled. Passionate didn't even begin to describe her. It was like she'd been lit on fire from the inside, desperate for something—or someone—to put out the flames before they consumed her.

And as much as she fought for control, it wasn't what she wanted. Or needed.

Five minutes into meeting her, he'd pegged her as a total control freak. She organized her life and the people in it like feng shui enthusiasts organized their living spaces. A place for everything and everything in its place, his mom had been fond of saying. For as carefree and fun as she was on the outside, she was as rigid as any soldier on the inside.

She was one hell of a strong woman, used to taking the lead and giving the orders. It was probably one of the reasons she and Lucie were such great friends. Lucie wasn't a mindless sheep by any means, but she'd always been more comfortable letting others forge ahead so she could stay comfortably in the shadows.

Well, that was until Reid got a hold of her. Though

she still didn't enjoy being the center of attention as much as Reid, she'd definitely broken free of her cocoon. When he'd seen her a few months earlier she'd been absolutely radiant, finally comfortable in her own skin, and very much in love.

But his sister was the last person he wanted to think about right now. What he really wanted was to know more about the enigmatic woman in his arms. A woman who lived by a set of strict rules. A woman who could flirt and tease one minute, then shut down completely the next. A woman who needed control and yet so desperately wanted it taken from her.

More of those opposites that continued to draw him in as much as they'd possessed him on the first day to make up the crazy shit that put them in this scenario. As her soft breaths feathered across his chest, he couldn't bring himself to regret the lies. After all, without them he wouldn't be holding her like he was. What he did regret was that as soon as he told her the truth, she'd probably never speak to him again. And kick him in the junk for good measure.

"Hey, V?" he asked softly.

"Mmm-hmm."

"Mind if I ask you a personal question?"

"Shoot."

"Where did you get the idea for your rules?"

She stiffened in his arms and the lazy patterns she'd been drawing on his chest with her nail stopped. "I told you I won't talk about it."

"So you did." He continued stroking her arm until he felt her relax again. "What's the deal with the starfish?"

"Sea star."

"Whatever," he said, feeling a wave of déjà vu.

"But they're not fish, so it's inaccurate."

"Well, they're not stars, either." He immediately

wanted to smack himself upside the head. He was making light of something that obviously held meaning for her. He wouldn't like it if she made fun of him for inking his body with flowers.

To his surprise, though, she let out a short giggle and a, "Touché," yet again keeping him on his toes. Every time he thought he knew what to expect, she proved him wrong. He liked that.

"So what's the story?" he asked.

"Why does there have to be one?"

"Every tattoo has a story. Even if it's, 'I got bored, walked into a parlor, and pointed at the first pretty thing I saw.'"

She didn't respond for five back and forths of the hammock. He figured it was another topic not up for discussion.

"In high school, we had a unit on ocean life in science. The teacher talked about all different types of sea creatures. So many of them had features that were truly remarkable, but when she got to the sea stars I became fascinated with them."

"Why's that?"

"They're small with soft, vulnerable underbellies, so the tops are tough with tiny spines that protect them from predators. And if that isn't enough, they're able to drop one of their arms—literally leave a piece of them behind—so they can escape. It takes a long time, but eventually they grow a new arm to replace the one they lost."

She'd only listed facts. No different than reading a paragraph out of a National Geographic article. And yet, it wasn't hard for him to read between the lines. "You relate to them."

Jax felt her tense briefly, and then relax herself piece by piece, like it was an exercise she practiced often. "Yes," she answered. "I do."

He thought as much. Her admission was a crack in her resolve to push him away. But he didn't want a hairline fissure. He wanted her to open to him completely. To trust him with her secrets so that maybe she could unload some of them and feel a little lighter for doing so.

Who the fuck are you kidding? You're the pot to her kettle.

Taking a deep breath, Jax said something he'd sworn to himself he'd never say to anyone for as long as he lived.

"I was adopted. It's the reason I moved here—to find my birth parents. It took several years, but eventually I learned that my birth mother got pregnant by a man staying on the island for business for several months. He left somewhere in her third trimester and never came back. So she gave me up for adoption. I found out she died from some sort of infection the year before I came here."

"Jackson, I'm so sorry. Lucie never told me."

"That's because she doesn't know. No one does."

Her head angled up so she could look at him, but he didn't meet her eyes. He couldn't. A deafening silence surrounded them. Even the waves seemed to pause and the palms above them no longer swayed as Vanessa processed the fact that his own sister didn't know the most vital piece of information about him. The sound of his heart beat in his ears, its tempo increasing the longer she failed to respond in some way.

"I don't understand. Why would your parents have kept it a secret from her?"

"They kept it a secret from both of us. I didn't find out until after the accident when I found the adoption paperwork." He let out a mirthless chuckle. "Of course, how I didn't come to the conclusion on my own I'll never know. Physically speaking, I'm nothing like them and Lucie."

Her brow furrowed. "After all these years, why haven't you told Lucie?"

"In the beginning, I didn't want to add more to the pile of crap she already had to deal with. She'd just lost both of her parents at a crucial age and wound up being raised by her barely legal older brother. Saying, 'Oh by the way, I'm not really your brother,' didn't feel right. I mean, I couldn't even wrap my head around it, so how could I expect her to?"

"But it's been more than fifteen years since your parents died, so why not tell her later?"

Jax scrubbed his free hand over his face and then shoved it under his head as he let out a heavy exhale. "I don't know. Every time I thought about telling her I just . . . couldn't."

His throat closed up and the stars began to blur. Swallowing hard to get past the lump, he blinked a few times until the world came back into focus. He hated talking about this. Hated how weak it made him sound. But he couldn't expect Vanessa to let him in if he stayed locked down like Fort Knox. So he sucked it up and continued to verbalize the things that until now had only lived in his head.

"I guess I felt like I'd already lost my status as a son to my parents. Lucie's all I've got left in the world. She means everything to me. I couldn't handle it if she didn't think of me as her brother anymore."

"Jackson, look at me." When he didn't move, she palmed the side of his face and coaxed him to turn his head. "Lucie would never in a million years look at you any differently than she always has. As her big brother who took care of, protected, and loved her with all his heart. That's who you are to Lucie, no matter what your DNA says."

His knee-jerk reaction was to argue with her—or at

least agree to disagree—but the conviction of her statement stared back at him from the depths of her eyes. So instead he dipped his head and captured her lips for a kiss meant as a thank-you and a punctuation mark on the topic. He didn't regret opening up to her, but now he needed some time to let the open wound scab over.

Vanessa settled back into his side, tucking her head between his neck and shoulder again. The hammock was close enough to their privacy fence that he could reach it with his fingers, so he gave them a tiny push, closed his eyes, and tried not to think about what he'd just revealed about himself to a woman he barely knew.

He didn't know how long they lay like that, but he guessed it was long enough for her to fall asleep. She hadn't moved and her breaths were even. So he was lucky he didn't accidentally flip them over when she spoke unexpectedly.

"NCIS."

Jax gave his heart a minute to regulate and made a mental note to spank her later for nearly causing him to go into arrest. "What's NCIS?"

"It's one of those crime dramas on TV. You know, like CSI, but it's based on the Navy unit."

"Oh, right. What about it?"

"That's where I came up with the idea for my rules."

His eyes flew open, but he didn't move a muscle. Now she had his attention. The question was, how much would she open up to him? He genuinely wanted to know what made her tick. Why she was so caught up in her rules that she refused to even bend on them most times. Not wanting to push the issue, he remained quiet and waited for her to reveal more.

"See, the main character's wife had these rules that she liked to use. He thought it was cute and endearing. But then she was killed, along with their only daughter, and he became a tortured individual who carried on her rules and then added to them over the years. By the time the show starts, he already has some forty plus that he teaches his agents as life lessons."

"So you saw the show and liked the idea so much that you made up your own?" He might not know her very well, but what little he did know of her didn't match up with such an impulsive act. "No offense, V, but that seems a little extreme."

"Yeah, well, when you've had an entire bottle of tequila by yourself after having a particularly shitty conversation with your mother, lots of extreme things tend to sound surprisingly normal."

Very carefully, Jax situated himself in the hammock on his side so he could look into her eyes as they talked. With her head resting on the inside of his bicep and their bodies naturally falling into the middle, they were as close as they could get without removing the sheet covering her from breasts to hips.

He tucked a stray curl behind her ear and let it glide through his fingertips. "From what I understand, every girl goes through a time in her life when she butts heads with her mom."

Her bitter laugh made the hairs on the back of his neck stand on end and the tone in her voice was flat with a knife's edge. She stared straight ahead at his chest, but he knew she saw something else. Something in her past. "I would've given anything to have the stereotypical misunderstandings and petty fights over what I had."

Initially, it'd been simple curiosity about what made her tick that prompted his questions. Then it turned into a challenge because she refused to tell him and made him agree to ridiculous stipulations. Later, the incident at the gym left him unsettled about the reason she reacted so strongly to him punching a guy who deserved it. But now something that felt a lot like the need to protect spread through his chest.

The warning bell sounded in his head. It was the bell that told him he was about to end the playful wrestling session he'd been having with Vanessa and step into the cage with her demons.

He always listened to that bell.

It warned him when things were about to get too serious. When there was a chance he was walking into a situation he had no chance of winning. And right now it told him if he went any further, there was a damn good chance he'd get beaten to a bloody pulp.

He always listened to that bell.

Jackson used his finger under her chin to angle her face up to his, then waited patiently for her to meet his gaze. Looking into her haunted green depths, he decided the bell could go fuck itself.

"Tell me."

His eyes were in shadow, yet she knew their intensity matched that of his command. A command that reached into her very core and knocked on the walls she'd constructed around her past. Was she really considering letting him in? A virtual stranger?

"Hey." Jackson's fingers trailed a soft path over her cheek before tunneling into her hair just enough to give his thumb the freedom to continue a back-and-forth caress on the side of her face. "It's okay. Nothing you tell me leaves this hammock. I swear it."

People had said similar things to her before, but their words had rung hollow in her ears, whether they'd meant them or not. She'd learned at a young age that just because people made promises didn't mean they would keep them.

But Jackson's declaration was different. He said it

with such strength and sincerity. It was then Vanessa realized he was no stranger. Despite only knowing him for three days, she felt she truly knew him. Not in the sense of knowing all his habits and favorite things. But more in the sense of knowing who he was as a person. Without a doubt she knew he was loyal and honorable. And no matter if they ended up despising each other tomorrow, he would never repeat anything she told him tonight.

Focusing on the hollow of his throat, she took a shaky breath and a leap of faith.

"My biological father left when I was six and my sister, Kat, was barely three. I don't remember him, and my mother never talked about him other than to bitch about the debt he left us in. She worked three different waitressing jobs to try and keep a roof over our heads and food on the table. But she wasn't a robot, and it was only a few months before the stress and lack of sleep started to really get to her. That's when one of the girls she worked with introduced her to coke."

"Shit."

"Yeah. It kept her awake and gave her tons of energy, but it also gave her an addiction, and sometimes scoring another bag took precedence over that week's groceries.

"By the time I was eight she'd abandoned the workforce for a lucrative career as a stay-at-home prostitute for her dealer. So instead of her having to worry about a babysitter, all her Johns came to our apartment at all hours of the day and night. I can remember Kat and me playing with our toys on the living room floor as they snorted their lines before taking care of business in her bedroom."

"Damn. That had to have been a nightmare for you and your sister."

"No, not really. Those were the times when things

were still fairly decent. I mean, even though my mom was drugged-out more often than not, she was still pretty conscientious of her kids. For the most part, she wasn't too bad at taking care of the essentials, and she never let any of her clients go anywhere near us. But then she married Carl."

"Who's Carl?"

"Originally he was one of my mom's regulars. For years he tried talking her into leaving her dealer-pimp for him, but since he wasn't much better off than we were, my mom couldn't justify it. Then his grandmother died and left him her house and a ton of money. Needless to say, the next time he made the proposal, my mom had a change of heart."

"How old were you?"

"Twelve."

"So what happened after you moved in with him?"

She shrugged her shoulder, not knowing how to put her past into words that wouldn't cause him to look on her with pity. "On the plus side, my mom stopped hooking. But the longer we lived with Carl, the more controlling he became. And when he drank—which was more often than not—he liked using his fist if he thought anyone even looked at him wrong. I did my best to keep Kat out of their way. It wasn't often, but if Carl set his sights on her, I'd provoke him so I got the brunt of it. I made sure we got to school, stayed on her to get good grades, and signed us up for any activities that kept us out of the house as much as possible."

"Sounds to me like your sister was extremely lucky you were there for her."

"But I wasn't. Not always." Vanessa swallowed, trying to prevent her throat from closing up. "My senior year, Carl was arrested for possession of cocaine. He had some priors so they sentenced him for six years. We were finally safe. That was a good eight months. Kat even started coming out of her shell more."

She wished that were the end of the story. For her and her sister, that was as close to Happily Ever After as they could get. But that wasn't the end. And there was nothing happy about any of it.

A thin veil of tears filled her eyes until it spilled over, one trailing across her temple and the other falling off the bridge of her nose. Jackson pulled her in a little more and pressed a kiss to the top of her head. The firm strokes of his hand on her back soothed her enough to continue.

"Second semester I received a letter that I'd gotten a scholarship. Originally, I hadn't planned on going to college. I don't even know why I applied. Maybe to pretend, I don't really know. But since Carl was gone . . . It was my ticket out of there. Away from a mom who'd never been there for me. Away from a life I wanted to forget. Just . . . away."

"Who can blame you?"

It wasn't a true question. It was one of those things people said when they didn't know what else to say. Unfortunately, it had an answer.

"Kat can," she said softly. "She doesn't, but she should."

Vanessa started to feel restless, her brain firing commands at her body to run. Her skin itched to be free of contact and the muscles in her legs jumped, needing to pace, to put distance between her and her past.

"What are you talking about? You took care of your sister her whole life and set a good example for her to follow. Why should Kat blame you for getting out and making something of yourself?"

"Because . . . I—" She shifted her legs and raised her head to look around, unsure of what she hoped to find. Someone to interrupt them? A magical portal to suck her into a parallel dimension? Despite being outdoors with the night sky stretching out above them, she felt stifled. Trapped.

"Hey, hey, hey." A large, callused hand palmed the side of her face and redirected her attention. "You're getting kinda flighty on me, Red. Come on, stay here with me." He stroked her cheek and brushed her hair away from her face. "That's it, honey. Take some slow breaths for me."

She hadn't realized just how close to a panic attack she'd been until he said that. She hadn't had one of those since her college days when she learned what her sister had gone through. Oh, God . . . Kat. Vanessa closed her eyes and focused on Jackson's deep voice, encouraging her to continue the deep breaths. His strong arms now banded around her, offering her comfort and a sense of security.

His lips touched her forehead in a chaste kiss, relaxing her like a dose of Valium. "That's better. Tell me why you think Kat should blame you."

Steeling herself for the onslaught of emotions she knew would accompany the admission, she spoke through a clenched jaw. "Because I left her behind to fend for herself. I wanted out so badly that I convinced myself she'd be okay without me."

"She only had three years left of school, though, right? And since Carl—"

"My mom found a replacement," she said sharply. "Tommy. From what I gathered, he was another alcoholic. He wasn't an angry drunk. But I think he was worse. And Kat was the one who suffered."

She felt him tense, the muscles under her cheek bunching and holding. "What happened?"

"H-he . . ." Vanessa shivered in his arms as the dark memories slithered along the walls of her brain, steadily making their way toward the light. She couldn't stop them now. They were too close to the surface. There was nothing left to do but let them come and trust that eventually she could shove them back where they belonged. "I think he abused her . . . sexually."

"Christ." The vehemence lacing his voice sent shivers down her spine. He must've felt it because his arms gathered her close. "I'm sorry, honey, I didn't mean to scare you."

"You didn't." He had. And she hated it. This woman—this girl—she became when she unlocked the past was not her. Not on the outside. Not anymore. Not since she created her Rules.

"So you're not sure about what happened?"

She shook her head slightly. "One of Kat's friends called me and said my mom's 'new boyfriend looked at Kat like she was his next meal' and that Kat had started acting more withdrawn than usual. I called Kat and tried to get her to tell me what was happening, but she just kept saying she was fine and to focus on school. That I'd gotten out, and that's where I needed to stay.

"So I called my mom. I told her I suspected Tommy was molesting Kat, but she refused to believe me. I screamed. I begged. But nothing I did made a damn bit of difference." Vanessa took a deep breath and let it out, the tightness in her chest sharpening as her ribs contracted. "I called Kat again. Told her as soon as I could afford the ticket I'd be flying home, but she freaked out. She made me promise I'd stay. S-said she'd h-hurt herself if I came home because of her."

"Oh, baby, I'm so sorry. I know you must have felt helpless, but she did it because she loved you and wanted the best for you."

Yes, she knew that. But it didn't absolve her of the

suffocating guilt. The tears streamed continually now and her breath hitched on every inhale. Jax tucked her closer against the solid wall of his chest and the steady beat of his heart coaxed hers to slow and match it, until at last the hysterics disappeared and she had calmed enough to finish the story.

"That was the night I drank an entire bottle of tequila while watching NCIS with Lucie. The night I decided to make a set of Rules that would keep me as far away from the kind of life I'd had growing up as possible." She tipped her head back to make eye contact. "That's why my Rules are so important to me. Where the inspiration came from might be a little strange, even silly . . . but I know if I follow them, I'll never be like them, and I'll never get involved with anyone like them, either. Not ever."

"Oh, honey . . . I still won't say I agree with your rules, but I understand now why you have them."

"And do you understand why it's so hard for me to forgive lying? Of all my Rules, that's the one I feel most strongly about. Most people might think it would be the one about choosing fists over words, based on my past with abuse." She swallowed past the lump in her throat, remembering the constant disappointment she lived with as a child. "But physical pain goes away. You know that as well as anyone. It's the emotional pain that does the most damage.

"My mother made so many promises to me and my sister. Every damn day was another promise: she'll take us to the park, see our school play, get clean . . . stop seeing men." She tried blinking them away, but another stream of tears escaped. "They weren't just broken promises. They were empty words. All of them, nothing but lies."

Jackson gathered her tightly, tucking her head beneath his chin. "Baby, I admire you so much. More than ever I know you're the strongest woman I've ever met."

Vanessa shook her head, but he quickly put a stop to it.

"Yes, you are." He prevented any further dispute by capturing her mouth with his for a sweet kiss. Pulling back, he studied her, his brows drawn together as though turning a thought over and over in his head. He opened his mouth to speak, but then hesitated and shook his head. "We can talk more tomorrow. Right now I want you to close your eyes and get some sleep."

His words added weight to her lids, making them too heavy to keep open any longer. On a deep sigh, she did as instructed, tucking her head firmly under his chin. He set them into a slight rocking motion again, and moments later, she drifted off to the sounds of the waves on the beach and the steady beat of his heart.

DAY 4: WEDNESDAY

Jax woke up to a red-haired angel draped over him, her soft breaths fanning his chest. Late last night, after she'd fallen into a deep sleep, he'd carried her into the room and settled them into bed. As soon as he'd tucked her back firmly against his chest, he let his eyes drift closed and didn't remember a thing after that until the sun crept over his face just minutes ago.

He reveled in letting his fingers play with her curls until the sun eventually woke her, too. She looked up at him, her lids still heavy with sleep and questions in her eyes. He suspected she might feel vulnerable after sharing so much of her past with him the night before, so he didn't hesitate to reassure her with a tender kiss.

When he pulled back, she rewarded him with her bright smile. From the very first, it had penetrated his armor as nothing else. But this one in particular did more than that. It managed to wrap itself around his heart, and the strangest part of all . . . He didn't even mind. It actually felt pretty damn good.

She gave him one more quick kiss and then leveled him with a stern look. "I expect coffee to be ready and waiting for me by the time I get out of the shower. And if you also happen to have bacon and eggs with it, I wouldn't turn them down."

It was so damn cute how she thought she was in charge. He saluted her with a, "Yes, ma'am," and watched her saunter naked into the bathroom, causing his cock to give a salute of its own. As soon as he heard the shower spray, he called room service, ordered a breakfast fit for a queen to be set outside their door, and then strode into the bathroom.

The shower was a large open stall, big enough for four people, with no door. The three shower heads—one angling down from either side and one straight above—were set in the back third of the tiled walls to prevent the water from splashing out. They had individual handles to allow the user to choose their preferences. Currently she only had the side ones on. Her hair was still dry and she was busy washing her body with a soapy loofah.

Facing away from him as she was, she hadn't heard or seen him enter. Which was perfect.

As she stepped into the shower sprays, soapy bubbles trailed down her pale, lithe body. His eyes watched in rapture as they flowed over the curves of her hips and the round globes of her ass. The room became thick with steam and the scent of oranges and something else invaded his senses to the point of distraction.

She turned on the overhead spray and ran her fingers through her long hair. The bright red curls straightened with the weight of the water and fell down her back like flames licking at her skin. She looked otherworldly, like something out of a James Cameron film.

Unable to stand by any longer, he sheathed himself in the condom he'd grabbed on the way in and stepped into the stall. Without warning, Jax wrapped his arms around her. Anticipating her startled reaction, he held her tight. As soon as she heard his voice, the tension leaked from her muscles, and she tried turning around.

"No. Stay."

"Jackson Maris, I'm going to kill you for scaring me like that."

He pressed his rock hard cock into the crevice of her ass, causing her breath to catch. He chuckled. "I don't think so."

"Well, I'm definitely going to make you pay for it," she said without much conviction. "Now, get out of here so I can finish."

He moved his hands to encompass her slick breasts and gave them a little squeeze. "Unfortunately, I don't take punishments very well. But if you remember correctly, I do enjoy giving them out." At the mention of the previous night's escapades, a tiny moan escaped her lips. "And I have every intention of making you finish."

Before she thought of another weak argument, he pinned her against the back wall and snaked his right hand in front to reach her clit. This wasn't going to be a slow seduction in the least. His goal was to get her off and bury himself as deep inside her as possible.

"God yes right there."

He knew exactly where. Though they'd only had sex twice, Jackson had catalogued every moan, every gasp, and every arch of her body, learning what she liked and how she wanted it. Every woman was different. Only a fool would assume he didn't have to pay attention to know how to please one from the next.

However, he'd also thought moans were moans and gasps were gasps. That the responses were the same, and it was only when and where he got them that changed.

But Vanessa's reactions were like a different language. One he'd never heard before and yet mysteriously understood as easily as if it were his own. The sounds she made fired his blood, quickened his pulse, and made his cock harder than steel.

Circling the sensitive nub with a fingertip, he teased her mercilessly, holding her captive when she bucked into his palm to try and create more friction. She reached behind him, digging her nails into his ass. The sharp bites in his flesh were like spurs on a horse, urging him to go faster. With any other woman he wouldn't have thought twice about the action, but he knew with Vanessa it was her way of taking back some control. If she got the desired response from him, it was a point in her corner.

But this wasn't her rodeo.

"I don't think so, Red." Jackson grabbed her wrists and held them with one hand above her head. "I call the shots. The sooner you learn that, the better."

"I—"

His free hand closed over the front of her neck and braced her jaw on either side. His mouth crushing hers smothered anything else she planned on saying. His lips pried hers apart and his tongue pushed in, taking command with an urgent force.

She rubbed her ass against his cock. He groaned, a sound she swallowed greedily before he wrenched his mouth from hers and moved to her neck. Biting his way down the taut column, he reached around again and without preamble plunged his long middle finger into her slick, hot pussy. She cried out, her pleasure bouncing off the tile walls and reverberating in his ears, drawing his balls impossibly tighter into his body. In and out, over and over. His actions relentless, her moans his encouragement.

"Oh, God, I'm so close. Jax, please!"

He held his finger still inside her. "Please what?" he growled in her ear.

"Jackson!"

His little wildcat was getting feisty. He was glad she couldn't see his smirk at her frustration. She'd likely haul off and hit him just for that, if not for stopping when teetered at the edge of climax. But as easygoing as he was in every other aspect of his life, there were two areas he insisted on dominating. Fighting and sex.

"Please what, Vanessa? I don't make another move until you say it."

She groaned, the walls of her sex clenching around his finger in a silent plea of their own, begging for what she struggled to ask. Submitting was still a foreign concept for her, but that didn't mean she didn't want to. It just meant she needed someone who could give her what she wanted. Someone like him.

"Please, Jax . . ." Finally she said the magic words, softly and banked with a need that rivaled his own. "Fuck me. Let me come."

"Good girl." His lips blazed a slow path from her shoulder, up her throat, and over the shell of her ear before whispering, "I love it when you beg, V. I have half a mind to hold out on you longer just to hear more." She whimpered. "Shhh, don't worry. I want my cock buried inside you too much right now. Open your legs for me, baby."

He dragged his finger out and let it glide up and over her swollen clit, making her spasm between him and the wall. Grabbing his shaft, he gave the order, "Wider," as he lightly kicked her legs out more. Bending his knees to get himself under her, he rubbed the sensitive head of his dick back and forth over her opening. He felt her trying to bear down on it, aching to be filled. When neither of them could take the teasing any longer, he stood tall and impaled her body, sending them both into a vortex of overwhelming sensations.

Jax brought her hands down from the wall and placed them behind his head. "Don't move them." He dug his fingers into her hips for purchase, his chest pressing into her back. Her breasts smashed against the wall, the tops plumped and round. Remembering sucking and licking and biting them made his mouth water and tempted him to flip her around so he could relive the night before. But instead, he doubled his efforts to drive them both off the proverbial cliff.

He hooked his hand under her left leg and hiked it up, opening her that much more and allowing him to slide deeper. Her nails dug into his scalp, shooting fingers of pleasure and pain down his spine that wrapped around his balls.

The spray of the shower still hit parts of them, making their bodies slip and slide without friction. The bathroom echoed with a cacophony of grunts, groans, moans, and cries, indistinguishable as to where they originated.

"So damn tight," he rasped, burying his head in her neck. "Feels so fucking good."

Releasing her hip, his right hand found her clit once more and began a feverish dance over it as he continued to pound into a heaven he'd never known.

"Oh! I'm going to—I'm—"

Screaming his name, she scratched furrows into the backs of his shoulders as she spasmed around him. The pain from her nails mixed with the pleasure of his cock being swallowed again and again by hot, clenching woman ripped the last thread he had on his control. With a powerful thrust, he buried himself balls deep and spent himself within her heat.

He wasn't sure how long they stood there, panting as the water continued to rain on them, but eventually he found the strength to slip from her body and dispose of the condom. He turned her around at last and drew her back into his arms. Her slight body was lax, but he had no trouble holding her up with one arm as his free hand delved into the hair at her nape, and he kissed her slowly, sensually.

When the kiss ended, she gazed up at him with crystalline eyes full of trust and utter contentment . . . and he lost a part of himself to her in that very moment. Which part of him exactly, he couldn't say.

The lie. It was eating him alive, especially in times like this. He knew he had to tell her, and the longer he waited, the worse he made things. But every time he thought he could do it, the fear of losing even one hour with her clawed at his gut until he chickened out. Damn those stupid rules of hers. Why? Because she wants to make sure anyone she's with is a moral and decent guy? No, damn him for being too big of a pussy to tell her the truth from the very beginning.

He would man up and tell her.

Later.

After they enjoyed their breakfast together, she went off to do wedding stuff with Robért for the next four hours, and he took advantage of the free time to hit training. Afterward, he talked with Coach for a while about getting him in the lineup for his next fight. Jackson was the last one to enter the showers at the gym, so all the guys were already getting changed or gone.

He winced as he reached across to turn the water on. Needing the mental distraction the pain provided, he'd told Corey not to hold back in their sparring session. The dude delivered and then some. Jax was thoroughly sore and aware of several areas on his body that would be sporting purple marks in the next ten minutes thanks to Corey's well-placed Muay Thai kicks.

He quickly finished up and was toweling his head dry with brisk movements on the way to his locker. He had to meet Vanessa soon and if he were late, she'd never let him hear the end of it.

"I think that knee to the chest you took in my last clinch was pretty fucking impressive."

Jackson whipped his head around to see Corey straddling a bench with a shit-eating grin on his face. "Fuck me," he muttered as he opened his locker and piled his clothes on the bench next to him. "Very funny, asshole. What are you still doing here?"

"Wanted to make sure you were able to walk out of here on your own after the beating I gave you."

Jax grunted in response. Normally he was right there with the guy, verbal jab for verbal jab, but he just wasn't in a joking mood.

"Seriously, brah, what gives? You're not yourself today. In the cage it was almost like you wanted me to break a few ribs for you."

After pulling his blue camo board shorts on, he straddled his own bench, facing the man who'd been the closest thing he'd had to a best friend since he moved to Hawaii. He dragged a hand down his face, vaguely noting the stubble he hadn't had the energy to shave that morning after the shower escapade with Vanessa.

"Have you ever had a belief or thought process that you've lived by for years, and then something happens to make you think maybe you were wrong? Or maybe you weren't wrong, but that it was time to look at things differently?"

"Yeah, sure. I think everyone does that at one point or another." Corey's eyes narrowed. "Are you giving up fighting? Were you trying to get injured out there? Because that's just fucking stupid, man."

"Fuck no. It's not anything like that." He sighed, stood up, and started taking his gym bag and things out of his locker. How did he tell his friend he needed his outside to match what his guilt was doing to him on the inside? He'd sound like a fucking lunatic. Hell, maybe he was. "Just forget it. It's nothing."

Corey crossed to his side and stood with his back to the lockers, arms crossed over his chest. "This have anything to do with that girl you brought in on Monday? Vanessa, right?"

Jax grabbed the top of the locker door and looked at the man, searching for any signs of interest on Corey's part. When he realized he'd been gripping the metal so tightly that he cut the underside of his forefinger, he snapped out of the crazy—and uncharacteristic—bout of jealousy. He did a mental shake of his head, sucked the blood from his finger, and pulled on his T-shirt. "Yeah, Vanessa. I also call her Red, Viper, Princess, and behind her back, Woman-who's-driving-me-fucking-insane."

Corey busted out laughing, but Jackson knew it wasn't due to his stand-up skills. "What's so funny?"

The man sobered up enough to answer, but that wide grin stayed intact. "Now it all makes sense. You've finally met someone who ties you up in knots, just like the rest of us mortals."

"The woman is a total enigma, so if she's tying anything up in knots, it's my brain, because nothing about her makes any damn sense."

Liar!

Jax told his subconscious to take a flying leap off a high cliff. It wasn't a total lie. Vanessa was enigmatic. He'd never met anyone like her before. And although he hadn't been able to figure her out right away like he could with most women, he was confident he understood her. Maybe even more than she understood herself.

"Come on, Maris, you can't bullshit me. I might not know you as well as Andrews does, but I've known you a long time. I've seen you with plenty of women, and none of them—even ones you had so-called relation-ships with—affected you any differently than a great steak would. Admit it. You're really into this girl."

Jax shut his locker and leaned back on it next to his friend. He couldn't deny it, nor was he the type to. He'd always been straight with people. Which was why any type of relationship he had with women always resulted in them leaving. He never hid the fact that for him it was more of a companionship with the bonus of sex. They always expected his feelings to grow over time, and when they didn't, they'd give him a Dear Jax letter.

"She's so different, man. She's stubborn and high maintenance and set in her ways . . ." He exhaled and let his head drop back, the banging metal sound echoing in the empty room. "And despite us living with each other the last few days, when I'm not with her all I do is think about her."

"She's living with you?"

"No, we're at the Mau Loa. It's a long story and not the point. The point is, I only have the rest of today and tomorrow to be with her and the thought of just being friends after that makes me feel violent."

"She's going back to the mainland Friday, huh?"

"No, she's here through next week, but she made me agree that our fling will only last three days." Corey opened his mouth, but Jax held out a hand. "Don't ask. Suffice it to say she's made it very clear she's not look-ing for anything more than that. The thing is, I think she might want more, but certain shit from her past has her scared."

"Listen, I'm no expert, but if you think there's some-thing more there than a few sheet dances—and it sounds to me as if there is—then you owe it to yourselves to give it a shot."

"She won't see it that way."

"So change her mind."

"You don't get it." Jax turned toward his friend, crossed his arms, and braced his shoulder against the locker. "She has these rules she lives by. Not just sayings. Rules."

"So get her to break them." Corey clapped him on the shoulder and walked over to snag his bag from his locker before heading for the door. Turning back, he said, "For what it's worth, man, I'd rather fight and lose than never step inside the cage."

As the door closed behind his friend, Jax dragged his hands down his face, Corey's last sentiment still ringing in his ears. Not only could the guy dish out a decent pounding, it turned out he wasn't half bad at advice, either, because he was right . . .

Win or lose, Jax was stepping into the cage.

The atmosphere at Duke's was a lot like Vanessa's beloved Fritz's back home. Hard-working locals who had probably lived in the area most, if not all, of their lives, kicking back with good friends and great beer.

The only real differences were the addition of tourists mixing it up with the locals and the aesthetics. Fritz's was dark with wood-paneled walls, black vinyl benches and stools, and little lighting to speak of, whereas Duke's Waikiki had walnut-colored wood furniture and surroundings, Tiki-style overhangs and table umbrellas, and open walls that looked out onto Waikiki beach and the vast Pacific beyond.

Jax had gone up to get them some beers from the bar while she grabbed a small table, ironically next to the only dartboard in the place. A piece of paper with scrawled marker was taped next to it informing patrons that the electronic aspect of the game no longer worked. But the darts were still in it, so it was usable. It'd just be a play-at-your-own-mathematical-peril kind of game.

Vanessa looked out through the open walls of the bar. Waikiki beach was absolutely stunning. She'd spent the afternoon on the back of a Jet Ski, her arms around Jackson, touring the different coves and having a blast as the wind whipped through her hair and stole the laughter right out of her mouth.

At one point a family of dolphins swam alongside them, jumping out of the water every few seconds. She'd been to SeaWorld before, but seeing them like that in the wild had been beyond magnificent. With their speed and grace, they were truly awe-inspiring, and she was disappointed when they eventually went their separate way.

However, her mood had brightened considerably when Jax claimed he needed a few minutes to rest his throttle hand and she realized they were floating in a very secluded bay, surrounded on three sides by high cliffs with a narrow mouth for an entrance. Somehow she managed to swing herself around so she sat in front, facing him.

"Mmm," he'd said as he wrapped his strong arms around her and gave her a kiss. "As much as I like this seating arrangement, babe, I'm not sure it's the safest idea to drive with you on my lap."

"Oh, I'm not planning on staying like this. I just thought maybe I could help you relax more than just your hand." When she palmed his cock over his shorts she felt him already halfway hard.

He sucked in a sharp breath. "If you're thinking what I think you're thinking, relaxing will be the last thing on my to-do list."

"Ah," she said before capturing his lower lip with her

teeth and pulling until released. "It might be last on the list, but if we take care of everything else, it's guaranteed to get checked off, too. Yes?"

His hands dropped to cup and squeeze her ass. "Very yes," he said, his voice gruff and low.

The memory making Vanessa smile, she waited for Jax to return with their drinks. She probably looked like an idiot, but she couldn't help it. They'd done some pretty inventive things on that Jet Ski. She'd only planned on fooling around with him, giving him a little taste of things to come and a little release. But after only a minute of having her mouth on him, he'd dragged her body up and her bikini top down.

He'd devoured first one nipple and then the other, then asked if she was on the pill. Since she wasn't a moron, she was able to answer him in the affirmative, to which he croaked out, "V, I want you right-fucking-now, but I'm obviously not prepared. So you can say no and I swear I'll respect it, but I want you to know that it's mandatory I get full-scale physicals on a regular basis and I'm totally clean. I would never do anything to put you at risk." His hands slid into her hair, his thumbs framing her cheeks. With his forehead touching hers and their short breaths mingling between them, he whispered, "Please say yes."

She replied equally as soft, unwilling to shatter the perfection of the moment. "Very yes."

In an instant he descended like a starved tiger let loose on its prey, consuming her completely—and carefully—on a Jet Ski in a small Hawaiian cove.

"What are you thinking about?"

Vanessa startled at Jackson's deep voice next to her ear. She gave him a dirty look as he laughed and sat down across the table from her. "Thank you for taking a year off my life."

"Sorry, Red. Couldn't resist. It's not often—or ever, for that matter—that I catch you daydreaming." He slid her Heineken across the table to her and leaned in close, his eyes darkening several shades. "Were you thinking about me bending you over the handlebars of a certain watercraft and taking you from behind?"

The tone in his voice had changed to one he always used with her during sex. So unlike his normal, playful tone, this was sexually charged and authoritative. They'd only been together a handful of times and yet she already responded to that voice like one of Pavlov's dogs. As soon as she heard it, she melted into a woman whose every goal was to follow his lead. She'd tried fighting it, tried taking back her usual control, but never succeeded. There was something about Jackson Maris that unraveled her control. No, she realized, that wasn't it. He unraveled her need for control.

Oh my God. That's it, isn't it? She half expected to look up and see a floating lightbulb over her head. Her need for control—for her rules—was because she didn't trust anyone to do right by her. If she controlled everything and everyone around her, she never needed to worry about that.

But almost from the first, she'd felt differently with Jackson. Outside the bedroom he was easygoing, laid-back. More than happy to let her indulge her need to hold the reins. But when it came to intimacy, he snatched the reins right out of her hands and refused to give them back until he was good and ready. And even though she'd fought it out of habit for a while, subconsciously she'd known she was safe with him. So she'd been able to let go. Finally.

She hadn't realized until now just how freeing that was for her. To let someone else take control, to give her what she needed without her having to take it or order it like she was choosing from a fucking menu. Yes, I'll have the Bites On My Neck as an appetizer and the Take Me From Behind, medium raw, as my entree, with Pull My Hair and Make Me Beg For It for my sides. Oh! And I'd love some Not-At-All-Awkward Snuggling for dessert. Thanks ever so much.

She met Jackson's dark gaze and answered him honestly. "Yes. I was."

"Good. Because I can't get it out of my head, either."

"Oh, yeah?" They were in a public place. Surely she could challenge him a teensy bit, right? "Which part exactly?"

The black of his eyes swallowed what little color was left and their intensity left her feeling as naked and on display as she'd been earlier in that cove. "Careful, babe. I've never been one for huge public displays, but when it comes to you, it won't take much to incite me into throwing you up against the nearest wall and taking what I want." He dragged the rough pad of his thumb over her lower lip. "Especially now that I know what it's like to have you bare. Goddamn, you felt so good."

A shiver of unadulterated desire swept over her body. All the moisture sucked out of her mouth and apparently ended up between her legs. He kissed her lightly and then leaned back in his chair, casual as could be, as if he hadn't just shaken her to her very core with nothing more than words.

She swiped her bottle up and quickly downed half its contents before setting it back on the table. Jackson chuckled as he lifted his own beer to his lips and did the same. Thankfully the waitress brought their food then, because she'd been in danger of leaning over and licking that sexy Adam's apple as he drank. What? Can those even be sexy? Mentally, she slammed her head against the table. She was soooo into this fling a lot deeper than she'd planned. The next thing she knew she'd be sighing over the guy's cuticles. Come on, Nessie, where'd you put your balls?

For the next hour they enjoyed their food, talked, laughed, and even debated politics. Turned out, Jackson was extremely intelligent and up on current events. He had a large database of useless facts stored in that gorgeous head of his. By the time they finished their Kimo's Original Hula Pie—which was absolutely sinful and totally worth the extra sit-ups she'd have to do—she was ashamed of herself for assuming he was simple-minded simply because he had a career in fighting and a hobby in surfing.

He set his fork down after taking his last bite and noticed her staring. "Do I have whipped cream on my face or something?"

She smiled, thinking of what she'd like to do if he had whipped cream anywhere on him. "No, you're fine. Want to play a game of darts?"

He shot a skeptical glance at the dartboard. "On that thing? It's broken."

She shrugged. "So we'll keep score in our heads, or else ask for a pen and notepad."

"I'm surprised you'd want to play without your own darts. You and Lucie take this game pretty seriously, don't you? You'll have to use bar darts. Could throw off your game."

"Then you'll actually have a chance of beating me. If I had my darts, I'd kick your ass down Waikiki beach and back. Then again, I'll probably still do that without my own darts."

The competitive glint sparked in his eyes. "Oh, you're on, babe. Let's go."

They played game after game as the sun turned the sky into shades of pink, orange, and purple. The waitress was kind enough to make sure they always had plenty of beer and replacement order cards to keep score on. Trash talking between them ran rampant, and they even collected a small audience who chose sides and cheered appropriately.

When they finally decided their throwing arms were sore enough for one night, the sun had long ago vanished and made way for a brilliant cast of stars surrounding a full moon. The patrons had grown and spilled onto the beach in front of Duke's and a band started playing music, signaling the start of the beach nightlife. Colored lanterns strung between trees and posts served as the only source of light other than the moon. People whooped and laughed as they gathered in the sand to dance, their drinks in one hand and a willing partner in the other. It looked straight out of a travel commercial. It was awesome.

Jax grabbed her hand and tugged. "Come on."

She happily followed him into the center of the dancers. Vanessa had always loved to be in the thick of a party, and she could scarcely recall a time when she hadn't closed down the dance floor. The music infused her body and compelled her to move and sway in time with its beat. She loved being mixed into the crowd, bodies brushing up on each other, sweaty and visceral.

As soon as they found a spot, she began to move, and so did Jackson. Not a lot of guys had rhythm, but he was not one of them. Placing one thick leg between hers, he pulled her close and rolled his pelvis with hers, their hips swaying to the beat.

She laced her fingers behind his neck and tilted her head back to meet his eyes. "Look at you, all Patrick Swayze and stuff."

"Dancing is no different than sex. It's all about moving with your partner. Finding a rhythm together. It's just like having sex while standing up." He dipped his head to speak into her ear. "Pretty sure I've proved my skill in that department once today already, but if you need a refresher, I'd be more than happy to oblige."

He nipped her earlobe before pulling away again. She was so tempted to yank him back to his Jeep and give him permission to break every speed limit from Duke's to the Mau Loa. But it had been so long since she'd had a chance to dance, especially with a guy as good at it as Jackson obviously was, and they had the rest of the night to bang each other's brains out.

"Right now I want you to show me your skills on the dance floor. But later you can refresh my memory as much as you want."

A wicked smile split his face. "You can count on it, princess."

For the next several songs they danced, sometimes facing each other and sometimes she'd turn and press her back against his chest. Every time she did the latter he'd grab her hips and pull her ass against his cock, allowing her to feel his hard length behind the thick denim. She'd rest her head back on his chest, and he'd tell her how he planned on hiking her sundress up as soon as they got to their room.

Between the dancing and the sexual tension, they worked up one hell of a sweat and a really big thirst. At the end of the fifth song, Jax kissed her neck and said he was going to get them something to drink. She waved him off and started moving with the next song, hands raised overhead, eyes closed, feeling the beat roll through her body.

It seemed like no time at all before he returned, pressing against her back, one hand spread over her stomach to pull her in close. He bent closer and spoke next to her ear.

"I knew you'd come around once you got rid of that asshole, baby."

Vanessa's heart skipped a beat, and not in the good way. Whipping around, she stared at the one person guaranteed to ruin what had been the perfect day so far. "What the hell do you think you're doing, Danny? Didn't your mother teach you to ask a girl if she wants to dance before mauling her?"

The dance floor was still crowded, so backing very far from him wasn't an option. Behind her people were ebbing and flowing with the music like the ocean waves, gently nudging her toward him. His breath reeked of alcohol and from the looks of the stains, so did his shirt. His would-be-handsome face was ruined by the arrogant sneer it held and the treacherous look in his eyes.

"Don't play coy with me. I know you're fucking Maris. I mean, the guy's generally happy-go-lucky as a rule, but that's not the face of a man who isn't getting some action." He reached out to touch her face. "You know what I mean?"

She slapped his hand away before it could touch her. The fact that his body had been pressed to hers without her permission made Vanessa's blood run cold. Even a hint of nonconsensual touching was enough to simultaneously make her want to throw up until she passed out and commit aggravated assault until he passed out. "Of course I know what you mean. A toddler would know what you mean, you monosyllabic imbecile. And if you don't want a repeat of the other day at the gym, I suggest you take your bullshit elsewhere."

The sneer on Danny's face morphed into rage, pure and simple. "I'd watch your tone with me, bitch."

"I disagree, Akana." Jax placed his massive frame between her and her pest. Her heart rate slowed somewhat. She was glad he showed up as a buffer, but she wasn't one to hide behind anyone's apron, so she stepped around to stand in front of him. Caveman that he was, he compromised by placing a hand on her hip and pulling her into his side. She decided it was a compromise she could live with. "I don't think she has to watch her tone with anyone. But if you don't leave her alone, you're going to have to watch your six. Feel me?"

Oh, shit. "Jackson, don't you dare," she said quietly to him. "I don't want you fighting because of me, or for me, or anything else."

Without taking his eyes off the other man, he replied, "Wasn't planning on it. I'm simply informing him that his company isn't welcome, and he should run along before he says something he'll regret." His eyes narrowed and his jaw muscles pulsed in aggravation. "Again."

It seemed Danny's face had only two settings because the sneer was back again. "Yeah, that got to you, didn't it, Maris? Maybe because you know it's true?"

Vanessa felt Jackson's muscles bunch around her, and the hand on her hip tightened reflexively as though trying to make a fist but unable to part with her to do so. Not good. One more word from his teammate and Jackson was going to throw down in the middle of this crowd.

"Whatever gets you through the night, Akana. You know what? You stay and have fun. I think we've danced enough for one night. See you at the gym." And with that he took her hand and started to lead her away.

"Remember, Maris, lemme know when you're done with her. I'll fuck that little cunt so long and hard she'll have to beg me to stop."

Vanessa froze in her tracks. Memories of crying herself to sleep at night because she hadn't been able to protect her baby sister from a predator, a monster who gave no thought to ruining a girl's life, came rushing to the surface. Her carefully constructed walls that prevented them from seeing the light of day had been breached by a mere sentence.

Releasing Jax's hand, she closed her fist, spun around, and decked the man square in his nose with every ounce of hatred she had for him, Carl, and every other man like them.

Bright red blood exploded from Akana's face. His eyes flew wide, stunned as his hands flew up to his broken nose while it continued to gush between his fingers. But a second later, the initial shock was replaced with a venomous snarl and the deafening roar of retaliation.

Jax saw the move coming before Akana even thought about cocking his fist. He'd managed to somehow keep his cool earlier when he really wanted to pound this punk into the ground, but hell would freeze over before he ever let anyone lay a hand on Vanessa.

Grabbing the guy's swinging arm with one hand and clinching him behind the neck with the other, he used Akana's forward momentum against him, pulling him in hard. Jax's knee met his sternum, knocking the wind clear out of him and possibly causing some very uncomfortable fractures.

As Akana fell over gasping, trying to catch his breath, Jax turned back to Vanessa, who hadn't moved. She just stood there, stone still, oblivious to the blood spattered on her dress and coating her hand. Oblivious to the crowd that gathered around them. Her shoulders heaved with shallow breaths and if looks could kill, Akana would be nothing more than a pile of smoking ash.

He was still a little stunned—and frankly a lot proud—that she'd cold cocked the bastard in the first place.

Thankfully security stepped in and, after a brief summary of what happened from a few patrons, they hauled the cocksucker away.

Gently grasping her shoulders, Jax turned her away from her victim to bring her attention to him. "Honey, look at me." Her body had turned, but her head stayed where it was, her eyes not even focused on the man she bloodied, but probably things from her past only she could see.

With a finger to her chin, he guided her eyes to his. Once they connected, she took in a big rush of air, held it for a few seconds, and released it on a shaky exhale. It was like watching a fighter come to after getting knocked out—for a few brief moments, he's dazed and confused. Then reality sets in and he realizes what happened in those last seconds.

"Oh my God," she whispered. "What have I done?"

"You punched a bastard who deserved it."

She glanced down at her hand, knuckles red and starting to swell, and trembled. "But I d-don't—I—"

He grabbed her face in his hands and forced her to look into his eyes. "Baby, listen to me. You did nothing wrong. That guy's a fucking asshole with no respect for women, who said something I wouldn't say to my worst enemy." He brushed her hair away from her face and kissed her forehead. "He's a fighter; he's used to getting hit. What's really going to hurt in the morning is his ego when the guys find out a female civilian is the one who busted his face."

He gave her a wicked grin. "It might be worth showing up for training in the morning just to watch him shrink like a violet when you walk through the door."

A laugh escaped her lips. It was weak, but he'd take it. Anything other than that look of fear and shame in her beautiful eyes. Tucking her into his side, he led her away from the crowd to where he'd parked his Jeep.

She was quiet on the drive, staring up at the night sky as though contemplating the stars in the universe. But he knew her better than that by now. She was trying to wrap her mind around what happened. Trying to rationalize her actions and probably holding them up against her rules or even creating new ones as a result. Either way, he left her to it. She hadn't completely closed off from him as she allowed him to hold her uninjured hand, so he was content with that much for now.

As soon as he got her into their bungalow, he directed her to sit on the couch while going to the kitchen for the first-aid kit under the sink. He grabbed the ice pack, broke the seal, and shook the contents on his way over to his gym bag, where he grabbed one of his blue hand wraps. "Apparently they should call you Red Viper in and out of the courtroom. That jab was lightning fast, woman. Remind me to never piss you off."

Sitting next to her, he picked up her injured hand and slowly helped her to straighten her fingers. She hissed in a quick breath then stole a glance at him through her lashes as a slight flush tinged her pale cheeks. He hated that she felt she couldn't show any weakness around him. It made it damn hard for a man to take care of a woman who kept trying to prove she didn't need him.

He carefully checked her range of motion and strength while she gritted her teeth against the pain. When his inspection was done, he gingerly set the ice pack on her bruised knuckles and began securing it with the wrap.

"You're lucky," he said, giving her a reassuring smile. "I don't think anything is broken, but it'll be sore as hell for a while. The good news is it'll turn a different shade every day for about a week, so you'll have plenty of opportunities to color coordinate your accessories or handbags or whatever you girls do."

She started to laugh, but it got off with a wince that she then tried pawning off as a blink.

"You know, it's okay to show me that it hurts," he said. "You don't always have to be so strong."

Exhaling and letting her shoulders relax, she trained her eyes on her hand, focusing on his movements as he wrapped it. "It's just . . . I've never . . ." She shook her head. Either she was unable to put her thoughts into words or couldn't bring herself to say them aloud.

"I know." After securing the Velcro, he rested his elbow on the back of the couch and tucked her hair behind her ear. "I get it. You never wanted the violence that touched you as a kid to be a part of your life as an adult. But, V, just because you punched some asshole doesn't mean you are a violent person."

She made a sound that said she clearly didn't agree. "Just a person with violent tendencies, right?"

He stood up and held out his hand. "Let's go for a walk."

"I don't feel like going for a walk."

"Sand between your toes and the ocean breeze on your skin will do you some good. You'll feel better afterward, I promise." Her eyes moved to the bedroom, clearly wanting to bury herself and her worries with the promise of sleep. But she needed to stop burying her past behind her rules. She needed to deal with it. At least a little. "Come on, Red, don't leave me hangin'."

Vanessa let out a resigned sigh and gave him her left hand to help pull her up. He offered a smile, which she weakly returned, then he led her out of the bungalow to the edge of the water.

He intertwined their fingers as they walked in silence, the warm saltwater rushing over their feet to stretch over the sand before it was forced to retreat and try again. The waning moon hung high in the dark void above them, lighting their way along the beach.

"Ironic, isn't it?" she asked.

"What's that?"

"You managed to restrain yourself tonight, and I ended up losing control."

"I'd say you were in complete control. Not many people could pull off such a solid punch."

"That's not what I meant and you know it," she mumbled.

Spotting a group of large, craggy rocks, he led her away from the surf. Once there, he faced them toward the ocean, settled his hips back against the formation, and positioned her between his legs. She took a deep breath and exhaled, letting her body sink into his. For several minutes they didn't speak. Just listened to the inky waves rolling over themselves as they raced toward the shore before being pulled back for yet another run.

Jackson slid his hands around her waist, reveling in the easy way she laid her arms over his and let her head fall back on his shoulder. Bending his head, he used his chin to push her hair to the side and nuzzled the smooth skin of her neck. Though he still felt the sadness that held her in its grasp, she at least accepted his affection and even returned it to some degree. The idea of her punishing herself for things in her past that she had no control over churned like acid deep in his gut.

He wanted to say something—anything—to take her thoughts away from the one dark spot of their day together. But the only two distractions he was good at when it came to women—joking around and hot sex—weren't even close to appropriate. So, for now, he figured it was best to just hold her and let her take the lead on any conversation.

Another few minutes passed, but eventually she broke the silence. "My sister would love it out here. I'd always been perfectly content with city life, but Kat hated it. She liked to read books like Anne of Green Gables or The Chronicles of Narnia. It didn't matter if the fiction was based in reality or fantasy. As long as she could imagine herself on a farm or in faraway lands, she was happy."

"Where is she now?"

"I don't know exactly. Last time I talked to her she was somewhere near Memphis, Tennessee. She might still be there, but chances are Lenny probably burned all of his bridges by now so they would've had to move to a different city. Again."

"Lenny her boyfriend?" She nodded. "You don't sound too thrilled about him."

"He's not anyone I'd want dating someone I care for, much less my sister, but he did get her out of my mom's house a year earlier than she could have. Regardless of the fact she was only seventeen and it was illegal for her to leave home, she was still better off with Lenny the Loser."

Jackson thought about how he'd have felt if some guy had swept Lucie off at the tender age of seventeen. The very idea made him violent. No way would he ever be down with that. Hell, it'd been hard enough to swallow the news of her dating Reid, and they'd been like brothers their whole lives.

"Okay, so Kat leaves home with Lenny at seventeen. Then what? Where'd they go?"

"All over the place. He's made a career out of taking advantage of his friends or his friends' friends. Kat usually picks up any odd job to get them by and Lenny starts to run whatever his latest racket is to get rich quick. But he always ends up screwing over the wrong people, and they have to pick up and move to a new city to start all over again."

"Is she happy with him?"

Vanessa's cynical laugh dropped in front of them like a dead weight. "No. At least not for several years now. But she'd never tell me that. She's too proud to tell me anything that isn't positive or necessary. I've tried to convince her to come live with me, but she won't. She thinks I'll see her as a huge screwup. I've tried assuring her I could never judge her when it isn't even her fault, but it never makes a difference. She's as stubborn as our mother."

He placed a kiss on her cheek. "Sounds like someone else I know."

She turned in his arms, placed her hands on his hips, and gave him a sly smile. "If you think you have me so figured out," she said in a sultry voice, "why don't you tell me what I'm thinking right now."

She was switching the topic to sex for reasons that had nothing to do with being horny. He saw it for what it was: a defense mechanism. He'd seen other women do the same thing before, and he'd only been too willing to follow their lead. Who was he to force them to discuss something they didn't want to?

But Vanessa was different. She wasn't just some girl. With every hour he spent with her, he realized more and more just how much she meant to him. And he'd rather deal with permanent blue balls than ignore her pain for a quick fuck.

As she stretched up on her tiptoes to kiss him, he laid his hands on her shoulders to stop her. She furrowed her brow.

"What happened to your sister . . . ," he began in a

gentle tone. "No matter what you think, it's not your fault."

"Ummm, o-kay," she answered sarcastically. "I don't know if you missed it or what, but I was trying to come on to you just now."

Not a smile, not a wink. He wouldn't react to her playful attempts. He wouldn't help her bury her feelings. "Honey, listen to me. It's not. Your. Fault."

"I don't want to talk about this."

"I know."

"Then why are you pushing something you know nothing about?"

She took a step back, trying to extricate herself from his grasp, but he wasn't making it that easy. He circled one arm around her back and shoved his free hand through the mass of curls to cradle the back of her head.

"There's a lot of shit I don't know in this world, but this," he said with emphasis, "this I do know."

Tears filled her eyes and a single drop slipped over the edge. In the moonlight it shone like a fluid crystal trailing over her cheek. She shook her head slightly, still trying to deny his claim. "Jackson, please . . . don't . . ."

"Do you have any idea how amazing I think you are? You practically raised her when you were a child yourself. You protected her, sheltered her, from as much as you could while growing up in conditions no child should ever experience."

"I know," she said, her voice trembling, "but I . . ."

"Made her into a strong, proud, self-sufficient woman. She might not have the life you want for her right now, but that doesn't mean she won't eventually."

Releasing a shaky exhale, Vanessa curled into him, resting her forehead on his chest. He rubbed her back slowly, up and down, letting her work through her emotions as they inevitably flooded to the surface. When she spoke again it was soft, almost muffled against his shirt, but not enough that he couldn't hear what she said or the anguish behind her words.

"I'm just so worried about her all the time, and . . ." She sniffed back her tears, sighed, and raised her eyes to his once again. "I miss her so damn much."

"I know you do, baby." Framing her face, he gently kissed away the new tears streaming from her moonlit eyes then wrapped her in his embrace again. "I know you do."

For several minutes he just held her as she cried. He rested his cheek on the top of her silky hair and ran a hand over her back, soothing her as best he could. When she at last seemed like she'd worked through the worst of it, he pulled away and said, "Let's go back to the room and get you taken care of."

She didn't object to his coddling like he expected. Exhaustion lined her face, and she was only too willing to let him lead her around the room as he finished taking care of her hand and instructed her to go through her nightly before-bed routine. When she finished, he humored her by letting her face away from him as he helped her into her pajamas, since her hand was too sore to do certain parts.

Once she was all set for bed, he sat on the couch and let her lay down with her head in his lap while they watched the old eighties movie Say Anything on the local cable channel. He idly played with her hair while Lloyd Dobler tried desperately to impress the girl of his dreams, Diane Court. By the time Lloyd thoughtfully pointed out broken glass for Diane to step around, Vanessa was sound asleep with one hand tucked under her cheek and the other resting on his thigh.

After covering her with the lightweight blanket he'd

set off to the side, Jackson settled in to watch the rest of the movie while making plans for his last official day with her. If all went according to plan, tomorrow would be just the beginning.

Day 5: Thursday

"Don't I even get a hint?"

Vanessa looked over at Jackson from the passenger seat of his Jeep. She held her hair in one hand to avoid the inevitable snarl wars in her curls as a result from traveling in a vehicle with no roof. Or doors, for that matter.

He spared a quick glance in her direction with what could only be described as a model-perfect smile. All gorgeous white teeth, laugh lines behind the dark shade of his stubble, and she'd bet laughing topaz eyes behind his dark wrap-around sunglasses.

"Nope."

That was it. He wouldn't say anything else no matter how many guesses she tossed into the wind. Considering she wasn't fond of surprises—after all, one can't prepare for what one doesn't know is coming—it was utterly infuriating. And really sweet. Damn him.

Finally giving up, she slid on her own sunglasses and let her head drop back. The late afternoon sun bathed her face and upper body, and she wondered how many new freckles she'd come away with by the time she flew home. She didn't have any on her face like Kat did, but she sported some light ones on her arms and shoulders. It was a damn good thing she'd slathered herself in suntan lotion before they left. She'd have to remember to reapply later if they were going to be outdoors.

Not that she knew if they were or not because someone wasn't coughing up any answers.

She sighed and thought about all that had transpired over the last several days. In a million years, she never would've guessed what the week had in store for her. Last night had been even more of a surprise. Not only did she actually punch someone in a fit of rage, she'd cried on Jackson's shoulder to the point of exhaustion then let him take care of her until she fell asleep in his lap.

She tried to think back to the last time anyone had taken care of her . . . and came up blank. Even as a child she'd been the one caring for herself and Kat. Hell, she'd even taken care of their mother when she was too far gone on God only knew what to perform the simplest of tasks.

But last night had been completely different. She'd opened up to Jackson more than she ever had with anyone else. Even in her more vulnerable moments with Lucie, she'd still had a thin wall around herself, allowing a modicum of control. And Lucie, being the sweetheart she was, never pushed for anything more than Vanessa was willing to give.

But Jackson had taken her thin wall and chipped away at it until he made a sizable dent. Then kept going until the dent became a crack and the crack became a gap, and that was all he needed to release the raw emotions he'd been looking for. The experience had been terrifying. And also cathartic.

She spent a good deal of her morning wondering why he was so intent on breaking through her barriers, though.

What was he getting out of it? It certainly wasn't some sleazy way of making her vulnerable enough to get into her pants. Technically speaking, he'd had backstage passes to her pants for a full three days. And it sure as hell wasn't because he was looking for some deep, meaningful relationship with her. They'd both agreed that this was a one-time-only fling.

Yep. Nothing but some fun in the sun and then they were done, and all that other rhyming mantra crap. Little did she know she'd be haunted by the phrase "be careful what you wish for" as she tried to ignore the pang of sadness and regret on their last day together. So much for her women's intuition.

Maybe Jackson was just one of those rare guys who was genuinely sweet. Plus, she was his sister's best friend, so he had an added incentive to be nice to her. At any rate, though they'd started off more than a little rocky, Vanessa was really glad for his company the last several days. She had fun with him, he made her laugh, he was playful and charming . . . and wicked talented in bed. And on the couch. And in the shower. And on Jet Skis.

"What are you smiling about over there?"

Vanessa pressed her lips together. She hadn't realized her wayward thoughts had gone rogue with brain signals to her mouth. But since they had, there was no sense in letting an opportunity go to waste.

Reaching across the short distance between them, she placed her hand high on his thigh and started tracing the inside hem of his shorts with a tip of her nail. His muscles bunched beneath her palm, and he groaned when her finger crept closer to his crotch then retreated without touching anything fun. She stifled her laugh.

"If you tell me where we're going, I'll tell you what I was thinking." Taking things a step further, she leaned over, pressed a moist kiss just under his ear, and whispered, "And even reward you with some in-the-car fun."

"Sorry, babe. No dice." Jackson grabbed her roaming hand, kissed it, and then intertwined their fingers before resting them on his lap. He did a bang-up job of pretending he wasn't affected, but the pulse in his neck told her it was his way of preventing any further threats of her handling his stick shift while he drove.

Sitting back in her seat, she huffed from defeat and considered the phone conversation she'd had that morning with the only other person besides Lucie she felt she could go to for advice. Fritz, the grizzled owner of the local bar she and Lucie had frequented ever since their freshman year in college, was the closest thing Vanessa had to a father figure. He was the type to show his affection through the fine art of teasing and mock arguments. It was rare for the man to have any serious moments, but the fatherly affection he had for her and Lucie was obvious in every fake barb he threw their way.

Vanessa had woken in Jackson's arms that morning groggy and content. As she lay there, listening to his even breaths and the steady beating of his heart, she turned her focus inward and analyzed her feelings. Something she rarely allowed herself to do. What she found astonished her. Not only did she feel safe and cared for, but she swore there was something that felt an awful lot like . . . love.

She'd given herself ten points for managing not to freak out. Instead, she'd suppressed her crazy and gone through their morning routine of drinking coffee and eating breakfast. Then he'd left to go run errands, and she'd frantically dialed the number for the bar, knowing with the time difference that Fritz would be getting ready to open.

"We don't open till four."

The surly, gravelly voice was like the beacon of a distant lighthouse in a blinding fog. "Fritz! It's Nessie. Do you have a minute?"

"Well, now, you know I'll always have time for my favorite redhead, but ain't you supposed to be in Hawaii?"

"I am, but I need someone to talk to, and I can't talk to Lucie about it." She paused and then amended it with, "Yet." One of the things she'd decided was that she was going to come clean with Lucie about the fling with Jax after her honeymoon was over. Vanessa didn't think it would upset her friend, but in case it even bothered her in the slightest, she didn't want it to ruin what should be the happiest week of her life.

"That's not like you, Red. What you got goin' on? Someone givin' you trouble, girl? You tell me who it is and I'll set 'em straight when I get down there tomorrow."

"No, no, it's nothing like that. Um . . ." She took a breath, closed her eyes, and spit it out. "I'm sleeping with Lucie's brother, Jackson."

A slow whistle came through the cell speaker. "Keepin' it in the family, are ya? Okay, so what's the problem? He not giving you the cunny quakes?"

It wasn't easy to shock Vanessa, especially when it came to the outrageously hilarious things that often came out of the retired Naval rescue swimmer's mouth, but that was definitely a new level of outrageous. The fun thing about her relationship with Fritz, though, was the smartass—and often crass and inappropriate—comments they tossed back and forth. It had caused more than a few bar patrons to look at them strangely over the years.

She welcomed the smirk on her face at the familiarity of their banter. "Just because you have issues getting the ladies to scream your name, old man, doesn't mean everyone else does."

"Hah! When I'm with a woman the sex is so good my neighbors need a cigarette. So don't you go accusin' me of not satisfyin' the ladies."

Vanessa busted out laughing and felt some of the tension leave her body. "All right, so we've established that both you and Jackson have no issues in the sack. Gee, I can't tell you what a relief that is. Not to mention the spectacular imagery that gave me, thank you very much."

"At least you don't sound like a scared little rabbit anymore," he said with tenderness in his voice. That he'd sensed her anxiety over the phone and tried to quell it the only way he knew how truly touched her. He really was a big teddy bear at heart. "Now, tell me what's really botherin' ya."

She raked a hand through her hair and fisted a chunk until the sharp pain at her scalp forced her to relax her grip. Say it, say it, say it! "God, this is crazy," she muttered. "I can't believe I'm actually going to say this . . ."

"Speak up, darlin', my hearin' ain't what it used to be."

"I think that maybe . . . I mean, it's possible . . ." Somewhere in the back of her mind Vanessa knew she was acting ridiculous. For shit's sake, she was actually wincing as though the words dangling off the tip of her tongue could actually cause physical pain. ". . . that I might be—just a little—infatuated, in lust, or whatever you want to call it, with Jackson."

Her breaths ceased, remaining trapped in her lungs as she waited for a response, a guffaw, a something. But the only sound that came through was the rasp of his fingers running over the ever-present gray stubble on his jaw. She'd bet he had his elbows on the bar, one hand holding the receiver of the old rotary phone, the other creating the sandpaper noise that seemed to get louder with every passing nanosecond.

"Fritz, say something," she pleaded. "Tell me I'm crazy because I've only known him a few days. That getting involved with my best friend's brother is asking for trouble. That I'm a hypocrite because he practically breaks every one of my Rules."

"Well now, Red, why would I have to say any of those things when you're already thinkin' 'em?"

"See? I knew it." She slumped forward on the couch and dropped her head into her hand. "Oh, this is bad. Bad, bad, bad."

"Now wait a minute. Just because I pointed out you're already thinkin' those things doesn't mean I agree with any of it."

Vanessa swore she heard a needle screech its way across a vinyl record somewhere. "You don't?"

"Hell no, I don't. Now you listen to me, and you listen good. You know I love you like my own, but Jesus Christ, yer the dumbest smart woman I know."

"Beg your pardon?"

"I've watched you turn down more fellas in this bar than I can count. Now, don't get me wrong, most of 'em weren't worth the time it took you to brush 'em off. But some were mighty nice gentlemen, and all that stopped you was those damn rules."

"My Rules are solid. They keep me from getting involved with anyone who isn't good for me," she argued as she crossed the room to stare out at the bright blue water beyond the white sand.

"Oh, that's such horseshit. Your rules ain't nothin' more than a way of making sure no one gets close enough to hurt you." She was about to contest that point when he said something that made her mouth slam shut. "If you keep goin' as you are, Nessie girl, yer always gonna be alone. An' I know that's not what you want."

No, she thought sadly. It isn't.

"No one's perfect, kiddo. Not even you, hard as that is to imagine."

A hint of a smile curved the edges of her lips at his mild jab, but the fear of contemplating all that he said kept her joviality at the baseline. Was she truly destined to be alone if she held every man she met against her Rules?

Fritz added one last thought, holding back the avalanche of questions she was about to inundate herself with. "I've never met Jackson, but from everything our Lucie's told me over the years, he sounds like a pretty good guy. After all, he practically raised her, so he can't be all that bad. Maybe you oughta give him the benefit of the doubt and yourself a shot at being happy and see how things turn out. You might just be surprised."

"Since when did you get so smart?"

His raspy chuckle warmed her heart and even made her a little homesick. Fritz's Bar had been a huge part of her regular routine for the last decade of her life, and so had its owner. "Since always, but I try to keep it in check, 'cause I hate to see a pretty girl cry when she's been outsmarted by an old-timer like me."

She'd laughed and then changed the topic with a bit of small talk about the wedding before hanging up and spending the rest of her morning trying to focus on her casework as opposed to her conversation with Fritz.

"Where you at, V?"

"Hmm?" Blinking, she looked over at Jackson to find they'd stopped.

"You seemed miles away just now." He stretched his arm over the back of her seat and leaned in as he shoved his shades onto his head. The golden brown of his eyes pierced through her flashback haze. "Where were you?"

She gave him a confident smile. Or at least what she hoped was confident. "Trust me, it's nowhere you want to be."

"I wouldn't be too sure of that, honey." He closed the distance between them and pressed his lips to hers in a gentle kiss. When he pulled back, he added, "As long as you're there, I'm thinking that's exactly where I want to be."

Vanessa sat stone still, her brain analyzing at hyperspeed while a warmth like she'd never known spread through her heart. Could he possibly have feelings for her like she'd started having for him? Did he want more than what they'd originally agreed to?

No, that didn't make any sense. He must be referring to the here and now. Today was their last contractual day together, and he probably wanted to make the most of it, just as she did.

"Come on, princess, get the lead out. We have a decent hike in front of us."

For the next half hour, they trekked through some of the most beautiful country she'd ever seen, even on TV. Seeing the jungle up close and personal as opposed to a two-dimensional picture was like the difference between seeing Jax in pictures (oh, he's cute) and knowing what it was like to make love to him (oh my fucking God he's heaven). No contest.

Jackson led the way, making sure he held the brush aside for her as she trailed behind him or held her hand to steady her when they went over a slippery area. Little by little the sounds of rushing water grew louder. At last she caught sight of the light at the end of their foliage tunnel. Anticipation bubbled in her chest at what she would find. Maybe surprises weren't so bad after all.

"Here we are," he announced, taking her hand and leading her out into the clearing. "Welcome to Maris Falls."

"Oh, Jackson!"

A clear pool of water surrounded on three sides by high cliffs dressed in lush greenery, and in the very center, a majestic waterfall draped itself over the edge, ending in a spectacular show of white spray and rainbows from the refracting light of the sun.

She turned to look at him. "This is your favorite place on the island."

"Yeah. I come here to think, relax, contemplate existentialism. You know, the norm."

She laughed and gazed back at the scene before her. "I've never seen anything so breathtakingly beautiful."

"I have."

At the husky sound of his voice, she found him staring at her, his meaning obvious in his heated gaze. Normally she'd throw out something saucy like, "Flattery will get you everywhere," but suddenly her throat was dry and her wit seemed to have taken a hike up a different mountain.

"Um, so . . ." She cleared her throat and tucked her hair behind her ear. "Now what?"

"Now," he said, shucking the heavy backpack from his shoulders and setting down the small cooler he'd carried, "we set up camp and go for a swim."

"That's the best news I've heard all day. Give me the pack," she said, holding out her hands. "I'm an excellent camp setter-upper."

"You are, huh?"

"Yep. It was my minor in college. I'll have us in the water in no time."

"I have a better idea." He dropped the pack behind him and stepped in front of her, grabbing her hips. Her hands gravitated to his pecs like magnets, the solid muscles fitting the curve of her palms as his full lips distracted her. "Why don't you hop in the water and cool off. I'll get stuff situated out here and join you in a minute."

She bit the corner of her lip and glanced over at the cool, clear pool beckoning her, then back up at Jackson. "You sure?"

A huge smile split that glorious mouth right before he bestowed her with a searing kiss. "I'm sure."

She couldn't bring herself to argue any more. The humidity of the jungle they'd trudged through had definitely taken its toll on her during their hike. Sweat and grit covered her skin, and she felt truly disgusting. Allowing Jax to be so close to her while feeling so grimy shot way past her comfort level, but for some reason when it came to him, she found herself acting out of character a lot.

Vanessa wasted no time in stripping off her shorts, T-shirt, tennies, and socks until all that remained was her cerulean string bikini. It was her personal favorite. The suit was basically a collection of triangles: two that barely covered more than her nipples, leaving cleavage and side swells exposed, and two skimpy inverted ones to form the bottoms, which were joined only by strings tied in bows on her hips and showed plenty of ass. It left pretty much nada to the imagination.

"What in God's name is that?"

"What is what?" Fearing he saw some sort of dangerous jungle animal, her heart leapt into her throat as she spun to see what he'd found. But he was staring at her. Air whooshed out of her lungs, and she took a few steadying breaths. "Don't do that! You scared the crap out of me."

"That is not a swimsuit."

"Don't be ridiculous. Of course it is."

"No," he said, his gaze trapped between her shoulders and her thighs. "That's a torture device. Do you wear that thing in public?"

She actually didn't. It was reserved for pool parties with her friends or sunbathing on her balcony. "Why, Jackson?" Sauntering over to him, she ran a finger down the center of his chest and looked up through her eyelashes. "Would it make you jealous if other men saw me wearing it?"

"Try murderous," he said through clenched teeth. "You're damn near naked."

She gave him a wicked grin and filed that information away for future reference. "Well, if seeing me in this barely anything bikini is actually torturing you . . ." She brought her hands up to the strings hanging at her hips, ready to release the bows. "I should probably just get rid of it."

Jackson grabbed her wrists, holding them captive. "Don't even think about it, V. It's rare I see anyone up here, but that doesn't mean it won't happen. And no one but me gets to look at what's mine."

Shit. Way to give her your back, Maris. He hadn't meant to say that last part out loud. Putting any kind of claim on Vanessa would spook her. He might as well have just pushed her away with his hands. Today was supposed to be his day to show her how he felt about her—that he wanted more than just the three days he'd agreed to. But if he couldn't keep his inner Neanderthal locked down, he wouldn't have much of a chance.

She canted her head slightly and studied him. He could almost see her wheels spinning, but which way they took her remained to be seen. At last she smiled and said, "Since you put it that way . . ."

Rising up on tiptoes, she pressed her lips to his. Just

when he planned to take it to the next level and to hell with setting anything up, she pulled back, gave him a brilliant smile, and walked away with a little extra swing in her hips. When she reached the edge of the water, she tossed him a look over her shoulder just before diving into the clear, cool water.

Why hadn't she closed down or reminded him he only had claim on her for another few hours? Was it possible she felt something more for him than just someone to fool around with on vacation? She broke the surface several yards away, laughing and treading water.

"Now this is heaven," she said, turning around to study the surrounding area, then diving back under.

"Pretty damn close," he said to himself. The only thing that would clinch it in his eyes was if Vanessa wanted to be with him. For good. He'd never felt a fraction for any woman like he did for her. They completed each other with a perfect balance of give and take.

She needed control in her daily life. She was a woman who knew what she wanted and didn't stop until she got it. It was damn refreshing to be with someone who preferred to make the plans instead of waiting to be told an agenda. She also thrived on being the center of attention, and he was more than happy to sit back and watch her command a crowd.

Jackson had tried shedding his natural tendencies to take charge of things when he moved to the islands. After playing parent to his sister for five years, he longed for a life where someone else took the lead for a change. Except every time he tried the relationship thing, the women looked to him for everything from positions in the bedroom to what they should have for lunch. The former he didn't mind. The latter drove him fucking crazy.

Jilli had once told Jax that on a subconscious level, he

purposely chose more submissive women, despite wanting the opposite. That way he never had to worry about a long-term commitment because deep down he knew they weren't compatible. At the time, he'd called "bullshit" on her female relationship psychobabble. But now he realized just how right she was.

The truth of the matter was, he had been afraid of finding someone he could get serious about. He'd grown rather fond of not having responsibility for anyone other than himself. And regardless of how strong either person was, when it came to relationships, they were a shared responsibility for the other person. As much as he'd loved his sister, for the years he'd taken care of her, he'd felt trapped. He never let her know that, of course. But with the sudden deaths of their parents, finding out he'd been adopted, and then putting his life on hold for half a decade to raise Lucie . . . Well, it'd been hard not to feel a little overwhelmed.

So yeah. Once he settled on Oahu, the last thing he'd wanted to do was chain himself to another human being, no matter the reason. He'd been perfectly content with his three-month average for keeping the occasional girlfriend and the friends-with-benefits situations he'd enjoyed while they lasted.

Which was why it was a total fluke that he and Vanessa were together in any sort of intimate capacity. Hell, under normal circumstances, even though his dominant demeanor might not have chased her off, her rules would've had her running in the opposite direction for sure.

But here they were. Like two halves of a puzzle that filled in the other's empty spaces, making them whole for the first time. Jax knew in his soul there would never be another woman who completed him so perfectly.

And now that he'd found her, there stood a damn

good chance he'd lose her. And he'd have no one to blame but himself.

It wouldn't matter that things between them had worked out. That they'd had an amazing five days so far and, if his suspicions were right, that they both wanted more time with each other. She'd made her rules to protect herself from ending up with someone who could hurt her in any way like her parents did, and that included someone who lied. Vanessa wouldn't see only the lies he told that first time. She'd see every minute they spent together as a deception. Everything he'd said to her. Everything he'd done to her. Everything he'd made her feel.

Jax knew he had one shot at this. He needed to show her just how much she meant to him—show her how much he meant to her—and hope like hell it would be enough.

It only took him a few minutes to spread out the blanket and check that all the snacks he'd brought with them hadn't been jostled open and were still safe in their containers. He planned on cooking her dinner later at his place, but until then, he'd brought fun finger foods to keep their energy up. Because one thing was for certain: he planned on burning through a whole lot of their energy.

Jax shucked everything but his shorts in record time. To say he was anxious to play in his favorite swimming hole with Vanessa was a gross understatement. Turning around, he found her relaxing on a large, flat boulder on the other side of the natural pool. Propped up on her elbows, one leg bent, head hanging back, and a cascade of dark red hair spilling onto the rock below like the waterfall not far away. She looked like a water nymph, sunning herself and tempting men with the strongest resolves to fall under her spell. And he was no exception.

But just as he was about to get in, she said something that had him stopping with one foot hovering over the rippling water.

Without opening her eyes or breaking from her cover-shoot pose, she yelled to him to be heard over the splashes of the waterfall. "You're taking forever over there. I didn't realize you had to actually make the blanket before setting it out."

Oh, really. Her smack talking put a big-ass grin on his face and brought out his playful side.

"Be right in!"

Jogging around the edge of the pool to the path he knew well enough to navigate blind, he climbed up the rock formation to the top of the falls. Once he stood firmly on the large rock that jutted above the flow of the fast-moving water, he cupped his hands around his mouth and called out for the attention of the bathing beauty some thirty feet below.

When she caught sight of him, she scrambled to her feet and yelled something that sounded an awful lot like a dig on his intelligence.

Pretending he hadn't jumped from this very spot hundreds of times before was probably cruel, but the mischievous teen inside him couldn't resist a little prank. "Don't worry, I'm sure I'll be fine! It doesn't look too bad!"

Without another word he leapt far away from the rock wall's edge and reveled in the sensation of free falling alongside the rushing water. Feet first, he plunged into the cool depths, feeling instantly revitalized as he sank to the bottom and then pushed up to break the surface.

"Are you out of your mind? You could've slipped and cracked your skull open."

He looked over to see a livid water nymph kneeling

and gripping the edge of her rock, glaring at him for all she was worth.

"What's the matter, Red?" he asked as he swam over to her. "Afraid you'd lose me over a little cliff jump?"

"Of course not. I was worried about finding my way back down the mountain by myself after you bled out like an idiot."

Damn, he loved that smart mouth of hers. Laughing, he yanked her into the water with him. She squealed in surprise and tried wresting herself from his hold, but he refused to yield. Soon she was laughing with him, and they spent a good half hour splashing and dunking each other in a back and forth game of cat and mouse.

Breathing heavily from their play, they hoisted themselves onto the rock platform she'd been sunning on earlier. Their legs dangled in the water as they leaned back on their hands. She exhaled heavily and stared out at the scenery before them. "This place is magical, Jackson." She turned to look at him. "Thank you for bringing me. For sharing this part of your life with me."

Her words had his gut clenching and his heart swelling. He wanted to share so much more with her if she'd let him. And he planned on telling her. But not now. Now he just wanted to lose himself in her smell, her taste, her body. Her.

Leaning over, he kissed her, slow and gentle, savoring the eager response she gave him. He wondered if she had any idea how easily she unraveled him.

He pulled back. "Ever stand under a waterfall?" She shook her head. "Come on."

Jax guided her over to the right of the main falls where water still fell down the rock wall, but without the amount and force it had in the center. It also had a decent ledge to stand on, being closer to the shoreline.

Holding her hand to keep her steady, he helped her until she had secure footing.

A wide smile broke over her face as she lifted her arms in the air to cut through the thin curtain of water spilling behind her. Jax was spellbound, watching her tip her head back and laugh with the sheer joy of experiencing one of Mother Nature's wonders.

Growing up in a landlocked state, he'd never known he had such an affinity for water until he moved to the islands. The first time he ever saw the Pacific, it called to him like the moon to a lone wolf. And ever since, water had become as much a part of him as his fighting. Which was why sex with an element of water—whether in a shower, hot tub, rain, or waterfall—was such a huge turn-on for him.

And why his cock was thick and straining against the confines of his board shorts.

Jax stepped in to her, crowding her against the rocks that had been smoothed by hundreds of years of streaming water. Her smile died with the firm grip of his hands on either side of her neck. Her breaths turned shallow, her pulse jackhammered under his touch, and her pupils nearly swallowed the green of her eyes.

He brushed a thumb over her lower lip, the way the plump flesh gave way to his touch so goddamn erotic. "Do you have any idea what you do to me?" His voice sounded harsh and broken, like he'd lost it the day before and it was only now starting to come back. "Every time I look at you, I fucking lose my mind."

"Good." She raked her nails down his abs, leaving trails of heated desire in their wake. Then she nipped the pad of his thumb. "That makes two of us, then."

Needing her kiss like he needed to breathe, Jax descended and laid claim to her mouth. He moved his lips over hers, pushing her onto the rock until the water cascaded around her body, a fluid outline of the soft curves that tempted his baser self. Her arms hooked under his, her hands gripped the backs of his shoulders, and she pulled him in so not even air could pass between them.

Shifting the lower half of his body, he positioned one of his legs between hers, grabbed her ass in both hands, and hauled her onto his thigh. Without further instruction, she rolled her hips to slowly grind her sex over his solid muscle. His tongue danced with hers to the music of the rushing falls surrounding them. She tasted of mint, coffee . . . and her.

No one tasted like her. No one felt like her. No one touched him—physically or emotionally—like her.

"Make love to me, Jackson."

Fuck, yes. Wait . . . Gathering every shred of will-power he had, he said, "Not here."

She retaliated with a, "Yes, here," and bit his bottom lip before her tongue swept in and scattered his resolve to the four winds.

The woman was dangerous. She had the power to make him lose control, something he'd never experienced before with anyone else. He could easily lose himself in her emerald eyes, from the scent of her skin or the power of her kiss. And he wasn't sure he'd care if he never found his way back.

Jax shifted his weight and felt his foot slip a little on one of the rocks, reminding him of exactly why he'd said no to begin with. He wrenched his mouth from hers, but before he could reiterate his earlier statement and tack on the safety explanation, one of her hands snaked down to run the length of his stiff cock before lightly squeezing his balls.

He took a sharp intake of breath through clenched teeth and let it out on a groan as he pushed himself into her palm. She looked up at him with an impish smile, clearly proud of herself for eliciting such a reaction from him.

"You think it's funny when you get me to lose my shit, don't you?" he asked. She nodded, a glimmer of mischief in eyes framed by wet, spiky lashes. Her lips, swollen and red from his kisses, held the barest hint of a smirk, as though she knew enjoying the moment too much would get her into worse trouble than she already was. Smart woman.

Willful woman.

"Let's see how funny you think it is when the roles are reversed, princess."

Vanessa became weightless as he picked her up and cradled her in his arms. She wrapped her arms around his neck and looked up to find him staring down at her.

She could almost see the flurry of thoughts in his mind; he looked that intense. But no matter how hard she tried, she couldn't begin to guess what they were. Did they have to do with what just happened? Or something about her? Were they good or bad? Shit, when did she become so neurotic?

"Everything okay?" she asked.

He blinked, then gave her the smile that made her insides melt. "Better than okay. You hungry?"

"Famished."

"Good. I brought some things I think you'll like."

He carried her over the rocks as easily as if they'd been flat, dry, and she weighed little more than a feather. Such grace in a man so large not only defied basic physics but spat in its face. It also turned her on something fierce.

Once they reached their blankets, Jax set her down and started to rummage around in the small cooler. The sun bounced off his tan skin and the dark images in his tattoo. The waves almost looked as though they rippled from the way his bicep moved with the simplest of motions. She loved his arms. So strong and sure, Vanessa couldn't remember ever feeling so safe and protected as when Jackson wrapped his arms around her.

Lowering herself to the blanket next to him, she said, "I'm suddenly hungry for something other than food."

His mouth quirked up in the corner as he turned to look at her. "That's the dessert menu you're talking about, babe. That typically comes after the main course."

She bit her lip for a second and then remembered that one of her coworkers told her that she has special days with her kids where they have dessert for dinner and then watch movies. "But it's a special day, right? So on special days we should be able to have dessert first."

"I don't know," he hedged. "That sounds an awful lot liking breaking the rules."

Her jaw dropped a second before he started to laugh. She retaliated by smacking him on the arm and pushing him away when he tackled her for a makeup kiss. She lasted all of two seconds before releasing a fit of giggles from her chest and giving in to the magic of his mouth.

A minute later he set them both to rights again and said they could indeed skip to dessert. So she was confused when he went back to the cooler instead of building on the amazing lip-lock they had going on.

He held up a bottle and two plastic flutes. "Thirsty?"

"Ooh, champagne. Absolutely."

Holding it over the grass, he freed the cork and waited for the initial foam to stop running from the bottle. He poured both of them half a glass and handed her one, then set the bottle on the lid of the cooler and turned back to her holding a small white box. When their eyes locked, all humor had been replaced by an intense seriousness. Something she hadn't seen much of from Jackson.

His natural settings were Charm and Flirt. She had a feeling most people rarely saw his serious side. He covered it up with the jokes and playful personality he portrayed so well. But he'd shown her what lay beneath in their talks about their pasts. And he was showing her now . . . but for what reason this time?

"Champagne and a gift?" she asked, raising an eyebrow. "Someone's stepping up his game."

"I'm not playing games with you, Vanessa. It's important to me that you know that."

For a long time she studied him, hoping his underlying meaning would appear in his caramel eyes or in the stern set of his stubbled jaw. She didn't find it, but what she did find was sincerity. Something honest, something pure, letting her know she wasn't just another conquest. Another notch on his headboard.

"I believe you," she answered softly.

A palpable relief settled over him. "Open it."

She removed the lid and pulled out a beautiful silver necklace. A two-piece pendant hung from the bottom. At the top, a square aquamarine sea glass bead dangled from its corner, and beneath that was a pewter—

"Starfish."

She smiled up at him through watery eyes. "Sea star."

He flashed her that brilliant white smile that hinted at his dimples. "Whatever. Here, let me help you put it on."

A few seconds later it was fastened and the cool metal of the sea star warmed where it rested in the center of her chest. "I love it, Jackson. Thank you so much."

"You're very welcome. Now we can have dessert." Setting his glass on top of the cooler next to the bottle, he kissed her long and slow. "Take off your suit, then lean back on your elbows. You can leave your legs straight or bend them, but I want them open. "

"What happened to worrying about spectators?"

"Chances are slim to none, and I find that right now I wouldn't care if we had a studio audience. I'm taking what's mine. Now."

The commanding tone he used during their sexual encounters both surprised her and sent a rush of heat between her legs.

What she hadn't realized until a couple days ago was that her need for control exhausted and frustrated her. After years of never letting up, her brain desperately needed a break. A chance to let go and trust that someone else could take over and give her what she needed without taking advantage of her vulnerability.

Jackson gave her that.

He was so in tune with her and her body. He'd known she secretly craved to submit her control even before she did. He knew how far he could push her and when it was far enough. And in only the few days they'd been together, he'd somehow trained her subconscious to instantly let go of her need for control when he slipped into his more dominant role with her.

Gazing up at him through her lashes, she did as she was told.

Jax watched Vanessa untie all four bows that held her suit to her lithe body and set the dangling scraps to the side. Though she'd used a ton of sunscreen all week to prevent burning her fair skin, she'd still gotten enough sun for a light base and a few new freckles. He'd never thought tan lines were particularly sexy, but he loved how her breasts and the triangle over her sex were still milky white against the light tan everywhere else.

She leaned back as he'd asked, holding herself up on

her forearms. Her legs were bent at the knees but only separated by a few inches. He narrowed his eyes just enough to make his point. "Wider, wahine. I want to see how wet you are for me."

Slowly she spread her legs, and he fought the urge to gulp in breaths of air. Breathe, Jackson.

He needed to make this count. To create a memory so powerful it would stay with her forever, even if the rest of their days together slipped away over time. He could say it was ego, but he knew better than that. It was fear, plain and simple. Fear that she didn't feel for him as he did for her. Fear that she would leave, and he'd be nothing more than a collection of memories. But memories faded, and the thought of not even having that small place in her life rattled him to his very core.

Jackson locked eyes with her and stretched out on the blanket between her bent legs. The intoxicating scent of her arousal made his mouth water.

His hands gripped her ass. She bit her lip.

His face lowered and held. She held her breath.

His lips met the soft flesh of her inner thigh before his teeth nipped her.

She gasped before dragging in short bursts of air, her hands fisting in the blanket.

He'd normally make her wait, make her beg. Build the anticipation until she was dripping and writhing without him even touching her sex. It sounded cruel, but in reality it only made her orgasms that much more explosive.

But he couldn't hack it this time. He didn't have the strength to hold out on her like he should. He needed to taste her, to drink of her, and he needed it right fucking now.

Feeling weak and selfish, he took exactly what he wanted.

Vanessa cried out the moment his mouth met her wet core. As he feasted, he watched her throw her head back, bowing her body, her pale breasts thrusting up to the sky like an offering to the sun.

Nothing else in the world compared, nor would it ever. Everything about her was unique, and this was no exception.

She felt like silk on his lips as he explored her moist folds, and when he fucked her with his tongue he thought he'd burn up from her heat and the way her body clamped around it.

"Oh, Jesus, Jax," she said on a harsh exhale. "You're killing me."

Not yet, I'm not.

He moved up slightly and found her clit. He flicked over it with the tip of his tongue, then sucked hard, then repeated both steps until her hips began to rock instinctively, searching for that final thing that would make her see stars in the middle of the day.

And he was only too happy to get her there.

He eased three fingers into her opening, knowing she could take them, but staying aware of how tight she was in the beginning. Slowly but firmly he pressed forward, feeling the walls of her channel clamp down on the welcome invasion. Once she'd taken their entire length, he met the rhythm of her hips thrust for thrust and went back to work on her clit with his mouth.

She reached through her legs and fisted a handful of his hair like grasping the horn of a saddle as she galloped toward her climax. His dick throbbed, wanting the friction his fingers currently had the pleasure of feeling.

Her breaths became moaning pants, keening cries, and finally a scream that rent the air as her entire body curled into itself, her muscles contracting and then convulsing with the pulses of her release.

Before she had a chance to come down, Jax yanked his shorts off, gently laid her the rest of the way on the ground, and poised himself at her entrance. As her body kissed the sensitive head of his cock, he groaned and pushed in to the hilt. Again her back bowed, but this time her breasts pressed into his chest until she relaxed beneath him.

"Vanessa, baby," he said, his voice no more than a rasp. "Open your eyes."

Long auburn lashes fluttered open to reveal lust-hazed eyes the color of wet moss. Her hair had dried partially in the sun, giving it multiple hues from brilliant red to deep mahogany. She was beautiful and amazing and . . .

"You're mine. Right here, right now. Only mine."

She reached up and trailed the tips of her fingers over his brow, down his nose, across his cheekbones, his lips. Finally, she placed her palms on the sides of his face, looked up at him with her heart in her eyes and whispered, "Only yours."

Two words. Three syllables. Nine letters.

Something so small shouldn't have such a tremendous power over him. Shouldn't be able to bring him to his metaphorical knees or make him want to climb mountains if she asked.

But it did. And it felt . . . right.

Jax took her mouth and then her body. He wanted as much of himself in her as possible. To mark her. Brand her. Claim her.

They moved as one, as though they'd made love thousands of times rather than only a handful. And this time they were connected more than just physically. Everything about being with her like this felt different, more intimate, more . . . just more.

Holding himself up on one forearm, he let his other hand roam. Over her breast, down her side, her hip. A quick squeeze of her ass, then down the outside of her thigh before hooking under her knee and pulling it forward to allow him in that little bit more.

Their kiss broke off as they both needed more air. Her hands found his back and her nails found his skin. When he dragged his teeth down the cord in her neck and bit, he felt a shudder ripple through her.

As he continued to pump into her, their hands and mouths and tongues and teeth explored every inch they could reach. Somewhere along the way he'd lost his mind, unable to gather a coherent thought to save his life. Their movements became more feverish, the coming together of their bodies more explosive. It was like a runaway train heading toward the unfinished bridge that would send them careening into space before they knew what had happened.

But Jax didn't want that. He wanted to be aware of every passing second, to hear every hitch of her breath and see every emotion on her face.

He deliberately slowed his rhythm and lifted his head to peer down at her.

"No," she whined. "Faster. So close!"

"I know, baby. I'll get you there." She opened her mouth to argue or maybe even beg, but he cut her off. "Vanessa, trust me. Let me make love to you."

She drew the center of her lip between her teeth for a moment then nodded her head.

Though the pace had lessened, the intensity had not. He thrust hard and still hit deep. Her heat and the way her body gripped his cock on every withdrawal killed him over and over again. It was the sweetest death he hoped to never survive.

"You're so fucking perfect, you know that?"

Her eyes filled with tears until they spilled over her temples. She grabbed onto the back of his neck, her fingers splaying into the hair at his nape. "Jackson, I think I might . . . Oh, God, I think I—"

"Shhh. No more words, baby." He was pretty sure he knew what she'd been trying to say, and though he wanted to hear her say it more than he wanted his next breath, he wouldn't handle it well if later she told him it was a heat-of-the-moment thing. Those words should never be uttered for the first time during sex. Ever. "Feel my skin on yours. Feel me inside you. Feel how perfect you fit me. Just feel, okay?"

Again she nodded, losing more tears. Jax adjusted his position, lifting up slightly to make sure his weight wasn't crushing her. When she gasped on his next thrust, he realized he'd found the bull's-eye. Keeping the slow and steady pace, he hit it again. And again. And again. Each time pushing her closer and closer to that waterfall edge, and each time feeling himself follow her that much more.

Her eyes started to drift closed as the tension consumed her. "Keep them open, Vanessa. Watch me. I want to look into your eyes when I make you come. I want to see you acknowledge who does this to you, who makes you feel this way."

She didn't argue, didn't deflect. She simply obeyed. And knowing she did so, no matter how far from her comfort zone it led her, was the last addition to his perfect storm for both of them.

This time Vanessa's cry stuck in her throat. Her body tensed, eyes widened and lips parted, but nothing came out. She was a living, silent work of art. The feel of her pussy milking him hurtled him over the edge, and with one last drive forward, he buried himself as far as he could go and spilled himself deep inside, branding her the way she had already branded herself on his heart.

* * *

As they lay on the blanket, her back to his chest and legs intertwined, Vanessa released a long exhale and snuggled into him a little more.

"You know," she said, her eyes still closed and a lazy grin on her face, "the last few days have been great. But today . . ." Her head turned, her bright green eyes searching his. "Today has been absolutely perfect. Thank you so much for this."

Bending his head, he placed a tender kiss on her swollen lips. "Believe me, it's been my pleasure."

Jax tightened his arms around her, wanting to obliterate any space between them as if it could prevent her from putting it there once he dropped the bomb he had to tell her.

There'd been plenty of times in Jax's life he should have been nervous. When he was eighteen and had to appear before the court to fight for his right of legal guardianship over Lucie, he'd been prepared to win. When he picked up at the age of twenty-three and moved halfway around the world on his own, he'd been determined to start fresh. Before every professional match in his career, he'd been hungry for the fight. But he'd never allowed himself to feel nervous in any of those situations. He believed in mind over matter and in being in control of his own destiny.

And telling Vanessa that he wanted more from her—that he wanted a shot at something real with her—was no different than any of those. He loved her. Convincing her of his feelings and to listen to her heart instead of her rules was a challenge he was confident he could win.

There was only one thing standing in his way. One thing that had the potential to take that "win" and blow it right out of the water.

His lie.

And that's where the nerves came in. For the first

time in his adult life he was more afraid of losing a "forever" relationship than getting in one.

He should've confessed the truth to her a dozen times over the last five days. In the beginning, he'd been worried about pissing her off or pissing his sister off. But after kissing her that first night, he'd been afraid of pushing her away. Of losing something he couldn't even identify at the time. All he'd known was he didn't want to take the chance, and that hopefully he could win her over enough so that her feelings for him overshadowed his deception.

And now that the time was here, he held on to that hope with both fists as he pushed open the door to the lion's den.

"Vanessa," he finally forced past the lump in his throat. "I want to talk to you about something, but I want you to let me finish before you say anything."

"No interruptions? You're asking quite a lot of me, big guy."

He kissed her shoulder. "I have faith in you."

She shifted on the blanket until she lay fully on her back, but the sun glaring across her face caused her to squint and lift a hand for protection. Jax propped himself up on his elbow to cast her in his shadow. Being able to look down on her was simply a bonus.

Lowering her arm, she sighed dramatically. "My hero."

His smile matched hers. Easy and carefree, the way a smile should be. He'd never seen her more beautiful than she was at that moment. Areas of her body glowed pink where his beard had irritated her skin the way she loved, dark pink nipples showed signs of his mouth's attention, and true contentment shone in her half-lidded eyes and lazy grin.

But the sexiest thing ever was his bite mark in the

front of her hip. He traced the red outline with his finger and felt a shudder run through her body.

Mine.

"I love seeing my marks on your skin, you know that?"

She bit the corner of her lip and gave a slight nod. He captured her chin and used his thumb to free her lip before tracing it once, twice. "If it weren't for the wedding in a couple of days, I'd have marked you so everyone could see it. So they know you belong to me."

Jax knew he took a big risk using dominant phrases with a woman like Vanessa. In her daily life she prided herself on her independence. On being in charge of herself and her life. On submitting to no one, especially a man. And he loved that about her. Her spunk, her drive, her stubborn streak. They were all things he found incredibly attractive.

But he needed her to understand she didn't always have to be that way. It wasn't completely who she was, but rather the way she'd built herself to be for her own protection. With him, she could let her guard down and let him take the lead. Trust in him to always take care of her, to know her needs and her wants, and know he'd always be loyal.

"I've never belonged to anyone," she said softly. "Not even my mother. Not really, anyway."

"That's because there's never been anyone in your life worthy enough to claim you."

"And you?" She reached up and placed her hand along his cheek. "You are worthy enough?"

"Hell no," he said, grabbing her fingers and pressing a warm kiss to the center of her palm. "But I promise I'll always give you what you need. And whether you're calling the shots or I am, you'll always come first."

A mischievous grin sprouted and her eyes twinkled. "I definitely like the sound of that last part."

He chuckled, catching her meaning. "That's not what I meant—which you well know—but, yes, in that respect as well. I couldn't count myself a man otherwise."

"Certainly not my man, that's for sure," she said, laughing.

She hadn't said it—not really—but it was so close that his heart tripped over itself. He sobered and gazed deeply into her eyes. He needed to hear her say it. At least once before he ruined everything. "Am I yours, V?"

Jax saw the warring thoughts behind those deep green pools. Walls of tears gathered, and yet nothing fell from the corners when she blinked and a heavy sigh escaped her lips. His gut twisted into a mass of knots and his entire body tensed.

Just as he feared the worst, she whispered, "I can't think of anything I want more."

He'd never anticipated hearing such sweet words. His heart pounded so hard he felt the vibrations in his ribs. Smiling like a complete idiot, he prepared to kiss her breathless.

She held a hand up between them. "But—"

"No," he said firmly. "No 'buts.' We can hash out details and logistics and whatever else later. What matters is how we feel and that we want to be together."

That I love you. But he couldn't say it out loud yet, even though he felt it in the very marrow of his bones. So much had happened so fast. What they just said was a huge step for both of them. When they finally reached the point of admitting to love, it would be monumental, and he wanted the moment to be perfect.

"Okay," she said. "No 'buts' . . . yet."

"Fair enough." And with that, he kissed her breathless. Arms and legs wrapped around each other, hands stroked, tongues danced. Adrenaline from the victory coursed through his veins like a potent drug.

He hated to lose that feeling, and yet he knew it was time for the last part of the conversation. The part that could irrevocably shatter everything he'd just gained.

Drawing back, he pressed his forehead to hers. One side of her face was cushioned by the inside of his upper arm, the other side framed with his free hand. The knots and tension crept back into the fibers of his muscles, causing them to burn like he'd just worked the bags at the gym.

"Hey," she whispered. "What's wrong? You've gone all hard on me. And not in a good way."

"There's something else I need to tell you."

"You're not looking to bring Jilli into this equation, are you? Because I've gotta tell you, as hot as she is, I'm extremely selfish where you're concerned, and I refuse to share."

Despite his nerves threatening to give him a stroke, he actually chuckled. "Never. You're more than enough for me, pupule wahine."

"I keep forgetting to ask someone what that means. Are you ever going to tell me?"

"Maybe someday. The literal translation kind of ruins the beauty of the words. Why, don't you like it?"

She shrugged her shoulder. "It sounds pretty, and I like that it's something you only use with me." Black lashes narrowed over green eyes. "Right?"

"Only you, I promise."

"Then I guess I can wait. Or maybe I'll remember to ask a native," she finished with a sly grin. "Now, what is it you wanted to tell me?"

Jax took a deep breath and let it out, trying to release his tension without success. "Remember our encounter at the airport?"

"How could I forget?" she said wryly.

"I went there expecting . . . Well, I'm not really sure. But I sure as hell wasn't expecting a fiery Scot who refused to be charmed and made it a point to call me out on my bullshit."

"You underestimated me. That was your first mistake," she said very matter-of-factly with a single haughty brow raised. He'd found her arrogance sexy back then, and he found it the same now.

"You're right. But I made a much bigger mistake after that. It's just that I'd never met anyone like you. You intrigued the hell out of me, and when you tried taking your bag back and you fell into me, I lost it. It was like a switch that I didn't even know I had got flipped, and I wanted—no, needed—to spend time with you."

He closed his eyes briefly, ordering himself to continue when all he wanted to do was forget the whole thing as he buried himself deep inside her again and again. But starting something based on a lie was destined to crumble, whether it was a month from now or in ten years.

"You dismissed me, V. Said good-bye and that you'd see me at the wedding, so I—"

A short, tinny melody played from the direction of his backpack. He recognized it as the text message alert on her phone. She reached over to grab it from the side pocket, but he held her arm. "Don't worry about it. You can check it later."

"Jax, what if it's Robért with a wedding emergency? Lucie and Reid will be here tomorrow and if everything isn't taken care of, she's liable to have a panic attack. It'll just take a second."

She planted a firm kiss on his mouth and then rolled over to retrieve the phone. He blew out a heavy breath and ran a hand through his hair. He felt like he'd been trying to tell her the truth for two hours instead of two minutes. Confessions fucking sucked.

Vanessa gasped and cried, "Oh my God."

Her tone was one of terror, her fingers covering her mouth as she stared at the screen of her phone with tear-filled eyes. There wasn't a wedding problem in the world that garnered that severe of a reaction.

"What is it?"

"My sister. She's in the hospital." V looked at him like he'd never seen her. Lost. "She was s-severely beaten."

Five minutes to pack up camp and another thirty minutes to hike back down the mountain to where she finally got full cell service again. Up at the falls she didn't have enough for a call to go through, but thankfully she heard her sister's text coming in.

Instead of wasting more time heading back to the Mau Loa, Jackson suggested they hang out at his place so she could talk to her sister and find out what the situation was.

When they'd parked earlier, he'd done so next to a small white cottage with bay windows. It was old with wooden siding and weathered shutters, but it had a certain quaint charm about it. She hadn't asked whose it was, and he hadn't offered. But now she had a pretty good idea, since he was unlocking the front door and letting them in. He flipped the lights on and closed the door after her.

Sky blue paint disguised what appeared to be wood paneling and a worn Berber carpet the same color as the sand on the beaches covered the floors. The kitchen to the left was small but functional-looking for a bachelor. The living room had a set of tan couches and a matching easy chair facing the TV. Down a short hallway looked to be a couple of rooms, most likely the bedroom and bathroom. He didn't have much as far as decor. No window treatments, no paintings on the walls. Though he did have a small shelving unit with pictures of his family and trophies.

Vanessa wasn't sure what she'd expected Jackson's home to look like, but she hadn't pictured this. She had no idea what a UFC fighter made, but apparently they fought for love of the sport and not the money. Not that it mattered one way or the other. He could live out of his Jeep for all she cared. But if this was how he had to live as a champion, what would happen when he couldn't fight at all anymore?

Rule #3: Never date a man without a stable future.

Shut the hell up, Rules!

"Uh, I know it's not much, but I don't really require a whole lot." He started picking up a few stray pieces of clothing and threw them into what she assumed was his bedroom. "I wouldn't have given the maid the day off if I knew you were coming."

She blinked in surprise. "You have a maid?"

His amber eyes softened. "No, baby, it was a joke," he said, gathering her into his arms. "Sorry, now isn't the time. I was just trying to break the tension."

Vanessa held on tight, her face pressed against his strong chest, and inhaled his unique scent as though he'd thrown it to her as a lifeline.

"Why don't you try her again?"

She shook her head and pulled back to stare at the silent phone in her hand. "I left a voice mail and several texts already. She must not be able to call back yet. I just have to wait."

And she'd never felt more helpless. Knowing her baby sister was in a hospital somewhere alone, bruised and battered . . . It was tearing her up inside.

"Come sit down with me before you collapse."

He sat in the corner of the couch, and then tucked her into his side with her legs draped across his lap. One arm wrapped around her back, and he rubbed the outside of her leg in gentle, reassuring strokes.

"If I could have one wish—anything at all—it would be to go back in time and never leave home until Kat was out of school. Then I could've taken her with me." Tears scalded her cheeks. "God, why didn't I think of that back then?"

"Because you needed to get out of that house, too. You deserved a chance at a future, Vanessa. You weren't Kat's mother. It wasn't your responsibility to put your life on hold for her."

She pulled back to meet his eyes. "Why the hell not? You did."

He frowned. "I did what?"

"You put your life on hold for your little sister. You did the right thing."

"Baby, it's not the same, and you know it."

Vanessa pushed off his lap and stood. She felt like a thousand watts of electricity were zipping through her veins, evaporating her blood cells along the way.

"Bullshit it's not. And look what happened," she said, pointing to the door as if her best friend stood there plain as day. "Lucie is a well-adjusted, successful adult because you didn't leave her with people who couldn't care less about her."

"Vanessa," he snapped, unfolding to his full height in front of her. "You need to stop blaming yourself for Kat's life. Lucie didn't turn out as she did because of me. I can't take credit for her accomplishments, just as I can't take the blame for when she made the worst mistake of her life and married that asshole in Vegas."

Vanessa tried turning to walk out the door, but he grabbed her arm and held fast. "Let go, Jackson. You don't get it. You'll never understand because you didn't fuck up."

"No, damn it, I won't let go. I'm not letting you walk away from this just because it makes you uncomfortable. I'm here for you, whether you like it or not." Without releasing her arm, he lifted his other hand to hold the side of her face. "I get that you've had a lot of people let you down in your life, but I am not one of those people."

An overwhelming concoction of emotions twisted inside her. Fear, helplessness, anger, regret . . . They expanded as they swirled, threatening to burst from her pores to taint everyone around her. But as she let Jackson's light eyes penetrate deep into her soul, she felt the devotion, faith, and trust they had for each other overpowering the others until they were only a murmur in the back of her mind.

She tried smiling but failed as more tears spilled over. "I'm really scared for her."

"I know you are, baby. Come here."

Again, Vanessa let him envelop her in the safety of his embrace. Listening to the steady beat of his heart seemed to regulate hers, as if it couldn't stand not to be in sync with his. Though she was still worried sick for Kat, Vanessa knew there was no other place she'd rather be in that moment than in Jackson's arms.

"Are you hungry?"

She shook her head. "I couldn't eat now if I wanted."

"Then let's go back to the couch while we wait for her call. I'll try to rub some of the tension out of your shoulders."

He kissed the crown of her head and pulled her to the couch again, only this time he situated her between his legs and facing away from him. Sitting sideways, she pulled her knees up to her chest, let her head drop down, and tried to relax as his hands worked under her shirt on the knots in her back.

They stayed like that for what seemed like an eternity but had only been ten minutes when her phone rang with her sister's caller ID. Leaping off the couch, she pressed the green button and shoved the cell to her ear.

"Kat! Where are you? What happened?"

"Nessie, calm down or you'll give yourself a coronary. Then we'll both be in the hospital."

The weak and raspy voice of Vanessa's baby sister was almost unrecognizable. Chills formed goose bumps on her flesh, immediately chased by the heat of righteous anger.

"I'll calm down as soon as you tell me what happened and where to find the soon-to-be-dead asshole responsible," she ground through a clenched jaw.

Kat sighed on the other end, no doubt resigning herself to the fact that Vanessa had no intentions of calming down about anything. "I'm okay, Nessie. Just a little banged up." There was a pregnant pause, and then a mumbled, "This time."

"What do you mean, 'this time'? So help me God, Kat, if you don't start spilling your guts I will hire every P.I. in the country until I find you, upon which I will kidnap you and hold you prisoner for your own damn good."

"I don't need your protection, Ness," Kat bit out.

"Oh, really? Then why the hell are you in a hospital?"

Another sigh. "This is a special situation. Lenny got mixed up with owing money to the wrong people. When he couldn't pay . . ." Vanessa almost heard her sister shrug through the phone. "They said they wanted to put a little fear of God into him. So they roughed me up so he could find me when he got home."

"Oh my God." Vanessa sank back onto the couch. Her mind barely registered Jackson rubbing her back, but her body lost some of its tension and her heart didn't race quite so fast. "How much does Lenny owe them?"

Silence.

"Kat! How much?"

"Twenty thousand dollars."

"Holy—"

"I'm so sorry, Nessie, I know it's a lot of money, and it absolutely kills me to have to ask you. You know that. But I don't know what else to do. They said they'd kill Lenny if he didn't come up with the money and they'd just take me as payment instead."

Kat's words had become less coherent every second until at last all she could manage was broken, choking sobs. Vanessa's heart rent in two. She wanted to sob right along with her sister, but she took a deep breath and used her big-sister voice.

"Okay, Kitty Kat, take it easy. Listen to me now." She kept her tone soft but firm, just as she had when they were younger and Vanessa needed Kat to follow her instructions. "I want you to take some deep breaths. That's it, settle down. Everything's going to be all right. I'll fix it, I promise."

Kat's shaky breaths were followed by sniffles and then finally silence.

"Good. Now how much time do you have before they come to collect again?"

"Two days."

"Two days? I've never understood that about thugs. If you don't have the money now, what makes them think you can magically make it appear in two goddamn days?" She put her head in her hand and rubbed absently at her temple. "Okay, let me think. I have some in savings, but the rest will have to come from my 401K, but that'll take a few days to even process. Will they take a down payment as an act of good faith? What am I saying? They're criminals; they don't know the meaning of good faith."

"Tell her she'll have it by tomorrow."

Vanessa spun around on the couch and stared at Jackson. "What did you say?"

"You heard me. Tell her."

"Jax," she said, "maybe you thought you heard her say two thousand, but—"

"It's a cell phone, V. The conversation might as well be in the room. I know she needs twenty Gs."

Vanessa glanced around the cottage as inconspicuously as possible, looking for signs that the man she loved wasn't in fact as destitute as he seemed.

"I know it doesn't seem like it," he said with an amused smirk, "but I'm doing pretty well for myself. Trust me when I say I can give her the money."

"Loan," Vanessa argued. "You're loaning me the money, with interest, and I'm paying you back."

"We'll arm wrestle about it later. Just tell her to find a place nearby that accepts money transfers—No, you know what?" His eyes narrowed and his jaw set like he'd been challenged and was now readying for a fight. "Find out where she is. We'll fly out there to make sure that man of hers doesn't fuck it up again. That way the debt gets paid without any more problems."

Vanessa's heart swelled ten times its normal size. At any moment, she expected to see it pushing between her ribs, it was so full of love for the man in front of her. She kissed him hard and fast and mouthed the words thank you before resuming the conversation with her sister and getting all the information needed to carry out Jax's plan.

After going over the details several times to be sure there was no room for miscommunication, and then telling Kat she loved her and would see her soon, Vanessa hung up the phone and collapsed back against Jackson's chest.

He wrapped his arms around her and rested his cheek on top of her head. "If you have her cell number, why aren't you ever able to talk to her?"

"That's a cell phone that's programmed with only my number in it. Lenny doesn't know she has it. Since she's always refused my help, it was the one concession I got so she had some way of reaching me in case of emergency or to just let me know when she moves to a new city. She doesn't use it as often as I'd like, but it's better than nothing. When she's not using it, it's turned off and hidden so Lenny doesn't find it."

A sad smile attempted to curve her mouth up but didn't quite succeed. "Sometimes I call it just to leave her a voice mail about my day or to let her know I'm thinking of her and miss her."

"I bet she likes that."

"I don't know," she mused. "She's never mentioned them."

"Sounds like she's stubborn and has a lot of pride. Kind of like someone else I know."

That, along with the kiss he placed on her neck, brought a genuine smile to her face. For him to accomplish that in one of her darkest moments said a lot about his effect on her. And it didn't even send her into a panic. Apparently miracles were possible.

Jackson got up from the couch and grabbed his phone, letting her know he planned to have the travel agent at the resort book their flights. As he did that, she grabbed a bottle of water from his fridge and settled on the couch, letting her head fall back between sips of the cool liquid.

"Yes, departing Honolulu and arriving in Nashville . . . The next flight out . . . One ticket for myself and the other for Miss MacGregor."

Vanessa's head snapped up. Miss MacGregor?

"No, they're arriving tomorrow. Place them in their original bungalow and keep the other one for Miss Mac-Gregor upon her return . . . Great. We'll be there shortly to pick up our things and the itineraries. Mahalo."

Jackson hung up and looked over at her. "Ready to go? The next flight leaves in a couple of hours."

Something told Vanessa to not ask. To let it go. It was a minute detail in the grand scheme of things right now. But in her profession, she knew it was those seemingly irrelevant details that sometimes made the difference between guilty and not guilty.

"Jackson, why did the lady at the resort recognize my real name?"

Lowering his head to his chest, he scrubbed a hand over his head several times before meeting her gaze again. "That's what I was trying to tell you before you got Kat's text."

"You told the resort my real identity?"

"Not exactly." He leaned his hips back on the short kitchenette counter and gripped the edge with his hands like it was the only thing holding him upright. "More like the resort has known your real identity the whole time."

"I don't understand."

"I was trying to explain earlier that from the first time we met, you knocked me on my ass. Intrigue and lust are a damn potent combination that I'd never experienced before. You're not like anyone I've ever met, and when you basically told me you had no desire to see me until the wedding . . . I said the first thing that came to mind that would ensure we had to spend a whole lot of time together."

Vanessa's insides began to vibrate, her body's reaction to what her mind was processing. And still she didn't want to believe it. "I didn't have to check in as Lucie. Did I." She left off the inflection at the end. It wasn't a question if she already knew the answer.

"No," he said. "You didn't."

"Which means you didn't need to check in as Reid, or at all for that matter."

"No. They were aware you would be standing in for Lucie for the week."

"How deep does the lie go, Jackson? You fed me all that bullshit about the Mau Loa being such an exclusive resort with the high security and strict policies crap. But I'm sure there's more," she said, crossing her arms over her chest. "There always is."

"The part about guests needing multiple IDs is true, and no one has been allowed to accept someone else's reservation until you."

She actually snorted at the very idea. "It's one thing to lie, but don't insult my intelligence, too, Maris. I know Reid's a big shot in the world of MMA, but he's no Donald Trump or Brad Pitt. An exclusive resort—which you're adamant the Mau Loa is—doesn't lift one of their strictest policies for someone like him."

"You're right," he said, holding her eyes with a meaningful look. "Unless of course he happens to be friends with one of the owners."

"Who's the . . ." Her voice trailed off as it suddenly dawned on her. Vanessa squinted at him as if through a pair of X-ray glasses that allowed her to see him as he truly was for the first time.

No answer, other than a slight tic in his jaw, which was answer enough for her.

He was an owner of the Mau Loa? It didn't add up. He lived out of a run-down cottage, with a Jeep and a surfboard. She'd seen no evidence of any material items to prove he had much more than a pot to piss in, much less had the kind of net worth he was talking about.

"I'm a silent partner, V, and I don't even own half. But I own enough to make sure I have a real comfortable nest egg should I ever get injured and can't fight anymore. And it's enough to break the policies for my sister and her best friend if I need to."

"Wow." Staring at a nick in the paneling across from her, she let the familiar feeling of betrayal spread through her like a virus. "I can only imagine the laughs you and God only knows how many other staff members had at my expense all week."

"Vanessa, that's not how it was at all. No one there even knows I'm an owner. And to be honest with you—"

"Now he wants to be honest," she mumbled.

"I planned on telling you the truth when I bought you the drink at the bar, but I couldn't bring myself to do it. I was afraid you'd be pissed and wouldn't give me the time of day after that."

"You were probably right."

"See? So—"

"It doesn't matter. You lied to me, Jackson. And not just once, but every second of every day. And even worse, you made me lie, even after you knew how I felt about it," she shouted. "I've heard of guys doing some crazy things to get in a girl's pants, but you take the fucking cake."

"That's not what I—"

"Bullshit! Listen to how pathetic your excuse is. You couldn't stand the idea of not spending time with me, so instead of being yourself and trying to get back in my good graces, you manipulated the situation so your chances were better."

She pressed her fingers into her temples to quell the pain that had been a dull ache when she got her sister's text, but which was now about as dull as a scalpel. Taking some deep breaths through her nose, she tried sorting through the myriad of thoughts spinning in her head . . . and made a shocking realization.

"My God," she said softly, dropping her hands and looking up at him. "I broke all my rules for you." *Lying, relinquishing control, dating a man who used his fists when angered, dating a man whom I'd thought wasn't financially stable, willing to see him more than three days, and I shirked my responsibilities for work on multiple occasions. And then of course, there's the big one, isn't there?* "Every. Last. One. I need to get out of here." She sprang from the couch and brushed by him on her way to the door.

"V—"

True to his M.O., he grabbed her arm to prevent her from leaving until he decided the conversation was over. But she wouldn't go along with it this time.

"Let go of my arm, Jackson, or so help me God I will claw your goddamn eyes out."

His jaw clenched and nostrils flared as his instincts no doubt warred with her command. But after a moment, he released her.

"I'm going to call a cab and wait for it outside. If you so much as step a toe over that threshold, I'll scream bloody murder until half of Oahu comes, do you hear me?"

"What are you going to do?"

"I'm getting my things and going to Nashville, alone and without your money. At this point, it would feel like a payment for services rendered," she said thickly as she begged the tears in her eyes to wait just a little longer, "and I made it a point to never go into the family business."

He flinched, the look on his face a mix of shock and pain, like he'd just been sucker punched below the belt. But she refused to let it affect her and turned to leave. That was it; she was done. There was nothing left to say.

Then again . . .

She met his eyes in the reflection of the glass. Her voice shaky. "You were the only person to ever make me break Rule #1."

"I don't think you ever told me that rule," he said, his voice scratchy and barely audible.

She glanced back, and damn it if the motion didn't jostle the hot tears loose to spill over her cheeks. Swallowing past the painful lump in her throat, she smiled wanly and said, "You're right. I didn't."

The slam of the screen door against its metal frame echoed in the night sky, the death knell for both their perfect day and the small bit of hope she'd harbored for their future.

"What do you mean she checked herself out?" Vanessa demanded in her best prosecutor voice as she stood in the security line at the airport. "She has a concussion. Aren't you supposed to hold her there for observation?"

"I'm sorry, ma'am, but there's nothing more I can tell you," said the annoyed night-shift nurse. "She refused further treatment and checked herself out about thirty minutes ago."

The line moved forward all of ten inches. Vanessa readjusted the strap of her carry-on higher onto her shoulder, took a step forward, and pulled her suitcase to her side again. "Well, did she leave on her own or was someone with her? Check with the other nurses; maybe she left me a message."

In the distant background, she registered the voice of a teenage boy saying something to her, but she didn't have time to pay attention to him. Kat had vanished, seemingly without a fucking trace, if she was to believe this nitwit of a nurse.

"Again, ma'am, I'd like to help—"

"You don't understand," Vanessa pressed. "I'm about to board a plane to come see her. She's expecting me to come to the hospital for her, so why on earth would she leave? It doesn't make any sense!"

Again, the teenager called something out. Again she ignored him. "Is there someone else I can talk to? Perhaps the nurse who actually took care of her before letting a concussed and beaten woman leave your damn facility?"

"Hey, lady!"

Vanessa whipped around to slice the surfer teen to ribbons with her eyes. "What!"

He flinched, but then gestured to the now ten-foot gap between her and the man in front of her. "Can you please move forward?"

Just as she was about to pick up her suitcase and lay into the nurse again, she realized she no longer heard that sound of space that came through a cell phone even when the other side was completely silent. Taking the phone away from her ear, she glanced at the screen to see that her call had ended. Considering she had full service in the airport and the nurse had been speaking on a landline, chances were pretty good the nurse had used the opportunity to hang up on her.

Mumbling a weak apology to the people behind her, she backtracked through the several rows of winding roped-off path and exited the airport in a trance, finally coming to rest on a stone bench.

Fear and worry gripped Vanessa's chest, squeezing like a vise until she found breathing difficult. Why would Kat have left the hospital? Did those thugs come back to threaten her some more? She supposed it was possible, but generally when someone was given a time frame to come up with money by less-than-savory characters, they didn't show up a few hours later to reiterate the deal.

Which meant Kat either left on her own even though she knew Vanessa had been on her way with the money . . . or Lenny had shown up and convinced her it was time to run again.

Fucking Lenny. Her hands curled into fists so tight she'd probably find crescent-shaped bruises on her palms later. If she ever came face-to-face with that loser, she'd kick him so hard in the balls, he'd choke on his own dick.

"Can I get you a cab, nani wahine?"

Vanessa lifted her gaze to see an older man in a porter uniform smiling at her with kind brown eyes. "I'm sorry, what did you call me?"

"Nani wahine. It means beautiful woman."

"Woman," she said. "So then what does pupule wahine mean?"

He chuckled, his big belly jerking up and down with the small effort. "Pupule wahine means crazy woman."

Crazy woman. The beautiful-sounding nickname Jax had given her was . . . an insult? Didn't that just figure. New tears sprung, and she barked a short, hysterical laugh before covering her mouth with a hand.

The man sat next to her and spoke softly as though afraid of startling her. "You don't look crazy to me, ku'uipo. You look tired. Is someone coming for you?"

She absently fingered the sea star around her neck. No, no one ever came for her. She shook her head.

"Then let me help you to a cab so you can get wherever you're going and get some rest, hmm?"

Rest? While her heart bled for a man who wasn't worth it and her sister was injured and most likely on the run to God knew where? At this point, rest was a pipe dream, but she nodded anyway. She couldn't sit outside the Honolulu airport all night.

After instructing the driver to take her to the farthest hotel from the Mau Loa and a fifteen-minute drive, she checked in and slipped the guy at the counter a fifty dollar bill to change her name in the computer so she couldn't be tracked down. Just in case.

She found her room, entered, and almost jumped out of her skin when the heavy door slammed back into place and echoed against the artless walls. The hum of the window AC unit was deafening in the silence, the air shooting from the vents billowing the tacky window treatments covered in, what else, but—"Sea stars."

Swallowing past the tightness in her throat, she dropped her bags and sat on the scratchy bedspread that matched the curtains.

"Definitely the farthest thing from Mau Loa," she mumbled.

Vanessa toed off her shoes, grabbed a pillow, and curled onto her side. Her stomach hurt from clenching into knots all night, her eyelids felt lined with sandpaper, and her chest physically ached where her heart still beat. The slow and steady rap against her ribs defied her to claim it broken.

Logic told her it was no less healthy than the day she arrived in Oahu. But the tears streaming from the corners of her eyes to darken the faded sea stars under her cheek told a much different story.

Day 6: Friday

Jackson strode through the lobby of the Mau Loa and out into the lavish pool area. It was just past noon on a typically beautiful Hawaiian day. Not a cloud in the powder blue sky, sun beating down to warm the white sandy beaches, and the aquamarine waves ebbed and flowed in perfect rhythm. And Jax noticed none of it.

All night he'd paced in his trailer, out of his trailer. Laid down to sleep and only tossed left before turning right, punching pillows and adjusting his sheets as if they were the reasons for his discomfort and not his guilty-as-fuck conscience.

He should have never let her leave. Not alone. Not like she did. The hurt in her eyes and the tears on her cheeks had pierced him through the chest. He hadn't been able to breathe, much less move, for several minutes. And when he finally snapped out of it enough to get his shit together, he fought with himself on whether or not to act on his instinct and go to her or respect her wish for space.

After grabbing the door handle and releasing it at least half a dozen times, he watched her cab pull up and whisk her away from him once again. Only this time he wouldn't do anything to trick her into giving him another chance. He'd already learned that lesson the hard way. A lesson he knew damn well to begin with but was too much of a pussy to own up to, and look where that had gotten him. Hurting the only woman he'd ever loved other than his mother and sister.

His sandals sank into warm sand. He blinked and realized he'd somehow successfully navigated through the throng of guests without remembering a single step. He wondered if this was how prisoners on Death Row felt on the way to their sentence. Because when he reached his destination and told Lucie he was leaving, she was going to kill him. And if she didn't, Reid would. Jax mentally shrugged in resignation—it didn't matter who wanted him dead; nothing they could say would change his mind—and continued walking.

I just need one more chance. But honestly, did he even deserve one? That was the question that had plagued him all morning as he forced himself through a training session at the gym. Hitting the bags and running on the treadmill until puking had felt cathartic.

In the end, he made the decision he'd known he would all along. He was flying to Nashville to find Vanessa, help her help her sister, and take care of the money drop with the thugs. He just hoped to Christ he wasn't too late.

"Maris!"

Jax turned his head in the direction of a familiar voice coming from the Moana Bar on the beach. Changing his direction, he walked over to embrace his best friend in a manly, no-more-than-three-seconds, back-thumping hug.

"Lookin' a little soft in the middle there, Andrews. Is it retirement or my sister that's turning you into a marshmallow?"

"You're full of shit," Reid said, crossing his arms over his chest. "I'm still in top physical condition. Besides, you and I both know all it would take is one right hook from me and you'd be on your ass."

Jax scoffed. "You tried that once before and I caught you in a flying arm bar, if I remember correctly." He gave his friend a wicked grin and poured a little salt on the old wound. "Had you tapping out like a little bitch."

Reid narrowed his eyes and pointed a finger at him. "That happened once and it was a lucky finish."

Jax slapped his hand away and they both laughed, turning to the bar. "So why are you here and not with Lucie?"

"I'm playing the role of dutiful husband-to-be and getting her one of those blue drinks she saw everywhere. She said something about it officially kicking off her vacation."

Jax stared past Reid's shoulder to the azure water and grunted at the memory of Vanessa wanting the same thing.

"Hey, man, what's up with you? You look like pure shit."

Cutting his eyes back to his friend, he said, "Why did I want to see you again?"

"Cut the bullshit, Jax. What the hell happened between you and Vanessa?"

Jax nearly jumped Reid right then. "You talked to her? What did she say?"

"Whoa!" Reid placed a hand on Jax's chest and firmly pressed until he was out of his personal space. "I don't know anything, man. She called Lu just before I came out here. All I know is that she's not here like she should be and you're edgy as fuck, which tells me something went down between you two."

Jax leaned on the bar, ordered a beer, and picked out

a swizzle straw from the jar to give his gnashing teeth a reason to gnash. He didn't want to admit how badly he'd fucked things up with V to his sister or his best friend. It was bad enough he had to admit it to himself.

"Shit, dude." Reid blew out a heavy breath and leaned on the bar next to him. "You fucked her, didn't you?"

Jax pointed the thin red straw in Reid's face. "Shut up, Andrews; you don't know what you're talking about."

"The hell I don't." Where Reid's voice had lost some of its volume, it gained in agitation. "I asked you to make sure everything was taken care of this week as my friend—as Lucie's brother—and you couldn't keep your dick in your pants long enough not to chase off the maid of honor."

Straightening from the bar, Jax turned to face his best friend. Though they towered over everyone else around them, they met each other at eye level, and both pairs threw daggers across the space between.

"I'm warning you, Andrews. You don't know the situation—"

"I don't care if she was strutting around naked. You should've found yourself a piece of ass somewhere else."

Growling, Jax fisted his hands in Reid's expensive polo and spun him around until his back slammed against the trunk of a nearby palm tree. Reid grabbed Jax's wrists but didn't attempt to pull him off. "If you ever fucking talk about her like that again, you'll be walking down the aisle without a single goddamn tooth in your head."

"Jackson Thomas Maris! What are you doing?"

Jax didn't look away from Reid's narrowed glare to address the woman bearing down on them. "Just saying hello to your fiancé, Lucie." Releasing Reid, he finally turned to face his baby sister. "Hey there, shorty. You look thin. This joker feeding you?"

Lucie jammed her hands on her hips. "I just spent most of the week unable to eat, smartass. And don't 'hey shorty' me. What's your—" Her brows gathered with her frown. "Jesus, you look like hell."

Smoothing out the wrinkles in his shirt, Reid stepped to Lucie's side and put his arm around her shoulders. "That's what I said, sweetheart."

Jax scowled. "Fuck you, Andrews."

"That's enough," Lucie ordered. Her voice was stern, but those big gray eyes of hers softened. Suddenly, he felt stripped bare of all his defenses. A talent his sister had when it came to him. Sighing, she said, "Come here, you big jerk."

The tightness in his chest loosened some as he enveloped his little sister in a bear hug. The feel of her arms around his waist grounded him, giving him a few moments of peace from the incessant anxiety threatening to tear him apart at his seams.

"It's good to see you, girl," he said, kissing the top of her head. "And you look as beautiful as ever."

Leaning back to look into his eyes she said, "Mmm-hmm. Don't start trying to sweet talk me. I want to know what's going on with you."

"I bet I can guess," Reid interjected. "Our dearest Jax here is in love with your best friend, but he did something to fuck it up."

Jax wanted to lash out at the man, maybe throw a punch to knock that smirk off his face. But that wouldn't do anything but give him a split second of satisfaction and a pissed-off sister when her groom had a shiner in their wedding photos.

Lucie looked up at him for confirmation. "Jackson?"

Releasing her, Jax took a step back and scrubbed a hand over his face. He hadn't bothered grooming after his shower earlier, so his usual five o'clock shadow was now the start of a decent beard. Another couple of days and he could get a job as a model for lumberjack fashion wear.

He cleared his throat, glanced at Reid's smug face, then met his sister's inquisitive stare. "That pretty much sums it up, yeah." A slow smile spread over her face. Oh, shit. "Shorty, don't start getting all mushy on me, okay?"

"What?" she asked innocently. "A girl can't be happy her big brother finally found love? And with my best friend, of all people?"

"Yeah, well, I wouldn't get too excited if I were you. She doesn't even want to see me, much less date me. But she'll just have to deal with me today because I'm going to Nashville whether she wants me there or not." Then he remembered Reid had said Lucie had been on the phone with V. "She's not answering my calls. Call and tell her not to do anything until I get there. I don't want her around those criminals, and I sure as hell don't trust Kat's boyfriend to—"

"Jackson!"

Hearing Lucie yell his name made him realize she'd tried interrupting him a couple of times before that. "What?"

"Vanessa isn't in Nashville. She's still on the island."

Relief that she'd never left and concern for why she hadn't flooded his system from opposite sides of his body, colliding somewhere in the center of his chest. "Tell me where she is."

His sister's eyes turned sad. "I can't."

He took a step forward and lowered his voice just above a growl. He must have looked pretty menacing if Reid felt the need to place himself half in front of his fiancée. As if Jax would ever lay a finger on his sister. The dude had gone all Tarzan over her. He would've respected Reid for that protective instinct if he wasn't on the verge of losing his shit over Vanessa. "Lucie, I'm not playing. I want to know where she is."

Lucie stepped around Reid while giving him her famous back off, Cujo look she used to use with Jax when he got too parental with her. And just as Jax had done years ago, Reid gave in. A little. "I mean, I can't tell you because she won't tell me. And when I asked why she switched hotels, she told me about Kat and said she didn't want to bring me into her funk."

That sounded exactly like something she'd say. That was his V. Always trying to save the ones she loved in one way or another. "She was supposed to go to Nashville to bail her sister out of a problem."

"Yeah, I know." Lucie tucked her long brown hair behind her ears and looked as though she debated on how much she should tell him. "Before she got on the plane last night, she found out Kat had taken off. Vanessa got a text from her this morning saying that she didn't want Nessie getting mixed up in her problems."

Jax snorted in disgust. "In other words, her boy Lenny told her they were better off doing another cut-and-run instead of facing the music that could very well be his death march."

Lucie nodded. "More than likely. And if the future can be predicted by looking at the past, Kat will probably be off-grid for several months again. It's nothing Nessie's not used to. She'll be fine; she just needs some time to herself."

"Fuck that," he growled. That's not what she needed at all. Left by herself, she'd do what she'd always done: bury the hurt and the guilt until she couldn't see it anymore. Feel that somehow, no matter how hard she tried, she wasn't enough. And that was bullshit. She was more than enough. She was everything to him, and he needed to tell her. To show her.

But in order to do that, he needed to stop hiding.

Vanessa deserved a man who owned up to who he was in life. Not a fighter who pretended not to own part of an exclusive resort so he wouldn't have to deal with the publicity and responsibilities that came along with it. And certainly not a brother who hid his true identity for fear of losing his place in his sister's life.

"Lucie," he rasped. "I need to talk to you." He flicked a glance at his best friend, who gave him a nod of understanding. "Alone."

The corners of her mouth lifted slightly as she held out her hand. "Come on," she said. "Let's go for a walk, big brother."

Lucie's private bungalow sat on the outskirts of the resort property facing the crystal blue waters of the Pacific. Jackson sat on the wood steps that led to the porch, forearms resting on his knees, one hand clasping his other wrist in the middle. He closed his eyes and sucked the salty sea air deep into his lungs, then regulated his breaths with the sounds of the waves hitting the shore.

When Lucie had sat him down for their talk, he'd been prepared for the worst reaction possible. Not because he truly believed his sister would abandon him, but because he couldn't let himself hope for something more if she wasn't able to give him that much.

Now he was ashamed of himself for thinking she'd react any differently than with the compassion, understanding, and love she'd shown him. Lucie truly was one in a million. When he told her about finding his adoption papers after their parents' deaths, he expected her to quietly process the information in that Lucie way he knew so well. Not only did she surprise him by responding without thinking, but the first thing out of her mouth completely leveled him.

"I won't lie and say this isn't the last thing I expected you to tell me. But Jackson," she said, gazing at him with her dove gray eyes, "I don't care who gave birth to you. It doesn't make you any less of a Maris than I am. And it sure as hell doesn't change the fact that you're my big brother."

More than fifteen years' worth of keeping his secret crashed over him, and he'd been helpless to stop the tears from flooding to the surface. Lucie wrapped her arms around his neck and squeezed for all her tiny frame was worth. He wasn't sure how long they held each other like that, but when they finally separated he had himself back under control.

They spent the next hour talking about everything from the real reason he moved to Hawaii to learning to accept not knowing why their parents never told him the truth. They speculated some, but in the end they both agreed that it probably wasn't something they meant to keep to themselves forever. Neither of their parents could have ever predicted being taken from their children so early. Not telling Jackson sooner in life may not have been the wisest course of action, but they must have had their reasons.

Either way, Lucie was right. Just because his DNA claimed differently didn't mean he wasn't still a Maris.

The door behind him swung open and shut just before Lucie handed him the cold beer she'd gone inside for. "Here you go."

"Thanks, shorty." He took several long swigs, letting the cold liquid soothe the tightness still gripping his throat.

"Now," she said, descending the steps to stand in front of him. "Whaddaya say we stretch our legs on the beach, and you can fill me in on what happened between you and Ness."

Jax took in the folded arms across her chest and the single eyebrow hitched up between a part in her bangs. "This is nonnegotiable, isn't it?"

"Yep."

Sighing, he unfolded from the stairs and followed her lead down the beach. "How much do you want to know?"

"Might as well start from the beginning. I'll let you know when I get bored."

He smiled around the lip of his beer bottle and took a fortifying sip before launching into the whole story. She listened attentively as they strolled at the water's edge, the warm water occasionally lapping over their bare feet. She didn't even miss a step when he told her about being part owner of the Mau Loa, just told him she was proud of him for doing something to secure his future in case his career was cut short by an injury. He supposed that would be something in the forefront of her mind, since she was a physical therapist. The majority of her patients were injured athletes, including Reid. Or at least he had been one of her patients. Now that Reid had retired, he probably no longer needed PT unless he wanted to role play in the—

Gross! That was one of the downfalls of having your best friend hook up with your sister. All the "yeah buddy" thoughts of Reid getting some action were tainted by the fact that it was with his innocent baby sister.

"What?" Lucie asked when he gave her a sideways glance.

Yeah, right. No way was he opening up that conversation. "Nothing."

She shrugged and let it go. "So what did she say when you told her the truth?"

"Exactly what she should have said. That I was the worst kind of liar and took advantage of the situation to get . . . close to her. And she's right."

"Yes, but it's not like you were the one who made the first move, right?" She grabbed his beer and took a sip, then handed it back. "I mean, technically, she was the one who proposed the fling, not you."

"Doesn't matter, Lucie. I created the situation that instigated her proposal. She should've been free to have a fling with anyone she wanted. But she chose me because she thought she was stuck playing house with me all week."

Lucie stared at her feet as she put one in front of the other, hands in her pockets and chewing on her lower lip. Jax knew she was turning the information over in her head like a rock tumbler. She wouldn't say anything else now until she could pull out something shiny and worth showing.

"She said I was the only person to ever make her break Rule Number One, and then she walked away." He shook his head in self-disgust. "I should've gone after her."

Lucie stopped in her tracks and grabbed hold of his arm. Jax turned back to her with a questioning look.

"Why didn't you go after her?"

"You mean besides not wanting my eyes clawed out?"

Lucie frowned, telling him she wasn't amused.

"Because it doesn't matter that I never meant to take advantage of her or the situation. The truth is that I did. I should have come clean about my involvement in the resort, but I didn't. Vanessa felt used, and I can't blame her for that. She had every right to hate me."

"I think hate is a little strong, Jax. Especially when she just got done telling you she loved you."

"What are you talking about? I never said she said that."

"Yes you did," she argued. "The thing about her breaking Rule Number One."

His heart stalled in his chest. His lungs refused all air.

Understanding dawned on Lucie's face. "Oh, Jackson. She never told you what Rule #1 is, did she?" He shook his head once. She stepped toward him and laid a hand on his chest. It took everything he had to hold firm. "Rule #1 is 'Never fall in love,' and I know for a fact that she never has . . . until now. She loves you, Jackson. So what are you going to do about it?"

The knowledge filled him with hope and fear. And determination. "I'm going to search every last inch of this island until I find her. Then I'm going to get in her face until she accepts my apology and gives us a chance."

"I'm not entirely sure on the getting-in-her-face part, but who am I to judge? Reid had to buy me for a hundred grand before I gave him the time of day again."

"I hope I get off that cheap." Jackson kissed his sister on the forehead. "Gotta run. Thanks, shorty. I'll see you at the rehearsal dinner later, hopefully with a gorgeous redhead on my arm."

Jogging back to his Jeep, he started to formulate plans for finding Vanessa and making things right.

DAY 7: SATURDAY

As Vanessa exited the cab and walked through the main entrance of the Mau Loa, she felt like the worst worst best friend in the history of worst best friends. She'd called Lucie and ditched the rehearsal dinner last night because she couldn't deal with seeing Jackson. She knew he'd try to talk to her, and she wouldn't have any way to escape without making a scene.

In fact, she'd just barely escaped him at her hotel yesterday afternoon. The guy who worked the front desk third shift told her the girl who worked before him mentioned a guy calling in to ask for a Vanessa MacGregor and a bunch of other names he thought might be aliases. Good thing she'd used something totally off the wall or he may have found her.

So her plan was to show up at the last possible minute, get through the wedding, and get shit-faced drunk with Fritz and her friends Eric and Kyle at the reception. She was calling it Operation Avoid Jax (At All Costs Because He Has the Power To Utterly Destroy My Resolve, Not to Mention Completely Shatter My Heart).

Okay, so the title was a little lengthy, but it was also more than a little accurate.

Passing the front desk, she noted Jillian wasn't working. Happy, smiley, exotically beautiful Jillian. Vanessa bet she wasn't a neurotic mess when it came to relationships. She probably charmed men with her customer service smile and took everything in stride, rule-free.

Vanessa took a turn down the hallway on the right toward the wing with the ballroom and bridal suite. Her palms grew damp and her heart beat a staccato rhythm behind her ribs. She prayed Jax wouldn't be in the next hallway waiting to pounce. Another twenty feet . . . ten feet . . . five . . . taking a deep breath and holding it, she rounded the corner . . .

Her heart sank. No Jax.

Wait, her heart wasn't supposed to sink. It should be buoyant. Like, super-mega-extra buoyant. Stupid heart, get with the damn program. Before she did something truly stupid, like knock on the groom's room to the left and ask to speak with him, she opened the door to the bridal suite, slipped inside, and closed it with her back like the hounds of hell were on her heels.

"Nessie!"

She caught Lucie's gaze in the vanity mirror, mid-application of moisturizer, in the back of the room. Surprise melted into joy on her friend's face before the dark-haired woman spun on the padded bench and launched across the space. Vanessa met her in the middle and embraced her for several long moments.

"Lucie, I'm so sorry."

Lucie pulled back and held Vanessa's shoulders. "Stop. You don't have to apologize. What matters is that you're here now."

"Well, hello, Vanessa."

Looking past Lucie, Vanessa found a very stern-faced Robért dressed in white, cradling a clipboard in one arm and rocking a pencil in the air between his first and second fingers of the other hand. It wasn't until that moment that she realized the jig was up. She'd been so wrapped up in her own shit, she'd forgotten all about the switcheroo they'd pulled on Robért.

"Uh, what are you doing here? I thought you couldn't make it." That's it. Avoid the real issue. You're good at that.

"Oh, that?" He waved his hand dismissively. "Turns out instead of renewing their vows, that couple decided to get divorced. So my friend was able to cover for me after all. Imagine my surprise when I showed up for rehearsal to find an entirely new bride and groom."

She placed a hand on her forehead. Whether it was to make sure the rise in temperature she felt wasn't actually a fever or to brace herself for the headache that was surely on its way, she wasn't certain. "Jesus, Robért, I'm sorry. I never wanted to deceive—"

A huge smile broke over his face. "Honey, please, I don't care if you pretended to be as many people as Cybil had personalities. I'd still rather work with people like you over ninety-nine percent of my clientele. Jackson already spoke to me and took full responsibility. Now get over here."

Relieved, she did as ordered and stepped into his arms for one of their customary hugs. Then a flurry of let's-get-readys had them scurrying to their separate vanities. They only had about an hour before the sunset ceremony.

A knock sounded at the door, pulling Vanessa's stomach into her throat, until she heard, "Girl coming in!"

Jilli strode in pulling a rolling carry-on behind her and wearing a simple white sundress and her ever-present Employee of the Month smile. "Hui, everyone!"

Lucie and Robért greeted her with a "Hi, Jilli" and "Hui, girl" respectively as Vanessa blurted out, "What are you doing here?"

Real nice, MacGregor. Could you be more of a bitch, maybe? Her cheeks flushed and she muttered her third apology of the day.

"No worries," she said, smile still in place. "I'm here to help with hair and makeup. Robért and I usually take care of the small bridal parties. I actually went to cosmetology school before I went back for hotel management."

"Okay, great, then you can take care of Lucie and Ro—"

"Oh, no," the woman said as she set up her station next to Vanessa's vanity. "I'm good, but Robért's a pro, so he gets the bride. But don't worry, it won't take much to make you stunning."

Wonderful. Tension was making itself known in the base of her skull. It would only be a matter of time before it spread to the backs of her eyes and through her temples. Grabbing four ibuprofen from her purse, she watched Jilli plug in her curler, flat iron, and dryer, then organize enough cosmetics to make up Tammy Faye Baker for fifty years.

When she thought about it, Vanessa wasn't even sure why she felt a level of agitation with the manager. She'd always been very pleasant and helpful, but there was something about her . . .

Jillian stood behind Vanessa in front of the large mirror and got to work brushing through her hair and sectioning it with clips. Behind them, Robért and Lucie were busy chatting away, laughing and going over wedding details. And somewhere in another area of the resort, Jackson was . . . She sighed. She wished she knew how to finish that thought.

"Jackie's pretty upset."

It took Vanessa a second to realize Jillian had spoken and another to realize whom she was talking about. Jackie. A nickname. Holy shit.

"You two dated." It wasn't a question. It was a damn good guess, one that explained why the sweet woman bothered her. She was competition.

"A couple of years ago." Jillian glanced at her in the mirror and then refocused on her task of curling the bottom sections of hair. "We weren't serious or anything. More like a friends-with-benefits thing. In fact, in all the years I've known him, I've never seen Jax get serious about anyone."

Ouch. That smacked of truth with a hint of he warned you sprinkled on top.

"Until you."

Vanessa's eyes snapped up to the mirror. "I'm sorry?" Hell, now she was apologizing in the form of a question. She sounded like a broken record.

"He tried finding you yesterday, and then when you didn't show up for the rehearsal he came over." This time when she smiled, it was more sympathetic in nature. "No need to throw darts with your eyes, sweetie. He came over to talk to me and my husband." She held up her left hand and wiggled her ring finger with the wedding band on it.

"Ugh, I'm sorry—Shit! There I go again." She released a frustrated huff and pushed in on her temples where the pain was settling in. "If I never have to say that word again, it'll be too soon."

Jillian chuckled and grabbed another section of curls to straighten. "Don't worry about it. I can understand why you'd be a bit territorial about him." Chocolate brown eyes met her gaze, all hints of play falling away. "He's a really great guy. I know you're upset with him, and truthfully, you have the right. But he's not normally a dishonest person, and I think you should at least give him the opportunity to make it right."

"I appreciate your concern, Jillian, but there's nothing to correct. Even his lie aside, Jackson and I made an agreement for three days with no strings. It was fun, but now it's over. And I'd rather not talk about it anymore."

The woman gave her shoulder a light squeeze as if to say, I understand, then finished Vanessa's hair and makeup in silence, leaving her to her thoughts that had no intentions of following Jillian's example.

Jackson Maris seemed to be a permanent fixture in her mind. What was that saying Fritz always had? I'd rather have a bottle in front o' me than a frontal lobotomy. At this point, if it would rid her of the memories of the past week, Vanessa would take either.

Eventually, Robért and Jillian finished with their hair and makeup and packed their things up.

"O-kay," Robért said at the door, "I'm going to check on things, but Jillian will be right outside if you need anything. The next time I see you, it'll be to collect you for the ceremony, so get dressed, have some champagne, and relax."

Lucie hugged the planner. "Thank you so much, Robért."

Once the door closed, Vanessa turned to study Lucie in her wedding gown. "You look like Cinderella, Lucie."

The strapless Grecian-style sheath flowed to the floor like a chiffon waterfall. Intricate beading trimmed the sweetheart neckline and the sweep train added a princess touch. Her dark brown hair fell in soft curls around her shoulders with an aqua hibiscus hair comb holding one side back. Robért had done an excellent job with her makeup, using subtle tones to accentuate Lucie's natural beauty and highlighting her dove gray eyes.

"Really?" Lucie asked.

Vanessa offered her friend a reassuring smile and blinked back the moisture blurring her vision. "A more beautiful bride never existed. You look exquisite, honey. Truly."

Lucie beamed but then faltered. Pressing a hand to her stomach she said, "Oh, God, I think I'm going to be sick. I don't know if I can do this."

Oh, shit. Lucie and Reid were perfect together. If she didn't believe in love, what hope was there for the rest of the world? Namely me.

"Come sit over here," she said, leading the pale bride to the fancy settee. Once she was sure Lucie wasn't about to faint, Vanessa crossed to the sideboard table where the opened champagne was chilling in a bucket of ice and poured them each a glass. "Every bride gets cold feet, honey, but you're going to be fine, I promise."

Lucie accepted the glass and downed the contents. "What? I'm not nervous about marrying Reid. I love him more than anything in the world."

"I should probably cut you off after that, but since when have I ever been the voice of reason in this relationship?" She handed Lucie her champagne, too, and went to find her garment bag. "So what is it you don't think you can do?"

"Walk down the aisle in this gorgeous gown with everyone staring at me! Have you forgotten how klutzy I am and how much I hate being the center of attention? There's no way I'm not falling flat on my face. None."

"Damn it, Lucie, don't scare me like that," she said as she extracted her dress and went through the careful process of getting it on without messing up Jilli's hard work. "When you walk, gather a handful of your dress and hold it up so you don't step on the front. Plus, you'll have Fritz to hold you steady."

"If you say so." Down went the second glass.

Vanessa asked Lucie to zip her up and then checked herself in the mirror. The deep aqua chiffon dress ended at her knees in an asymmetrical hemline, and the strapless ruched bust drew the eye nicely to one of her better assets. Her hair was styled the same as Lucie's, but Jillian had had to straighten her tighter curls before making them into the large, soft ones they were now.

"Okay," she said, turning to face Lucie. "I guess we're ready."

Lucie stared pointedly at the spot below her clavicle. Then up at her eyes. Then down. Then back up.

"Luce, why are you looking at me like that?"

"Jackson mentioned he'd given you a necklace, so . . ."

"Oh, yeah, um . . ." She busied herself smoothing the front of her dress so she wouldn't caress the place on her skin that felt bare ever since she'd taken it off two nights ago. "I figured it wasn't part of the ensemble, so . . . we should probably go, huh?"

Which meant she'd be seeing Jackson very soon, and she was as sure as she was of her name that she'd want to wrap her arms around him and let him hold her until . . . until when? Tomorrow morning? When she left to go back home? The next time he decided to deck a guy because he said something Jax didn't like?

No matter what, their separation was inevitable. Prolonging it and giving her time to fall even more in love with him was the worst idea ever. And yet, the idea of seeing him and not walking into his arms made her physically ill.

"You love him, don't you?"

She put a hand to her forehead and nodded. "God, I never meant to, Lucie, I swear. I thought . . . Hell, I don't know what I thought."

"He looked everywhere for you yesterday. He's a

wreck, Ness. I've never seen him like this. You two should talk."

"I need a drink," she said as she quickly crossed the room, then, since Lucie had both glasses, lifted the bottle to her mouth and drank until the bubbles made her eyes water. "Lucie, I'm not feeling so hot. Would you totally and completely hate me if I excused myself after the ceremony?"

Vanessa felt like a schmuck for even asking. This was her best friend's wedding and she wanted to help make it the most wonderful and memorable day of Lucie's life. Being near him would be hard but not impossible. But the thought of dancing with Jackson, of being so intimately close . . .

Dancing is no different than sex. It's all about moving with your partner. Finding a rhythm together.

She'd never survive it.

Lucie joined her at the sideboard table and held out the two glasses. Vanessa refilled them and reluctantly set the bottle back in the ice bucket to take the flute thrust at her.

"I know this is going to be difficult, but you can't leave, Nessie. Stay at least through dinner, okay? And if after that you still don't want to stay for the dance, I'll understand if you leave. Okay?"

With as bright a smile as she could muster, Vanessa said, "Okay, let's go get you hitched." Then she raised her glass and said, "Salut, my friend."

Joining in on their time-honored drinking tradition, Lucie raised her glass and clinked it against Vanessa's. "Salut, Nessie."

As they tossed back their last glasses of champagne, Vanessa saw a glimmer of something oddly secretive in Lucie's smile.

* * *

"Jax, the groom is typically the nervous one at a wedding. If you don't stop pacing, you're going to wear a path to the bottom of the island."

Jackson threw a dirty look in Reid's direction but didn't stop his brisk walk back and forth across the room where they'd gotten dressed. His friend's placid disposition as he lounged on the couch was enough to aggravate him—he didn't need his smartass comments, too.

It was driving him insane that mere drywall was all that separated him from Vanessa in the next room. He hated waiting to see her, to tell her the things that had been like bullhorns in his mind for the last thirty-six hours. But he'd promised both Reid and Lucie he'd keep himself in check until after the wedding. That way, if things went badly, it wouldn't affect the ceremony.

The last thing he wanted to do was ruin his baby sister's big day. But the next to last thing he wanted was to let Vanessa run from what they had together. Because that's what she was doing. He'd had a lot of time to think about things since she got into that cab and seemingly disappeared off the face of the damn island.

He had no doubt the deception bothered her, but he did doubt that it was the main reason for her avoidance. When her sister called, everything from the past—the pain, the fear, the guilt—came rushing back from the dark place she'd buried it. And with the reminder of the past came the reminder of why she'd created her rules and why she needed to keep them.

Jax was certain Vanessa loved him. She'd admitted as much when she told him he'd caused her to break Rule #1. But even without that, he'd never been more sure of anything. They fit together, made sense together. As cliché as it sounded, they completed each other.

So now it was up to him to prove how much he loved her in a way he hoped would speak to her.

Reid stood and stepped in Jackson's path. His casual wedding attire of white linen pants and shirt matched his composure. Not even a hint of unease marked the man's face. This was a man who trusted in his love and the love of his bride. As much as Jax loved them both, a pang of jealousy twisted deep in his gut. Jax wished he could be as trusting, but right now things were a mess.

Reid clapped a hand on his shoulder and asked, "Got the rings, bro?"

Jax put his hand in the pocket of his pants and felt the cool metal of both rings. He nodded.

"Good," Reid said. "And how 'bout your best man speech?"

Sticking his hand in the other pocket, he almost shit himself when he came up empty. Then he remembered he'd moved it. Touching the breast pocket of his aqua shirt, he felt the outline of the folded sheet of paper and told himself to calm the fuck down. "Yeah," he said, his voice sounding strained. "Got it."

"Then relax. Everything'll work out. I got your back, all right?"

Jax inclined his head once.

A knock at the door announced Jilli before she entered, all smiles as usual. "Well, don't you boys clean up nicely. Looking good, Jackie."

"Jackie?" Reid said with a hitch of his brow.

Jax cut him a death look. "Don't even think about it. You can still get married with a black eye."

"It would totally be worth it, but Luce will kill me if I ruin the pictures, so you're safe. For now," he added with a smirk.

"Asshole."

Jilli held the door open wide. "Come on, children, time to take your places."

Reid turned to Jax and with nothing more than a look,

they said more things in three seconds than most women could say in three hours.

Thanks for always being there for me.

No problem, you've done the same for me.

I love your sister, man, I'll do whatever it takes to make her happy.

I know you do, and I know you will. Plus, if you don't, I'll break your fucking legs.

Fair enough.

Then let's do this.

Hell yeah.

Reid walked out first. Jax followed but paused when he reached Jilli. He knew she'd seen Vanessa. He wanted to ask her how she was doing, if she was okay, if she said anything about him . . . but he knew that if he let himself start, it would be a slippery slope.

She seemed to read his thoughts. Rising on her toes, she gave him a big hug that helped to somewhat calm his nerves. Then she kissed his cheek, pulled back, and said, "Good luck, Jackie."

"Thanks, girl. Let's hope I don't need it."

Jax walked down the hall, his heart tugging in his chest as he passed the bridal suite like a magnet being pulled to its other half. Clenching his fists, he forced himself to keep moving. To distract himself, he counted his steps. Forty-three to the exit. Twenty-two across the outdoor lounge area. And one hundred and seventy-one to the elegant setup for the beach ceremony and reception where the small group of guests mingled.

An aisle of smoothed sand, bordered by lit Tiki torches strung together with white netting, bisected the two groupings of six chairs. Blue and aqua sea glass pebbles were scattered along the edges in lieu of the typical rose petals that would just blow away in the ocean breeze. Reid stood at the front, speaking with the minister beneath an archway made from aqua and white netting draped among four wooden posts. Beyond them the setting sun was just beginning to inject the sky with pale shades of lavender and coral as the sea lapped lazily at the shore.

This was what his sister deserved: a wedding in paradise.

Just like Vanessa deserved to expect a hell of a lot more from a relationship than following her rules, half of which ensured she didn't date an asshole and the other half protecting her even if she did.

He understood why she'd created the rules—and he supposed they made sense to an extent and had served her well up to this point. But now she'd outgrown them and it was time she realized that she'd be okay without them.

Jax greeted the few guests he knew and introduced himself to the few he didn't until finally Robért shooed him into his place next to Reid.

The violinist was cued.

Reid and the minister stood at attention.

A hush fell over the guests as they turned in their seats.

Jax straightened . . . and lost his breath.

Vanessa. Her name whispered through his mind like a silent prayer as she glided in slow motion toward him. Words probably existed to describe her beauty but not in his vocabulary. Exquisite, flawless, timeless . . . none of those even came close.

She smiled at her friends Eric and Kyle—decent guys he'd heard a lot about over the years from his sister—and rolled her eyes when they blew kisses in her direction. Finally, she reached the end, putting her within reaching distance. His body vibrated with the need to touch her, to hold her, but he held firm, doing nothing more than praying she'd look in his direction. But she didn't. She greeted Reid with a quick hug and kiss on the cheek . . . then turned and took her place on the other side without ever acknowledging his presence.

He'd expected her rebuff, but that didn't make it sting any less.

The sound of muffled gasps brought his attention to the back once again as Lucie appeared on the arm of her grizzled father-figure Fritz. She'd originally asked Jax to walk her down the aisle, but he casually suggested she ask Fritz, saying the man was getting on in years and it would probably mean a hell of a lot to him since he thought of Lucie and Vanessa as his second and third daughters.

In reality, Jax knew he'd be a jacked-up mess if he had to be the one to give her away. The moment she asked, he knew what every father in the world must feel like. No matter how much you approve of or like the guy she's marrying, everything in you wants to throw her over your shoulder and haul her ass back to her bedroom and ground her for life. So for her sake, he was trying to focus on being the best man, because the best man's main concerns were not losing the rings and getting drunk at the reception. Way easier.

Though he tried to keep himself in that juvenile mentality, Jax's heart swelled with pride and love as his baby sister walked toward her future. He'd never seen her more beautiful or more sure of herself. The moment her gaze collided with Reid's was almost palpable. The rest of them could disappear in a puff of smoke and neither would notice.

Once they reached the archway, Reid held out his hand to accept his bride's, only the old man wasn't giving it up so easily.

Reid quirked a brow. "Fritz?"

Narrowing his eyes, the old man spoke so only those standing at the front could hear. "You ever break this girl's heart, Andrews, and I'll serve your balls to my one-eyed bulldog for breakfast."

Reid leaned in slightly. "If I ever break her heart, I'll serve them to Willy myself."

Fritz nodded with a satisfied grunt before turning to face Lucie. His weathered skin melted into a mask of wrinkles as he beamed with pride. She returned his smile, kissed him on the cheek, and let him place her hand in Reid's with a firm pat of approval.

Jax drank in the sight of his sister, overflowing with happiness and love for the man who was a friend by blood but a brother by bond. When their parents died, Jax had doubted more often than not that he'd see this day. A day when he no longer had to worry about failing her. That despite the fact he'd had no idea how to raise a teenage girl, she'd managed to come through the other side a well-adjusted, amazing woman. And if anyone could continue to love and take care of her as he'd done, it was Reid. She was in good hands.

Knowing that, it left Jax free to think about his own future. As the minister talked about the usual wedding stuff in the background, Jax studied the maid of honor.

Her eyes were trained on the minister. She appeared to be listening intently with a sweet grin on her face. But Jax knew better. Her eyes were unfocused. Her body was tense, grasping her bouquet in front of her like a shield, and the lines of her smile were tight, forced.

Someone said something about rings and Jackson retrieved them from his pocket and dutifully placed them in Reid's hand before his attention swung back to Vanessa again.

He could see the thoughts kicking up a storm in her mind, creating more pain, more doubt. Knowing he had any part of that felt like a hot knife twisting in his gut. He wanted more than anything in the world to kiss the tension away in that smile. To do whatever it took to make her happy, today and every day, for the rest of her life.

Hearing Lucie start her vows pulled Jax out of his ruminations.

"Reid," she said, her eyes already brimming with unshed tears as she pushed the ring onto his finger. "I promise to continue trying to see myself as you see me, no matter how blinded by love I think you are."

"I've got better than twenty-twenty vision when it comes to you, sweetheart."

"Reid, you can't interrupt my vows!"

"Sorry, Lu. Go on." He winked and gave her a smile that said he wasn't sorry at all.

The guests chuckled and Lucie did a horrible job of looking stern. A moment later she gave up, smiled, and continued.

"I promise to always rub the kinks out of your hands when you spend too many hours on a new drawing or sculpture. I promise to never let you forget how talented you are and to always support your dreams. Whether it's just to create things for our home or to sell pieces in your own gallery someday. But most of all . . . I promise to cherish, honor, and love you with all that I am, from this day forward, until my very last breath."

"Luce," Reid began as he slowly slid her ring on. "I promise to stop cracking jokes about rubbing kinks out of other places when you're trying to help with my cramped hands." Lucie turned about ten shades of red and this time everyone straight-up laughed. "I promise to never let you flirt with another waiter for as long as I live."

"You made me—"

He shushed her and pressed a finger against her lips. "No interrupting, remember?" Lucie released an exasperated sigh. Jax was finding the whole thing amusing as hell. He'd only seen their unique and playful relationship as a couple for a short time before this. If Lucie had thought Reid would forgo the teasing during their wedding, she'd been sadly mistaken. Though, from the twinkle in his sister's eyes, he didn't think she'd expected anything less than business as usual.

But then Reid sobered and lifted her right hand, placing it over his heart. The onlookers quieted and even the sea breeze felt more serious as it tousled Lucie's curls.

"I promise that someday you will shed every last one of your insecurities and finally see yourself as not only I see you but as the entire world sees you. I promise to never take your love for granted and to show you every day how very thankful I am to have you in my life. But most of all . . . I promise to cherish, honor, and love you with all that I am, from this day forward, until my very last breath."

Tears flowed unchecked over Lucie's cheeks, and as soon as they were announced as husband and wife, Reid gathered his bride up and kissed her like she was the breath of life, which was probably how his friend felt.

He could relate.

Now more than ever, Jackson knew how much he truly loved Vanessa. He wanted with her what Reid had with Lucie. A life together. A forever.

He couldn't tell her any of that now. But soon he would. Very soon.

Vanessa knew that everything looked stunning, that the food was exquisite and the cake was like little bites of heaven. After all, she'd been the one to choose all of it during her many meetings with Robért. But that was the only reason she knew it. Nothing seemed to quite come into focus, and she couldn't remember what any of the five courses tasted like.

From the moment she saw Jackson, she felt as though she'd been underwater. The world around her looked wavy, the conversations were muted and unclear, and no matter how hard she tried, she could never move fast enough to get away.

After the ceremony, she tried excusing herself to use the restroom, thinking she could sneak away long enough to avoid the dinner portion of the night where she'd be forced to sit across from Jackson and his stares that bored through her like fricking lasers. But she'd been swept along to pose for a million pictures where—thanks to the photographer, who was now on Vanessa's hit list— she was forced to stand with Jackson and endure the heat of his hands on her waist and the smell of him in the air.

She'd braced herself for him to try and talk to her, to pull her aside or speak his mind where they stood, but he never did. He also never stood close enough that their bodies touched. She found it sadly ironic that she felt more bereft standing a mere three inches away from him than when she'd been thirty miles away.

She reminded herself that he was giving her exactly what she wanted. Relief should be lifting the huge weights off her shoulders, making it possible for her to breathe easily for the first time in days. But all she wanted to do was cry into a pillow until her ducts dried up and she passed out.

Once the pictures were finally over, she again tried to excuse herself, but the tidal wave of wedding organization that was Robért herded everyone, including her, to their seats at the long table. Bride and groom sat at the head with Vanessa to Lu's right, Jackson to Reid's left, and the rest of the guests filling in the other twelve spots.

Lucie had asked that she at least stay through dinner, and despite her attempts at escaping sooner, that's what she did. And now she was getting the hell out of there before the first dance started and she was roped into dancing with her bridal party counterpart.

As the wait staff began clearing the table of dishes, several people wandered over to the small tiki bar, including Eric and Kyle, her two best guy friends and dart league partners. Perfect. Vanessa pushed back from her seat. Lucie's hand struck like a cobra, grabbing her wrist before she was even fully standing.

"Where are you going, Nessie?"

She smiled and nodded in the direction of the bar. "To talk to the boys and order a whole lot of something that rhymes with shequila."

"Oh, okay. Hey, will you bring me back a beer? If I have any more champagne, I'll have to look at my wedding album to remember anything."

"Sure thing." Or at least she'd send one of the guys back with one. Moving as fast as her beach shoes could carry her, she bee-lined it to the bar. After hugging the guys, she ordered a Patron on the rocks and didn't begin to relax until she downed the first and ordered the second.

Kyle, her buff, blond, and bound-to-state-the-obvious friend didn't disappoint. "So what's with Lucie's beauhunk of a brother staring at you like you're his last meal but you kicked him in the balls and ran away?"

Vanessa almost choked on an ice cube. "That's the dumbest thing I think you've ever said."

Eric, a solidly built Hispanic with black hair and too-observant chocolaty eyes, said, "No, the dumbest thing he ever said was when he told me certain things had become routine. He couldn't sit without wincing for a week after that."

"Which is why I consider it one of the smartest things I've ever said, babe."

Listening to the familiar back and forth of Kyle goading Eric eased some of her tension. They'd been to-

gether since their college days and were as tight as any
hetero married couple she knew. People who didn't know
them never guessed they were gay. Both men were extremely athletic and macho and neither were fans of PDA.
But just like any group of close-knit friends, when they
were hanging out with Vanessa and Lucie, not much was
TMI. At least it had gotten her out of answering Kyle's
ridiculous inquiry.

As the guys continued to play-bicker about who did
what intentionally, she glanced around, searching for
Robért, who would no doubt usher her back within the
reception parameters should she breach them.

"Good evening, everyone."

Even facing away, there was no mistaking who the
voice belonged to. Her body betrayed her the minute the
sound entered her ears, bypassed her brain, and traveled
straight south to settle between her legs. Clenching her
thighs together, she turned just as Jax stood and reached
into his breast pocket for a folded sheet of paper. The best
man speech. The perfect time for her to slip away. All
eyes would be on him and his would be on the happy
couple. She'd just wait a minute for everyone to get settled, and then she'd make her move.

A hand closed around her elbow as another landed on
her lower back and led her toward the reception table.
The Wedding Nazi had found her. "Robért, I was fine
where I was," she stage-whispered.

"Nonsense, it's toast time. The maid of honor has to
be up there with the best man."

Vanessa had no choice but to go along unless she
wanted to cause a scene. After depositing her next to
Lucie, Robért went off in search of his next mission. Letting out a discreet sigh of frustration, Lucie faced Jackson
and feigned a happy interest. The idiot winked at her and
turned to face the group.

"On behalf of Reid and Lucie, I'd like to thank you all for being here to help make their day special as they begin their new life together. As a fighter, I know that you can only do so much planning and prep for your opponents. You can study their moves, their strategies, learn how to defend and counter. But the truth of the matter is, when you step inside that cage, you never know what that guy is going to throw at you. You have to accept, adjust, and execute.

"Love is no different," Jackson said, the sound of his deep voice washing over her on the salty breeze. "Growing up, we imagine the type of person we'll someday fall in love with, and over time, we try our best to execute our plans to find—or for us commit-aphobes, avoid"—polite, muted laughter met his last comment—"that person.

"But just as a fighter can't predict what an opponent will do as he works to execute his plan, we can't predict what love will throw our way as we search for that perfect person." Eyes alight with the setting sun met hers, melting her resolve from the inside out. "And more often than not, who we think we need isn't at all who we really need."

Jackson turned his head to address the couple. "Case in point, our very own Reid and Lucie. If they hadn't accepted what love was throwing their way and adjusted their points of view, Reid would still be a miserable bachelor denying his passion for art, and Lucie would be married to a narcissistic surgeon who wouldn't know true beauty if it bit him on the ass."

Laughs and murmurs of agreement rose from the guests. Lucie's cheeks were moist from tears, but the smile she'd worn all day was still in place and the only way Reid could get any closer to her was if he pulled her onto his lap.

Clapping a hand on his best friend's shoulder, Jackson continued. "I'm incredibly thankful that my best friend and my sister were smart enough to adjust and accept their love for each other." His hand dropped and his eyes found Vanessa's again. "But what about the future? Relationships have ups and downs just like everything else. One minute you're winning and on top of the world . . ."

Jackson swallowed hard, pausing like he'd forgotten what came next. Or like it's too hard to say. A tightness spread through her chest just as he came back to himself, but the last part of his sentence only made the pressure worse. ". . . and the next minute you're knocked out, fighting against the darkness and wondering where the hell things went wrong."

Just when Vanessa thought she couldn't take any more—that she needed to stop him or she'd crumple where she stood from her bleeding heart—his speech took a left turn.

"So I wanted to give them some advice that might help them in the future, and I came up with a list of seven things. I guess you could call them rules . . ."

"Oh no." Vanessa clapped a hand over her mouth, but it was too late. She'd blurted it out and now everyone was staring at her as ice shot through her veins. He was going to mock her. Right here, right now, in front of all her friends. Seeing as she'd already made a fool of herself, she skirted around the happy couple to Jackson's side.

She tried not to notice the guests whispering guesses as to what was going on. The best man's hijacking the fucking wedding, that's what's going on. Damn him, this wedding wasn't about them or what they did or didn't want . . .

God, you are such a hypocrite, Nessie.

She'd been doing exactly that all damn day, trying to leave because she felt uncomfortable around Jackson.

How fricking selfish could she be? Lucie should have told Vanessa to take a flying leap off a tall cliff hours ago, hell, yesterday even, but her friend was too kind for that.

So, yes, she felt slightly schmucky about all that, but at least Vanessa only intended on excusing herself from the party. She never would've dreamed to make the wedding a public forum for her relationship problems like an episode of The Jerry Springer Show. The whole thing was so ludicrous, she didn't have the words.

Oh, who was she kidding? Yes, she did.

Stepping in close to keep her voice low, she angled her body away from the crowd and said, "Jackson, this is so completely and utterly unacceptable to do this to Lucie and—"

"It's okay, Nessie." Vanessa looked down at Lucie's hand covering hers, then sought the hurt that would surely show in her friend's eyes but found none. "Reid and I gave him the idea."

"You what?" she whispered.

"Bitch me out later, Ness. Right now you need to listen to my brother."

"Yeah, and make it quick, will ya? I'd like to dance with my wife." Reid pulled Lucie closer to his side. "Before I need a hip replacement would be nice," he added wryly. That earned him a discreet elbow to the ribs.

Speechless. They'd rendered her one hundred percent speechless. Which gave Jackson the perfect opportunity to carry out whatever asinine plan he had up his sleeve. Once again he addressed the crowd.

"As I was saying, I created a list of rules I'd like Reid and Lucie to have if they ever lose their way . . ." Jackson sought her out with intense eyes, and she was helpless to do anything but meet them. ". . . and need to find their way back."

Damn him. Damn him and his amber eyes and his silver tongue.

He faced her and, if it was anywhere in the realm of possibilities, almost looked . . . nervous.

And if that was the case, then it explained why she was damn near jumping out of her skin with anxiety. Countless scenarios—good, bad, ugly, and horrifying—spun in her mind like Tasmanian devils on speed. Her heart had somehow escaped her ribs because she felt it beating faster and faster just under the surface of her skin, and her lungs must have collapsed because she couldn't draw a full breath. Her organs were failing, the apocalypse was at hand, they were all doomed and holy shit what the hell is wrong with me!

Jax placed a large, warm hand at her hip and leaned in until his cheek kissed hers and his mouth rested close to her ear. "V, take some deep breaths for me, honey." His tone lacked the gruffness he used during more intimate times, but it was still heavy and commanding enough to trigger her desire to obey, to let go.

With him coaching her softly, she managed to slow her heart rate and fill her lungs to capacity, banishing her panic attack and preventing what would certainly have been an embarrassing moment if she'd completely lost it. She felt his hand brush her hair over her shoulder, letting his fingertips glide lightly over the shell of her ear and down her neck. "That's my girl," he whispered, before placing a discreet kiss at her temple and pulling away.

"Don't you mean 'crazy woman'?"

"Uh-oh. Someone's been talking to the locals." At least he had the decency to wince. "Come on, it's kind of funny. You thought it sounded pretty."

"I also thought pupule wahine was a term of endearment," she whispered a little too loudly. Snickers and giggles wafted up from the peanut gallery.

"Can you berate me for your nickname later?"

"Absolutely. I'll add it to the growing list of things I plan on berating you for later."

That time she heard a snort, pronouncing her best friend's amusement of the dressing-down of her big brother. Vanessa crossed her arms and arched a single brow, daring him to finish what he started, though she wanted more than anything for him to spontaneously lose the gift of speech.

Clearing his throat, Jax glanced at their rapt audience, took a deep breath himself, and began. "I call this 'Jackson's Lucky Seven Rules to Love By.' Rule #7: Always be one hundred percent honest. Even if it means you can't pretend to be engaged to the most beautiful woman on the island."

She inhaled sharply. He peered up from the paper briefly then continued.

"Rule #6: Always own up to your mistakes. Even if you weren't that late and planned on buying her lunch to make up for it."

"Rule #5: Always negotiate in terms of forever. Even if she gives you a little more Hyde than Jekyll." He gave their rapt audience an audacious wink. "The crazy just adds spice."

Everyone laughed at that one. If they kept this up, she'd wind up with them voting her off the island like a bad mash-up of Survivor and The Love Connection.

"Rule #4: Always use your fists in the cage and to protect her if necessary, but never bring violence into your life." Jackson picked up her hand and cradled it against his chest. "Even if she's strong enough to take care of herself."

Hot tears stung her eyes and her throat closed tightly on something the size of a Ping-Pong ball. It was the only thing preventing her from cursing him aloud at the moment.

"Rule #3: Always be willing to move out of the bachelor shack into a grown-up house." A grin hitched up one corner of his mouth where his dimple winked at her. "Even if said shack has bonus amenities you can't get anywhere else, like mind-blowing waterfall sex."

"Jackson!" she warned, sure her face was turning a bright red. The bastard ignored her and kept going.

"Rule #2: Always understand the balance of control and give as often as you take." His thumb traced circles on her hand. "Even if it means admitting your chivalry can be a little pushy."

"Little, my ass," she muttered under her breath.

He gave her a wink that promised they could discuss her ass later, then he turned his expression serious and her heart caught in her chest. "And, most importantly, Rule #1." He gazed deeply into her eyes. "Always, always, always . . . tell her how much you love her, now and forever, before it's too late."

Loved? Did he just tell her he loved her? Emotions rushed through her—joy, fear, relief, fear, happiness, did she mention fear—that she became lightheaded. She'd wanted so badly for him to love her. Half of her rejoiced, but the other half shrieked in terror like a B-movie vampire as the sun crept over the horizon.

It was in that moment Vanessa realized she hadn't made the rules to ensure she found the right man to love her. She'd made them to prevent accepting anyone who did. Because if she didn't allow herself to love someone in return, then he'd never have the power to hurt her. Her rules had been nothing more than a coat of armor protecting her from her past instead of a plan to protect her future like she'd thought.

She covered her mouth and nose with her hands, tears streaming on either side, unable to verbalize the over-whelming emotions coursing through her. He'd taken her coping mechanism and turned it into something positive and beautiful, each one of his rules directly correlating in some way to the ones she'd lived by for more than a decade. But whereas hers had held everyone at arms' length, Jackson's were vows of love, promises to her of how he wanted to treat her with respect and honor.

He could've written a hundred different speeches. Some may have worked, most probably not. But nothing would have made an impact on her like those seven rules did. And he knew that, because in the span of only a few days, Jackson knew her better than she knew her-self. She loved that about him. She loved him period.

"V, please don't cry." He shoved the paper in his pocket and pulled her hands away from her face, placing a kiss in both of her palms before holding them over his heart. "God, baby, I am so sorry. I swear I'll never lie to you again for as long as I live. Just please give me another chance. I love you so goddamn much—"

"I love you, too."

"—and I—What did you say?"

She couldn't resist. He'd taken her from depressed and cynical to ecstatic and giddy in point-oh-six seconds. Biting the inside of her cheek, she tried to keep the smile from her face. "If you weren't listening, I'm not going to repeat myself. You might want to make 'Always listen the first time' Rule #8."

His lashes almost fused together and she heard the familiar rumbling of a growl deep in his chest that set off a chain reaction of heat and wetness throughout her body. Stepping into her until she was forced to tilt her head back to meet his eyes, he gave her a command as she'd known he would.

"Tell me again, while I'm not in mid-sentence, so I can hear you properly."

Game, set, match went to Jackson. In a matter of forty-eight hours, she'd managed to forget just how much he affected her like this. She swallowed and wet her lips, desperately trying to regain some semblance of moisture, but apparently every last available drop had pooled between her legs to soak her expensive new lingerie.

"I love you, Jackson," she said as she slid her hands up his chest and clasped them behind his neck. "I love you so much I don't know what to do with myself."

A radiant smile spread across his face, showing the lines of his dimples and accentuating the wicked gleam in his eye. "Don't you worry about that, Princess," he said, wrapping his arms around her waist and hauling her up his body, "I promise I know exactly what to do with a pupule wahine like you."

Then, as their audience cheered—and Reid thanked God it was over—Jax gave her a little taste of his promise yet to come.

Epilogue

Vanessa sat at the vanity in her bedroom, putting the finishing touches on her makeup and rifling through her earrings to find a pair to wear with her ever-present sea star necklace, and wondering what the hell was taking Jackson so long. He'd said he had to run an errand after training and then was stopping to pick up Reid and Lucie on his way home.

They still hadn't figured things out logistically, with her job being in Nevada and his training being in Hawaii, but they'd been doing pretty well with switching off between states. When he wasn't preparing for a fight, he stayed out by her. When he had to go back for a camp, or if he was just plain homesick for the sun and the waves, she visited him as often as possible when she wasn't in court or if she could get away with catching up on paperwork and doing things remotely.

So far it seemed to be working well for them. They'd both discussed that neither were in a place to give up their current positions in their careers, but that once they were, they'd decide on the next course of action. But whatever they did, they would do it together.

Smiling, she looked down at the solitaire princess-cut diamond on her left ring finger and gave it a little wiggle. She'd had it a month already, but she still ogled it in private. She never thought she'd be a part of the fiancée club, but she was lovin' every minute of it.

From the front of the apartment, she heard the door open and close.

"Jax, where the hell have you been?" she called out. "I'm going to be late for my own birthday drinks, and that's entirely unacceptable."

"You're doing that thing where you talk like Robért again," he yelled back.

"Am not!"

As the devil himself stepped into her room, she caught his reflection in the mirror in front of her and almost swallowed her tongue.

Half of his mouth curved up in a wicked grin. "Are, too."

"Holy shit, who are you, and what have you done with my fiancé?"

A tux. Jackson Maris was actually in a tuxedo. Black and white with a bow tie (as yet untied), the whole penguin nine yards. The only time she'd ever seen him dress up was at Lucie's wedding, which was to say she'd never seen him dressed up.

"What, no good?" he asked, glancing down his front. "I told Lucie I didn't want the tie fixed until the last possible moment. How men don't choke with these things is beyond me." Then, almost as if he thought his attitude might ruin the moment, he quickly added, "But it's not a rental. Reid took me to some guy who measured me in ways that made me think he should've bought me dinner first, so this thing better look decent."

She spun on her seat and stood. "Are you kidding

me? You look so good I want to tear it off with my teeth and have my wicked way with you."

"Baby, if I'd have known letting some guy feel me up and putting on a monkey suit would do that to you, I'd be wearing one of these every damn day."

Laughing, she crossed to him and said, "Let's not get crazy. I enjoy seeing you strut around in nothing but your shorts."

"Listen, wahine, I don't strut. I simply walk in a manly way."

"Yeah, right, whatever. Now shut up and kiss me."

She slid her hands up the fine material of his jacket as he bent his head to meet her halfway, when suddenly he jerked his left shoulder back with a hiss.

Her brows drew together. "What's wrong? Did you get hurt at the gym today?"

"No, that's your birthday present."

"Wow," she said slowly. "A hurt shoulder? I don't want to hurt your feelings, too, honey, but you used to be better at this whole present thing."

"Well, it's too bad you don't like it because I don't believe in any of that laser removal shit. So I guess you're stuck there."

Laser removal? She stared at the place above his heart as though she could see through the layers of fabric. Did he . . . ?

Carefully, she pushed his jacket off his left arm, then undid the buttons of his shirt with shaky fingers. Though her focus was on her movements, she felt the heat of those topaz eyes trained on her as surely as if she'd been staring back.

Once she reached the bottom, she took in a slow breath and lifted the left side of his shirt in the same manner she did the jacket. A white square of gauze beneath plastic wrap was taped to his golden brown skin.

"Go ahead, V," he said softly.

She lifted three sides and peeled the covering back to reveal a coral-colored sea star with a capital V in script in the center, right next to one of the cherry blossoms riding the ocean waves of his tattoo.

"I gave you an engagement ring to show the world that I want you with me forever. But this . . ." He tapped a finger next to the fresh ink. "This is for you, for us. I wanted a tattoo of you on my skin, because I can't show you the one you've already left on my heart."

He was such a jerk. She hated crying. She'd cried more in the last six months of knowing him than she had in the last fifteen years. At least it was always happy crying. But he was still a jerk.

Taking slow, deep breaths to prevent an all-out sob fest, she gingerly secured the tape again and asked, "Where are Reid and Lucie?"

"Outside, waiting in the car. Why?"

Slipping her hand under his shirt, she pushed everything off in one fell swoop, then peered up through her lashes at the desire now flashing in his eyes.

"Well, we'd have to make it quick, but I thought maybe we could examine some different areas on my body where I could get a cherry blossom."

She stepped in close and pressed her hips into the growing erection in the front of his pants. Groaning, his hands found the short hem of her mini dress and bunched it around her waist to grab onto her ass.

"And what if I love every inch of you so much that I can't decide?" he asked, his deep voice sending shivers down her spine. Before she had the chance to answer, his mouth assaulted her neck, alternately sucking and scraping, shattering her thoughts as soon as they appeared.

"Then I'll get it next to my starfish."

He nipped her lower lip and smiled widely at her sharp inhale. "It's a sea star."

"Whatever," she said with an answering grin and then gladly let him take the lead.

Jax's "Lucky 7" Rules to Love By

7. Always be 100% honest.
6. Always own up to your mistakes.
5. Always negotiate in terms of forever.
4. Always use fists in the cage and to protect her when necessary, but never bring violence into your life.
3. Always be willing to move out of the bachelor shack into a grown-up house.
2. Always understand the balance of control and give as often as you take.
1. Always, always, always . . . tell her how much you love her, now and forever, before it's too late.

ACKNOWLEDGMENTS

As always, first and foremost, thank you to my wonderful husband and children who deal with, and work around, the crazy hours I keep to do what I love.

Thank you to my Maxwell Mob officers—Pat, Diane, Annie, Kristin, Laura, Aimee, Angie, and Andrea—who keep things running with my readers and the Mob when I'm stuck in Deadline Hell and can't come up for air. The Mob wouldn't exist without all your hard work and dedication, and I'd probably be in the loony bin.

To my amazing friend Kristin Anders who spent hours upon hours with me over IM, text, phone, and Skype figuring out the plot holes and conflicts for this beast. I would have given up on Jax months ago if not for her encouragement and middle-of-the-night sessions.

To Jilli Linnett and her family for giving me all my information on Oahu and the Hawaiian culture to make sure I got it right. Also for all the beautiful pictures and thoughtful gifts. You deserved a place in this story.

To Christa Cervone who coined the phrase "cunny quake." I knew instantly it was a Fritz-ism.

To Josh Williams, Parker Hurley, Ally Sturm, and Jeremy Austin: thank you for giving me not only one, but two gorgeous covers for this series.

To my editor, Liz Pelletier, who stayed up with me for several all-nighters in a row to make sure we had this book as perfect as we could get it, and for helping me love the story again.

To Kara Wiesmann and Courtenay Birchmeier of Sun-Tree Accessories for designing and creating Vanessa's Necklace as a continuation to the Fighting for Love jewelry tradition.

And last, but certainly not least, everyone who has ever said an encouraging, supportive word to me about my books, my characters, or my accomplishments. I take them all to heart. Thank you.

BONUS SCENE BETWEEN JAX AND DANNY AKANA FROM *RULES OF ENTANGLEMENT*

Vanessa stood at the entrance to the Neal S. Blaisdell Center in Honolulu where Jackson was fighting Danny Akana shortly at UFC 165. The jerk had switched camps after she emasculated him by breaking his nose with her fist and then made a career of publicly smearing Jax's name and challenging him in the media. Akana only had a few fights under his belt and in no way deserved to fight a seasoned and former champion like Jax, but even the UFC wasn't immune to the politics of ratings, and the bigger the rivalry, the bigger the ratings.

Jax, of course, couldn't have been happier when UFC president, Dana White, proposed the fight. Now he could finish what Danny started all those months ago when he'd sucker punched Jax after a sparring session in the gym, followed by a crass threat of what he'd like to do to Vanessa. Although she would never condone Jax going after the guy outside of the octagon, *inside* the cage was another story entirely.

At last the town car with her guests arrived, and she greeted Becca and Christine at the curb with a warm smile and big hugs. They'd interviewed her and Jackson the day before and now they were here to continue their exposé on the couple. Christine would be writing an article on the fight and Becca would be taking pictures and clips of video to accompany it.

Vanessa handed them their press passes to wear around their necks. "Okay, girls, are you ready?"

Becca adjusted the camera strap over her shoulder. "Absolutely. I'm hoping to get so close to the action I get sprayed with sweat."

Christine added, "You never know, Bec, it might end up being blood."

Becca momentarily paled as her friend laughed at her expense, then recovered with a shrug. "I don't care, as long as it's followed by Jackson kicking Akana's sorry a—"

"Ladies," said a deep voice from behind them, "if you'll follow me I'll escort you inside."

All three women turned to see a member of the arena's security team. The guy was massive and could have easily gotten a job as Duane "The Rock" Johnson's stunt double. Vanessa thanked him, then followed as he directed them through the throng of MMA fans to a door labeled as Restricted Access. After navigating several hallways, they finally arrived at a room with Jackson's name beside it.

Vanessa looked back at the girls. "Becca, you're fine to take pictures. Christine, Jax is going to be in pre-fight mode, so don't feel bad if he totally ignores you. Depending on what he's doing in there, he might be fine with talking or he might not. Just follow his lead, okay?"

Becca nodded and Christine added, "Got it." Big Man knocked and waited for someone to call out that it was okay to come in before opening the door and waving them in.

It looked like a typical green room where celebrities

might wait before appearing on a show or where a band hung out before their concert. A couple of couches lined the back and left walls and a large flat screen TV hung in the opposite corner, showing the fights as they happened.

"There she is." Corey, one of Jackson's good friends and teammates, crossed the room to greet her with a hug and kiss on the cheek. Vanessa introduced him to the girls and explained why they were there. He bestowed them with his signature boy-next-door smile and warm handshake. Then, jerking his thumb in the direction of Jax shadow boxing in the middle of the room, he said, "Have you finally come to dump this poor schmo and ask me for my hand in marriage?"

She laughed at the tall and lanky fighter with his All-American good looks and charm by the mile. "Isn't it the man's job to do the asking?"

"I'm all for the feminist movement. I support your right to pursue happiness, and in this case, I think you'd be happier with me," he said with a wink.

"Now, Corey, what did I tell you about thinking? It only gets you into trouble." She patted his cheek a couple of times. "Stick with fighting."

"Can't say I haven't given it the old college try. Why don't you have a seat on the couch over there while your golden boy does his thing."

All three women sat and watched the pre-fight routine. Corey and a couple of the other fighters who would be "cornering" for Jackson talked amongst themselves and watched the current fight on TV. Jax was now throwing combinations at the hand pads his coach was wearing. Vanessa loved watching him move. He wore a pair of black shorts that looked just like the dozens of pairs of board shorts he owned, only these had his sponsors' logos all over them. On top he wore a matching sponsor-loaded hoodie, hood pulled up to block out his peripheral vision, and ear buds blasting his favorite "get psyched" music straight into his brain.

He was focused. He was ready. He was damn sexy.

Becca took the occasional picture, and Christine watched and took down notes on her writing pad. Vanessa was eager to see what the article would say. Hopefully it ended with Jackson's hand being raised in the air.

Fifteen minutes later, Coach shed the pads and Jax removed the ear buds and his hood to listen to the plan one last time before the older man cuffed him on the side of the head as his own twisted way of showing affection. Apparently it was *everyone's* way. Vanessa's eyes grew wide as every man in the room proceeded to hit Jax on the sides of the head—hard!—as they yelled words of encouragement at him.

Glancing over, Vanessa found Christine's mouth hanging open and Becca giggling as she took shot after shot of the barbaric scenario.

"That explains so much about the male psyche," Vanessa muttered. "Come on, girls, let's leave them to their caveman rituals and find our seats. It's almost time."

The girls both made pouty faces at having to leave the testosterone-filled room, and Vanessa tried not to laugh as she ushered them toward the door.

"Wait!"

She knew that deep voice as intimately as her own. Turning, she watched as Jackson strode toward her. Normally her fiancé had a ready smile that showed his dimples and warm topaz eyes that reminded her of gooey caramel. He was a charmer by nature and no one was immune to his powers. But right at this moment, all of that was replaced with a feral intensity he only ever unleashed during two things: fighting . . . and sex.

He stopped in front of her, so close she swore she

could hear his heart beating a rapid tattoo against his chest. Or maybe that was hers. "You didn't think I'd actually let you leave without saying anything, did you?"

"I didn't think you knew I was here. I mean, I didn't think you saw me."

He challenged her statement with an arch of his scarred eyebrow. "I don't have to see you to know when you've stepped into the room, V. You should know that by now." A shudder ran through her as he lifted his taped-up hands and framed her face. "Tonight, this win's for you."

"You know I don't like the idea of you fighting for me."

"Yeah, I know. But just this once, I'm doing it all the same. You can yell at me for it later."

She rolled her eyes and released an exasperated sigh. "Fine. Now go on, get in the zone or whatever. I'll see you after."

Jax kissed her firmly on the lips and dropped his hands. He acknowledged Becca and Christine with a nod of his head before bouncing from side-to-side back to the center of the room. Becca opened the door and they started to shuffle into the hallway, but at the last minute Vanessa looked over her shoulder and called out to the man she loved. He stopped jumping around to turn and face her again.

Then she said the words she'd been secretly wanting to tell him since that first time he'd been in a cage with Akana. "Kick his ass."

A shit-eating grin split his face just before Corey shoved a guard into his mouth. The glint in his eyes shone brightly as he started jumping again with renewed energy. As Vanessa finally joined the girls in the hallway, encouraging shouts from the men of Team Titan echoed as the door swung shut behind her.

Thirty minutes later, Vanessa, Becca, and Christine

were seated in the front row behind the raised octagon platform where Jackson's corner would be. As Becca checked her camera's settings and took some preliminary shots, Christine leaned over to be heard over the loudness surrounding them. "Holy crap, I'm so nervous for him I could puke. How do you deal with this?"

Vanessa gave her a helpless look. "I have no idea. This is his first professional fight since we've been together."

Becca had just sat down and heard the tail end. "Oh my God, are you kidding? This is perfect! We're going to capture every nail-biting, jaw-clenching reaction!"

Christine and Vanessa stared at the woman who looked like she'd just won the lottery. Becca cleared her throat and schooled her face. "What I meant to say was, 'I'm sure everything will be fine. Despite how it can look, these fights don't result in permanent injuries all that often.'" Vanessa felt the color drain from her face and she thought she saw Christine jab her friend in the ribs. "I mean, just because there's blood and lots of things swollen ten times their normal size doesn't mean it's all that serious."

"I think I'm going to be sick," Vanessa muttered.

Christine used her notepad to fan Vanessa. "No, you're not, you're going to be just fine because we all know that Jax is going to rip Akana to shreds. Isn't that right, Bec?"

"Yes! Absolutely. That's what I was trying to say."

Vanessa laughed despite the knots growing in her stomach and gave Becca a reassuring shoulder squeeze. "Do me a favor, girl. Keep up the awesome work with making trailers and movies and leave the pep-talk business to someone else."

They all laughed at that point, but it was interrupted by the walk-in music for Danny Akana. She didn't recognize the song, but it was just as obnoxious as its fighter. When he got into the cage, he ran around it taunting the fans, sticking his tongue out, and finally making a lewd gesture directed at Vanessa. As much as she wanted to flip him off, she refrained. As the fiancée of one of the fighters, not to mention the publicly known reason for the rivalry, the cameras were sure to pan to her from time to time. She wasn't going to risk her reputation for a split-second of satisfaction.

Next came the music for Jackson. Another song she didn't know, but it sounded electrifying and empowering. After hugging his coach and teammates, getting greased up with Vaseline, and proving he wore a mouth guard and cup, he entered the cage and jogged around once with his fist in the air as a salute to the crowd. When he stopped at his corner, he found her in the fans, pointed to the sea star tattoo over his heart and then at her.

The crowd cheered even louder, eating up the brief attention he paid her. But the only thing Vanessa paid attention to was the easing of the knots in her stomach. With just one look Jackson had been able to reassure her. She was ready to watch the fight.

The music died down as the announcer rattled off the stats of each man. The referee brought them to the center and went over the rules. Jackson held out his fists to touch gloves in a show of good sportsmanship. Danny ignored it and backed away. The referee asked one last time if each man was ready . . . then clapped his hands and started round one.

The next five minutes were a flurry of fists and kicks as both men kept the fight on their feet. They bounced back and forth and circled each other, looking for the opening they needed to connect their next blow. The problem was that Danny seemed to be landing twice as many hits as Jax. Already Jax's lip was split open and bleeding along with a cut over his right eye. Vanessa had no idea what Jackson's game plan was, but if the shouted orders coming from his corner were any indication, he wasn't following it.

During the round, Becca followed the action with the other photographers and captured the damage with her camera. Christine wrote feverishly while glancing between the cage and her notepad. Vanessa's eyes were glued to her fiancé and her hands were wringing themselves in the hem of her shirt.

At the end of the round she watched Corey rub ice bags on his shoulders, back, and chest. One guy wiped the blood from his face and slathered more Vaseline over the cuts to prevent them from bleeding. Yet another guy pressed a cold, metal object to his face to keep the swelling down as much as possible. And all of that took place while they barked orders at him. But Jax didn't seem to be listening. His eyes were locked onto Akana the entire time.

Round two.

This time the fight went to the ground, but other than that, the outcome was the same. Five minutes of Akana taking Jackson to the mat, passing his guard, and trying to work submissions on him. He almost succeeded a few times, too, but each time Jackson managed to get out of it before Danny could lock anything in. His coach and teammates were screaming bloody murder at him to do this and that, but Jax either didn't hear them or decided to ignore them.

When the round came to an end, Vanessa watched helplessly as the earlier break played over again like a bad case of déjà vu. She understood enough by now to know that if a fight wasn't called by KO, TKO, or submission, it came down to points and who won at least two of the three rounds. And it would be obvious to even a newcomer to the sport that Akana had won both rounds so far. Jax needed to finish him in round three, or he'd lose.

Unable to stand by anymore, Vanessa ran past security to the black chain-link fence. "Maris!" she yelled. He twisted his upper body so he could see her. "What the hell are you doing out there? Stop toying with him and *finish* this!"

He gave her a wicked grin and a wink to match before heading out for round three.

This time things were different. Jackson came out with a vengeance, landing his punches and connecting his kicks. Whatever submission Danny tried to get him in, Jax easily maneuvered out of it. With each new thwarted attack the kid grew angrier, more volatile. But the more he let the emotions get the better of him, the sloppier his technique became.

Finally, the kid threw his hands out to the side in yet another taunt. And that's when Jax struck. His arm shot out like a viper uncoiling, hitting dead center on his target. Danny's eyes rolled into the back of his head and he fell boneless to the mat.

The crowd rose to their feet, their cheers deafening in the arena. Jax was joined in the cage by his teammates and coach as they congratulated him and helped him into his black T-shirt. All the while, the world could have been standing still for all Vanessa and Jax knew. Their eyes had locked onto each other the second he won the fight and hadn't broken since. She mouthed the words *I love you* and he responded by pointing to his heart, then her.

As the announcer named Jackson winner by knockout, Vanessa cheered and screamed with Christine as Becca captured each moment with her camera. She made a mental note to get each and every picture to make a coffee table album so they could look back on this night for years to come.

But she knew even without the pictures and article, this would be a night Vanessa and Jackson would never forget.

And the fight was only the beginning.

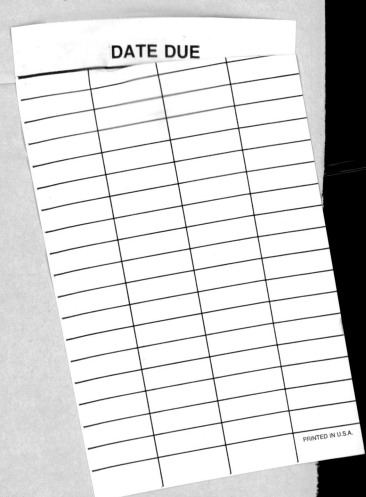

DATE DUE

PRINTED IN U.S.A.